THRICE SPARED

THRICE SPARED

REG RAWLINS, PSYCHIC INVESTIGATOR #17

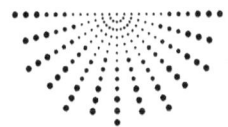

P.D. WORKMAN

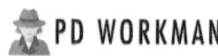 **PD WORKMAN**

ISBN: 9781774683255 (KDP Hardcover)
ISBN: 9781774683217 (KDP Paperback)
ISBN: 9781774683248 (Large Print)
ISBN: 9781774683262 (Lulu Paperback)
ISBN: 9781774683224 (Kindle)
ISBN: 9781774683231 (ePub)

ALSO BY P.D. WORKMAN

MYSTERY/SUSPENSE:

Reg Rawlins, Psychic Detective
Paranormal Mystery & Adventure
What the Cat Knew
A Psychic with Catitude
A Catastrophic Theft
Night of Nine Tails
Telepathy of Gardens
Delusions of the Past
Fairy Blade Unmade
Web of Nightmares
A Whisker's Breadth
Skunk Man Swamp
Magic Ain't A Game
Without Foresight
Careful of Thy Wishes
Time to Your Elf
Undiscovered Tomb
Missing Powers
Thrice Spared
Cloaked Campaign (Coming Soon)
Cat Tales in the Swamp (Short Story)

AND MORE AT PDWORKMAN.COM

For those whose wrongs were never avenged
And those who have scraped pizza from the ceiling

CHAPTER ONE

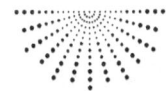

*R*eg watched Corvin walk away from her down the path out of the backyard. Almost as soon as he was gone, the back door of the big house banged and Sarah was striding toward Reg with great purpose. Reg was momentarily thrown back to her childhood when an older woman coming toward her like that almost certainly presaged a slap across the head and punishment for whatever real or perceived infraction the current foster mom thought she had committed.

And the red aura around her landlady was not a comfort.

Sarah stopped in front of Reg, a crease between her eyebrows, her mouth turning down in a stern frown. Her gray hair was in disarray, as if she had been running her fingers through it.

"What was *he* doing here?"

Reg sighed and let out her breath. She gathered her red box-braids in a bunch and released them behind her back. "Just came over for a visit, I guess."

"He came over for a visit. And you let him in!"

Reg shook her head. "I didn't let him in."

"The only way he could get by the wards that protect this yard and the guest cottage is if you let him in, one way or the other. What did you do?"

"I didn't do anything. I was just sitting here. I didn't invite him in; I didn't even call him on the phone. He just showed up here on his own."

"That isn't possible."

Reg raised her brows at Sarah. "I didn't do anything to let him in."

"Did you have something of his here that he could come back to retrieve? Or you gave him a key?"

"I know better than that now," Reg pointed out. She hadn't known all of the rules in the beginning when she had first arrived in Black Sands. But she knew all of the sneaky ways Corvin, a handsome warlock with evil purpose in his heart, could get past the wards that Sarah had set. He had managed to finagle his way around them a few times, and Reg had helped set the new wards, using her newly discovered gifts under Sarah's direction.

But now…

Sarah stared at her, expecting more information about how Corvin had managed to worm his way in again, sure that it had to be something that Reg had done wrong. Reg just shook her head helplessly.

The creases on Sarah's face deepened. Her normally pleasant, grandmotherly demeanor was gone. This new development was definitely of concern to her.

"But if Corvin got past the wards without any action on your part…"

Reg nodded. "You said before that it could happen. That you could not protect the yard from someone whose powers were greater than yours."

CHAPTER TWO

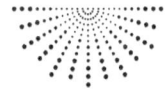

*S*arah sank onto the bench beside Reg. Her face went slack and Reg grabbed for her, afraid that she would faint and fall right off the bench.

"Sarah!"

Sarah held on to Reg's arm, steadying herself, then let go. "It's all right, dear. I'm fine." Even so, she put her hand over her heart, breathing heavily. "Is it possible?" She closed her eyes. "Of course it is. Corvin has been growing in strength. He has all of the powers that he has been able to absorb from others and from the artifacts he has acquired. And he has apparently grown enough…"

That he was stronger than Sarah.

Reg had relied upon Sarah's wards as she had gotten used to living in Black Sands, with all of the possible dangers that lurked there. Black Sands was home to a large population of witches, psychics, and other magical races, and not all of them were good. Sarah said that there was no black magic or white magic, just the intentions of the individuals who wielded the powers. And not all of the individuals who wielded powers in Black Sands had good intentions.

Reg had learned this the way she learned most things. From personal experience. She had always been told that she should listen to the advice of others, to learn from their experiences and trust that they knew better than she did. But she had not been able to trust. She always had to try things for herself.

The breaching of Sarah's wards meant that Reg was exposed to Corvin and his wiles and charms once more. She had to be able to withstand all of the pheromones and stolen magical powers that he could bring to bear against her. She had not always succeeded in the past and had been caught in dangerous circumstances more than once.

But *she* was stronger now too. She had grown into powers and gifts that she had known nothing about before moving into the guest cottage in Sarah's backyard. She had learned that there was more to her success in conning unsuspecting clients out of their money doing psychic readings than just being able to cold read them. She wasn't just observant; she had gifts that she had never understood or suspected.

"Corvin's star is rising and mine is waning," Sarah said in a soft, flat tone. As if she were talking in her sleep, unaware that Reg still sat beside her.

"No," Reg told Sarah sternly. "It doesn't have anything to do with you. It's just because Corvin has been able to drink the powers of the Witch Doctor and Kareem."

"It is only natural that sooner or later, my powers begin to weaken. Even though this body has lasted a long time…" She indicated her apparently middle-aged body. Reg would have put her in her sixties, but she knew that others had said Sarah was centuries old. Only magic had kept her looking so young.

Sarah rubbed her forehead, the third eye position between her brows. She looked suddenly tired and older than she had been since she'd been restored by her powerful emerald.

"You're not old," Reg insisted. "You're not weakening."

Sarah lifted her head and looked around the garden. "We will need to reset and strengthen the wards. You are young and strong and are growing into your powers. Together, we should be able to keep them strong. You have been able to resist Corvin before; that shows that you and he are nearly matched in strength."

Reg nodded. Though she knew it wasn't just her magical gifts that had allowed her to resist Corvin in the past. She had other weaponry in her arsenal. While Sarah knew about Reg's siren heritage, she didn't know that Reg had used the physical traits and instincts that came from that heritage to defeat Corvin the last time. She wasn't sure Corvin would try to seduce her again. Knowing what she could do and how he was just as vulnerable to her wiles as she was to his, would he dare make another attempt?

Who was she kidding? Of course he would. The fact that he had sat on the bench with her and not made any attempt to charm her did not mean that he was finished trying. He was just taking some time to reevaluate his prey and her weaknesses.

Sarah was quite a powerful witch. Her wards had kept Corvin at bay for quite a while and, if Reg helped, then surely he wouldn't be able to get past them again.

"You'll need to be more vigilant now," Sarah advised. "Strengthen the wards every day. I will do what I can to maintain them, but it will be up to you to see that Corvin can't get past." She shook her head, looking around at the peaceful garden, full of blooms and every imaginable shade of green, and the little burbling waterfall and pond in front of the bench they rested on. "He cannot have the run of this place. Not to access you and not to disturb any of the wildlife or the peace of the garden."

"Okay." Reg nodded. "If you'll show me what to do, I'll do my best."

She didn't point out that she wasn't particularly reliable. Remembering to strengthen the wards every day? Reg found establishing new habits, especially good habits, difficult. She remembered to feed Starlight, her black and white tuxedo cat, every day because he wouldn't let her forget, getting underfoot, yowling, biting her ankles, jumping up on the kitchen island. Whatever he had to do to get her to feed him.

If he had been a goldfish, it would be a different story.

Or a plant.

Sarah was constantly rolling her eyes and telling Reg she needed to take care of the plant that Fir had given her. Sarah watered it, turned it, and kept it close to the window so that it got enough light, but not so much that it would burn. She occasionally took it outside to the garden to be with the other plants, and for Forst, the garden gnome, to use his gifts to keep it healthy. Otherwise, Reg was sure that the plant would have shriveled up into a brown, crispy mass of leaves before she realized she had been neglecting it.

"You have to be diligent," Sarah insisted, perhaps understanding Reg's silence too well. "This could be a matter of life and death."

CHAPTER THREE

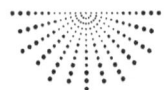

*D*espite looking so tired and pasty, Sarah walked around the garden with Reg and began weaving her spells. She talked to Reg about what she was doing, why she picked the spells that she did, in the strategic places she did, and how Reg could help. It was almost all Greek to Reg. She didn't have a lot of experience in spells, and the ones that she had performed had been simple, without any of the chants or arm-waving that Sarah was doing. All that Reg did was focus her intentions, stretch out all of her senses, and occasionally issue a short command or request. Sometimes it worked and sometimes it didn't. The magic that Sarah was doing was far more complex, learned over a lifetime of practice. Reg didn't know if she would ever be able to learn how to do all of those things.

She still saw herself as just a psychic, despite some of the things that she had been able to do in the past. She never thought of herself as a witch or as magical. She dressed in long, colorful dresses and headscarves, the garb of a fortune teller, and that was how she made a living.

She had gifts, but they were inborn, not something she had studied formally. The only formal training she had was a few tips from Sarah and the mentoring that she received from Davyn, the leader of Corvin's coven.

At least, the leader of the coven for a little while longer.

Reg wasn't sure when the election was set for, but Corvin was campaigning to take the leadership over from Davyn. And while Davyn wasn't keen on Corvin taking over, he was tired and ready to turn the responsibility over to someone else.

Reg shook her head at the thought of Corvin being in charge of the spiritual leadership of his coven. He wasn't exactly the best example of the maxim "an' it harm none." He might have a lot of scholarly experience and had grown up with magic in a practicing home, but he wasn't who she would choose as the best person to lead her to understand herself and her potential. And she didn't exactly feel at peace around him. Sedated sometimes, yes, drugged on his charms, but not at peace.

Sarah looked at Reg questioningly. Reg hadn't said any of this out loud, but she had been shaking her head and wasn't sure whether she had made any other gestures or sounds of disgust.

"Sorry. Off in my own little world." Reg's face warmed, flushing in embarrassment. "I was just thinking of Corvin... about the coven's election."

"Yes." Sarah nodded, looking grim. "I suppose he will get his way. It seems like sooner or later, he always does."

"You think they'll elect him?"

"I imagine so. Do you doubt it?"

"But even with what he does? Is? Being a power drinker. A predator. I wouldn't even want him in my coven, let alone leading it."

"He has been working for many years to weasel himself into the coven and then to preach that banning *his kind* from holding a position in the coven is unfair and an affront to his rights. I'm afraid that he and the others like him around the world have been working tirelessly to shift sentiments in their direction. As you know, there are now several covens who have not only allowed the accursed membership, but have elected them to leadership positions." She sighed and looked around the garden, perhaps checking if she'd missed anything or left any part of the yard vulnerable. "So far, there have not been any casualties. But I suspect it is only a matter of time."

"I can't believe that people would allow him to lead, knowing what he is. The core members of his coven all seem just fine with it. Some of the neophytes are opposed, but I just can't understand it. It seems only logical that you need to keep a predator like him out of leadership positions. Don't give him access to people who are vulnerable."

"Luckily, it is a traditional, all-male coven. They won't be as susceptible to him as women. But he can still influence the behavior of warlocks as well, and I imagine he has been subtly pushing them to accept him and change their minds about it for the past few years. If he is generous with his gifts, they will see him as an asset to the coven rather than a danger. What does it matter what method he uses to increase his powers, as long as he shares them with the group?"

"But *you* don't think that?"

"No, Reg. Of course I don't. The way that he treated you and continues to pursue you is despicable. Certainly, it matters whether his powers are something that he has put time and effort into increasing, or whether they were sucked from the witches who previously held them. Especially if it was done without their consent."

The first time Reg had encountered Corvin, she had not known what she was consenting to, which, as far as Reg was concerned, was not consent at all. Corvin had been able to steal her powers but had, unbelievably, returned them to save her from torture and possibly death. The time after that… there had certainly been no consent. And she would have succumbed to him again if she had not been saved by a group of fairies who saw what was going on and threatened Corvin's life to stop him.

Corvin seemed to be *ethically challenged* with regard to the issue of consent and what he was and wasn't allowed to do under the common law observed by the witches and warlocks in Black Sands.

Reg saw a movement under one of the bushes and walked over to it to see if she could spot what had made the leaves and branches shake. But whatever it was had apparently either run away or had frozen and blended in with the undergrowth. Reg prodded at the dirt with the toe of her sneaker. "What did this?"

Sarah moved closer and peered down at the dirt that had been disturbed by long, straight scratches. "I'm not sure," she said, lifting her glasses to look under the rims at the marks, and then settling them back into place. "Something digging. Maybe a squirrel or a skunk."

Reg's nostrils flared, and she sniffed at the air. Usually, if there were a skunk nearby, it wasn't easy to miss its musky scent. "Would a skunk be able to get into the yard? Wouldn't your wards keep it away?"

Sarah laughed. "Certainly not. There is nothing evil or dangerous about a skunk. They are quite shy. If they hear you coming, they'll go the other direction."

"They could spray you."

"They are not going to spray either of us. I extended the charms to cover animals who could do you harm. Poisonous snakes. But not skunks." She laughed again. Maybe she was a little more giggly than usual because she was stressed about Corvin being able to break her wards.

"And alligators, right?"

"Yes. No alligators allowed back here." Sarah looked down at the disturbed dirt. "It isn't like they would be digging for grubs or roots here. The only reason they would dig would be to lay eggs, as far as I know. And they wouldn't lay eggs so far from the water."

"You don't think it is anything to be worried about?"

"I don't think that anything digging for grubs is a danger to you. Unless you are planning to shift into a grub."

"I'm not a skin walker." Reg smiled and shook her head, remembering Bruce in the Everglades. She had never thought to actually see a shapeshifter in real life. She had never considered the possibility that they even existed.

Or fairies. Or elves. Or any of the other magical races that she had encountered so far in Black Sands.

Well, maybe it wasn't true to say she had never considered the possibility that they existed. As a child, she had assumed that such things did exist. They were on TV and in the books that foster mothers read to her at bedtime, so of course they existed, just like the ghosts that were part of her daily experience.

It wasn't until later that her parents, social workers, and therapists had started shutting down any talk of supernatural or paranormal experiences. The concrete world was the only thing that existed, and she wasn't allowed to live in or acknowledge anything but the world they could all see and touch.

"You don't need to worry about anything living in this garden," Sarah assured Reg, with a comforting hand on her arm. "Nothing at all."

CHAPTER FOUR

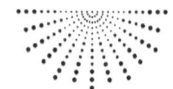

*R*eg put all thought of Corvin and the wards and whether she was safe in the backyard or her cottage out of her mind when she went to bed. She needed her sleep, not to be obsessing over her safety.

At least, she tried to put them out of her mind.

It didn't actually work that way.

As much as she tried just to push all of her worries away and chase the sandman, her anxious brain kept returning to her fears, offering up concerning scenarios. Reg called Starlight to her, and he cuddled up against her for a while, but he eventually returned to his perch on the bedroom windowsill to look out into the darkness and to his nighttime patrols of the house.

Reg was still recovering from her lack of sleep while looking for Davyn and trying to return him to his coven when he had been missing. Now that he was back, she needed to catch up again, but believing this and actually getting her body to cooperate were two very different things.

She slept fitfully from the time she went to bed after her last client departed until nine or ten in the morning, and finally got up. She normally slept a few hours later, but the time for sleep appeared to have passed her by, and there was no point in lying in bed fighting it for the next few hours.

"You know what I need?" Reg asked Starlight as he chowed down on a freshly opened can of tuna while she leaned on the kitchen island watching him. "I need a really good cup of coffee."

He stopped for a moment and looked at her, then turned his head to gaze at the coffee machine on the counter.

He really was too clever for his own good.

"Not homemade coffee. I need *coffeehouse* coffee."

Starlight seemed unimpressed by this. He returned to his breakfast.

Reg had been to a few coffee shops in the area, but one stood out over the rest. The Witches' Brew was, obviously, a cafe run for and on behalf of witches. And their specialty coffees were—Reg was almost afraid to say it—magical. She had been there a couple of times with Corvin or on a date and was always impressed. Maybe they added a little extra love and some special culinary spells into the brews.

Reg gathered her large purse and everything she thought she might need.

"Are you even going to say goodbye?" she asked Starlight.

He positioned himself in a patch of sunshine and began bathing.

"Burn!" Reg muttered. "Snubbed by a cat."

She opened her door tentatively and looked out before stepping over the threshold. Just to be sure Corvin wasn't lurking out there. Or some other person or creature that intended her harm. She wasn't convinced that Sarah's wards would continue to hold. Especially if Sarah herself didn't believe they would.

There was no sign of movement or feeling that she was being watched. Everything looked as it had. No one had egged her door. There were no remnants of candles or other spell work left behind. Everything seemed quiet, as she would expect it to be.

* * *

She had forgotten, when she decided to go to The Witches' Brew, that it was frequented by cops. Or at least, by one cop in particular.

Reg hadn't been there for ten minutes when Detective Marta Jessup appeared. At first, she was focused on getting her coffee from the barista but, once she received her cup and took a sip, she looked around the cafe and saw Reg sitting at one of the tables with her coffee. It was too late for Reg to duck down out of sight or take a trip to the restroom to avoid Jessup. Besides, she was trying to get over her antipathy toward Jessup. The detective didn't actually *want* to arrest Reg for anything, and maybe she couldn't help it that Reg kept landing on their suspect list. It wasn't Jessup's fault, after all, that Reg had broken into a cemetery and been discovered with a dead body. A recently deceased dead body, and not one that had been buried. Maybe Jessup hadn't really suspected Reg, but her hands had been tied and she had had to treat Reg as if she did. She didn't want to lose her job.

Maybe if Jessup had been in a different profession, the two of them could have been friends. That was what Jessup apparently wanted, but Reg wasn't the type who made friends easily. She had gone through her childhood being the new kid at school, the new girl in the foster home, a competitor for the limited resources that foster parents had at their disposal. And she'd been weird. She had to admit that her gifts had gotten in the way of making friends with the people who lived the closest to her. She couldn't suppress the voices all day; it was exhausting.

Erin Price had been one of the rare exceptions, a foster child who didn't see Reg as a competitor or damaged in some way, but actually looked up to her and could be bent to go along with some of Reg's ill-fated money-making schemes. After graduating from foster care, they had reconnected for a time but had clearly been headed in different directions. Reg had eventually gone off on her own. She didn't need to be burdened by someone who wanted to follow all of the rules and take care of other people. Reg had to take care of her own needs. She hadn't had that drive to look after those less fortunate. That was why Erin did so much better as a companion or home care professional. People quickly came to like and trust her. And though Erin had been accused more than once of taking advantage of one of her elderly clients, Reg didn't believe for a minute that Erin had ever taken anything that hadn't been given to her.

Reg's experiences in trying to provide companionship, cleaning, or care services to older ladies or gentlemen had been destined to turn out a little bit differently.

"Reg!" Jessup waved and walked over to Reg's table. She pulled out a chair and sat down. "Hi! I didn't expect to see you here."

"Well, no," Reg agreed. Considering that she wasn't usually even out of bed yet, it was probably a pretty big surprise for Jessup to find Reg at the coffee shop. Not only awake, but out of her house. "I couldn't get back to sleep and I couldn't face home-brewed coffee. So…" Reg looked around at The Witches' Brew and shrugged. "Here I am."

"Well, what a nice coincidence. I'm just taking a break… it was a pretty crazy night. Or early morning, I guess. It was after midnight."

Despite her night shift, Jessup looked fresh and energetic. Her golden skin was flawless, black hair neatly in place.

"Something big going on?" Reg asked. She looked away from Jessup, not that interested in the answer. She didn't want a whole long story about the police work that Jessup had been doing in the wee hours of the morning.

"You haven't heard yet?" Jessup asked.

Reg looked back at her face. Eager. Excited to tell her about whatever horrible thing had happened during the night. To share what her part in it had been, even if it was small.

"No, I guess not. I haven't heard anything since last night. I had some readings, a seance, and went to bed. Haven't checked out the news this morning. Not that any Black Sands news would be on the news channels I usually watch anyway."

"No, but I thought maybe Sarah had told you. Or… *he* might have."

"Who?" Reg saw the answer in Jessup's eyes before the words passed her lips. "Corvin?" Reg demanded. "What has he done now?"

It couldn't be the coven's election. Reg was sure that wouldn't be taking place for a few more weeks, though none of the warlocks had ever given her a firm date. She thought it was still up in the air. Or maybe that was the news. That a date had been set and the count-down had begun.

Jessup reached across the table to grasp Reg's arm, as if she needed comfort. Reg fought the urge to jerk her arm back. Jessup didn't intend to harm Reg, and her feelings would be hurt if Reg had responded that way.

"It's not what he did," Jessup explained. "It's what happened to him."

"Oh." Reg relaxed. She pulled gently back from Jessup and pretended she needed both hands to lift her cup to her lips for a forti-fying sip of coffee. Corvin wasn't dead, or Jessup wouldn't have suggested that Corvin might have told Reg what had happened himself. "Well, what is it? What happened?"

"Someone broke into his house last night and tried to kill him."

CHAPTER FIVE

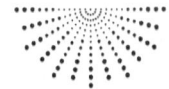

*I*t was a good thing that Reg wasn't eating breakfast or she would definitely have choked on it.

"Somebody tried to kill Corvin?" she repeated in disbelief.

"Yes. Crazy, huh?"

"Tried to kill him how?" Reg was finding it difficult to catch her breath, and her heart beat rapidly in her chest, making her feel like she was going to have a heart attack. Or maybe just faint. "What exactly happened?"

"He was stabbed in the chest," Jessup informed her with relish. "Whoever did it was not going halfway. No covert poisoning or trying to make it look like some kind of accident. They actually broke into Hunter's house and stabbed him while he slept."

"That's crazy. But he's okay?" She wasn't sure how Corvin could have survived being stabbed in the chest while he slept. His attacker must have been really inept, or he hadn't been as bold as Jessup assumed and had pulled back at the last moment.

"He's in the hospital, but I don't think they'll keep him very long. He didn't look like he intended to stay there very long, whether they plan to release him or not. He's bandaged up, and there is no damage to his heart." Jessup took a sip of her coffee. "Bet you thought he didn't even have a heart."

17

Reg knew that Jessup meant it as a joke, but she had been only too aware of Corvin's heartbeat on more than one occasion. When they drew too close together and, overwhelmed by his charms, Reg just wanted to curl up in his arms and put her ear against his chest, listening to the thudding of his heart.

And when Reg's siren instincts were triggered and she could hear and smell the blood pulsing through the arteries in his throat, making her mouth water.

She tried to tear herself away from both images. Forcing a smile, she raised her brows and agreed with Jessup. "Yeah, who would have thought? I thought his kind was born without hearts."

What would it feel like to prey on the weak if he let himself feel compassion for them? He couldn't let himself. He must have to hold himself separate from everyone else, acknowledging that they were different from him in order to attack and satisfy his needs without guilt.

"What about his lungs?" Reg asked, her fingers tapping on her coffee cup, trying to mask the sudden burst of restless energy and overwhelming desire to see Corvin for herself to ensure that he was okay. "And other organs? Everything was okay?"

"There was lung damage, but the doctors patched him up and said that he'll heal up just fine as long as he takes it easy and follows their instructions."

"Are they sure? Do they know how old he is?"

"Well," Jessup chuckled. "We can't exactly tell non-practitioners his real age, if he even knows what it is. But they can see what kind of shape his physical body is in, and it has been well preserved through the years."

"Do *you* know how old he is?"

Jessup shook her head. "Hard to even guess. And he's certainly never told me directly. Having heard him talk about historical events that he witnessed, certainly over a hundred. Probably a couple of centuries, at least."

"And he and Sarah were never a thing?"

"A couple, you mean?" Jessup grinned and shook her head. "Not that I know of. I know Sarah tolerates him, but she's old school. She doesn't think that letting his kind operate as part of our society is a good idea."

"No," Reg agreed. "It's not. It's definitely not."

Jessup tilted her head, giving Reg a bemused smile. "I'm sort of surprised to hear you say that, when you and Hunter seem to always be so involved with each other. I know you're not exactly dating, but you guys are always together. I would think that you would be on the other side of the fence. That they are just like anyone else and should be allowed free association with the rest of society."

Reg wondered briefly what life in Black Sands would have been like without Corvin Hunter. Would she have been bored? Would she be just like any other person, or any other psychic, just going about her daily business without the stress of someone like Corvin hanging around her and trying to steal her powers? Would she have grown as much as she had in her powers and figured out who and what she was if it weren't for the challenges that Corvin threw up in her way? Would she have been able to help all of the people she had without Corvin there to help her? How many times had she pulled from his powers when she hadn't been strong enough to defeat an opponent herself? Or how many times had he helped her when her power had been overwhelming and gotten away from her?

What would life have been like without Corvin around?

They weren't friends, exactly. They were much closer to being enemies. But she had a connection with him that could never be severed because of the powers and consciousness that they had shared in the past. Their lives were way too wrapped up in each other now for them to completely separate. Even now, she was worrying about what had happened to him, thinking of him lying in his hospital bed, and she wasn't doing a particularly good job at keeping herself from reaching out to him through that channel of consciousness that they shared to find out how he was really feeling and what he was thinking.

"Does he know who attacked him?" she asked Jessup.

Jessup blinked at her and Reg realized that she had changed the subject rather abruptly. But she didn't want to talk about her relationship with Corvin and what exactly they were to each other. It might make good girl talk, but she wasn't girl friends with Jessup yet. And she didn't want to share those things. Her connection with Corvin wasn't just an intimate one. It wasn't like she was trying to decide whether to go out with him or get engaged. The "it's complicated" label for relationships on social media seemed more than apt.

"He says he has no idea who it was," Jessup said slowly. "Of course, whether or not you believe that is up to you. I'm taking it with a grain of salt. I can't imagine there are hordes of people who would break into his house and kill him. Not like that. There may be a mob with torches and pitchforks at his door sometime in the future, but I think that the number of people who would make an attempt like this is pretty small."

"He didn't get a look at the attacker?"

Jessup shook her head. "It was dark and he had a knife in his chest. He had just woken up and was disoriented. Not a good situation for making an eyewitness identification. He couldn't even say whether it was a man or a woman."

Was it Reg's imagination, or was Jessup looking at her differently? Considering whether Reg could have been Corvin's attacker. She certainly had motive, when she considered all that Corvin had done to her over the past year. But why would she wait until now to try to kill him?

"I didn't do it," Reg told her evenly. "I was at home all night. With clients and then asleep."

"What time was your last appointment?"

"Midnight." Reg could argue that it was none of Jessup's business but, even if she didn't answer, Jessup would have a pretty good idea anyway. Midnight was almost always the time of Reg's last appointment, because that was the best time to hold a seance.

"How long did it go?"

Reg shrugged. "I probably got to bed around three. I don't remember what time everyone left. And then I slept until a few minutes ago. You know I don't normally get up this early." Reg sipped her coffee concoction.

"Which makes me wonder why you are up already," Jessup commented. She didn't say it like an accusation, but Reg didn't like it anyway. This was why it was so hard to have a law enforcement officer as a friend. Reg didn't appreciate the mix of friendliness and suspicion. She shouldn't have to give a friend an alibi or explanation. And if Jessup was just a police detective and not Reg's friend, she shouldn't have to sit there having coffee with her pretending otherwise.

"Can Corvin have visitors?"

Jessup gave her a blank look.

"At the hospital. Is he allowed to have visitors? Do you think they would let me see him?"

"I'm sure they would. Even if it wasn't normal, Corvin could charm them into letting you do whatever he wanted you to."

Reg nodded. She wanted to put an end to the interview but didn't want to just get up and walk away. She wanted to sit there alone a bit longer and drink her coffee, but not to have to talk to Jessup. She made a point of looking at the time on the front of her phone. "But I'm holding you up. I should let you get back to work now."

Jessup gave her a wry look, then, shaking her head, stood up. "Well, it was nice chatting with you. Say 'hi' to Hunter for me."

CHAPTER SIX

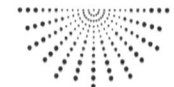

*R*eg told herself that she wasn't going to the hospital to see Corvin. She had just been asking Jessup about visiting out of idle curiosity. She would finish her coffee and then head back home and get started on her day. Since she was up, she might as well do some housecleaning. And she might sit in the garden for a while again to relax with nature and talk to Forst if he was around. She found it very soothing to sit in the beautiful garden, so full of lush, perfect growth. It helped reduce her general anxiety level and focus on the important things in her life.

For the first time in her life, she wasn't scrounging for money and had a permanent address. While it was a big relief, the consequences weren't all positive. She also found her anxiety ramping up for no reason. Things had never been easy for her so, whenever it was quiet, she worried about what was just around the corner and dreaded whatever evil was coming next. And she didn't have any hobbies, so there was a hole in her life when she was left with time on her hands and didn't know what to do with it.

She had partially filled that hole with Starlight, friendships, and lots of streaming videos. But she needed more healthy, productive stuff to do. Sitting meditating in the garden. Cleaning her house. Shopping at the store like a normal person. There wasn't anything to fix up in the house or the yard, so those pastimes were out, but she needed to find productive ways to fill the void so she didn't go crazy.

Or any crazier than she already was. Sometimes she wondered if her entire stay in Black Sands might have been a hallucination.

So even though she told herself that she wasn't going to the hospital like Jessup thought she was, she knew in the back of her mind that she was eventually going to end up there. Maybe if she put it off long enough, Corvin would no longer be at the hospital. They could run into each other somewhere else instead, and she could ask him casually about the attack that she had just happened to hear about.

By the time she finished her coffee and got back into her car, Reg knew that she wasn't going home to clean the house or sit in the garden with nothing to think about but her own circular thoughts. The nose of the car oriented itself toward the hospital, and she just followed its lead, eventually ending up in a parking lot with a few slots still available, close to the Black Sands hospital.

Black Sands wasn't a big city. But the hospital wasn't a tiny, single-story rest home that called itself a hospital, as she had seen in other small towns. It was a short, squat little building, a few stories high, built of plain gray concrete that made it look more like a prison than anything else. There was a knot in Reg's stomach as she climbed out of her car and approached the main doors. She did not like prisons. And she didn't like hospitals either. She had been held prisoner in enough of them that the differences between one kind of institution and the other was negligible in her mind.

"I'm here to see Corvin Hunter," Reg told the receptionist at the front desk with Information hanging over it in big letters.

The nurse looked her over. "I'm sorry, but we can't give out any information about patients."

"I just want to visit him. You have visiting hours, don't you?" It was the middle of the morning, certainly not too early or too late for a hospital visit.

"I can't tell you anything about him."

"Can you just point me in the right direction?"

She shook her head. "You will have to get that information from the patient himself. I can't give it out."

Reg looked again at the ironic letters above the desk. *Information.* "What if he is unconscious?"

The nurse shook her head. "Are you his next of kin?"

Reg toyed with the idea of saying that she was. But she didn't want to end up in the situation where everyone thought that she and Corvin were either related or a couple. That would be just the kind of news that would be bound to spread through a small town like Black Sands.

"No. But he doesn't have any relatives in town. I'm the only person here."

The only person? What, the only person who knew him? Who was friends with him? Who wanted to visit him? Reg had no idea who else might have stopped by to see him, other than the police.

"I'm sorry. If you're his next of kin, the doctor will be in touch with you." The nurse ignored the fact that Reg had already said that she was not the next of kin.

"How can the doctor do that if he doesn't know who I am?"

The receptionist rolled her eyes and sighed. "If you would like to leave your information here with me, I'll make sure that the appropriate person gets it."

Sure, she would.

Reg raised her brows and waited. The receptionist slid a small piece of paper and stubby pencil across the counter to her. Reg wrote down her information.

"Who would that be? What is his doctor's name?"

The nurse looked at her like she was crazy and there was no need for her to know that.

"I have to know the doctor's name so I know whether to answer the phone or not," Reg pointed out.

"You can just answer it if it is a name that you don't know. Or the hospital's name."

"You've obviously never been stalked."

The woman's neatly penciled eyebrows rose up into her fringe of bangs. "I beg your pardon?"

"I can't just answer any call that comes through on my phone. It could be the guy who is stalking me. I never know when he might call me or what number he might call from. I only answer calls if I know who it is."

"Then you can let it go through and he can leave you a message. Then you can call him back."

Reg was starting to get very irritated with the nurse, who seemed to have an answer to everything. All she wanted was to see Corvin. What was the problem with that?

"I don't have voicemail," Reg said precisely. "I don't want him to leave me any more threatening or lewd messages. Would you want to listen to that? I need to know the name of the doctor so that I can answer the phone when he calls me."

With a deep sigh, the nurse tapped a key to bring her sleeping computer to life. "What's the patient's name?"

"Corvin Hunter."

The receptionist clearly knew Corvin's name. Reg immediately felt a blossoming of warmth as the woman thought of him. At some point in his visit to the hospital, she had clearly run into him, and he had managed to charm her despite his injury. As the woman looked up Corvin's information on the computer, Reg could feel a thread of something else from her. Anger? Jealousy? Probably jealousy. If Reg were holding herself out as the only person who cared about Corvin enough to come and see him at the hospital, the nurse would see her as a rival for his affections.

Since the woman's mind was already open far enough for Reg to sense these emotions from her, Reg closed her eyes and stretched out her senses further to see what else she could find out when Corvin's admittance information came up on the screen.

"That would be Dr. Green," the nurse said crisply. "And that's all of the information I can give you."

"Is that what it will say on his caller ID?"

"I don't know. I am not his secretary."

"Could it be the name of his unit? What is his specialty?"

"If you see the name of a medical unit or specialty on your phone, you'll know who it is."

Reg leveled a glare at the woman, holding it for an uncomfortably long time and waiting for her to break down and give Reg the information she needed.

"He is a pulmonary specialist."

"Thank you. I appreciate your help," Reg told her sweetly. "And which way is the cafeteria from here?"

The nurse pointed to one of the hallways and indicated the sign on the wall. "Just follow the signs."

At least she could share *some* kind of information.

Reg nodded and headed off down the hall. Once she turned into another hallway that was out of the view of the so-called Information desk, she looked at the other signs on the wall and hanging down overhead. Pulmonary. If she found a unit that had the word pulmonary in it, she would be bound to find Corvin.

CHAPTER SEVEN

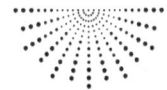

*A*s it turned out, all of Reg's subterfuge and attempt at mind reading were completely unnecessary. She looked around for an elevator, sure that all of the patient rooms would be on the upper floors, and painstakingly looked through the unit names on the board inside the elevator, trying to find Pulmonary as the elevator rose to the top floor.

But once she was up there, she could feel Corvin. The pull toward him was as strong as ever. Maybe even stronger. Maybe because he had been hurt or was on medication, he was not able to mask his mind from her as much as usual. Reg followed the pull like a dog following a scent in the air, through several turns of the corridor, until she walked into the unit. She didn't bother to talk to the nurses at the nursing station to see if she was right or ask how Corvin was doing, but started walking around the loop, looking for Corvin's name by the door.

Apparently, they didn't do names by the door anymore. Another casualty of the need to keep everything about a patient confidential. Go a little further, and pretty soon, the doctors themselves wouldn't be allowed to know a patient's name, and everyone would have to be treated under anonymous numbers. Everyone in the hospital would be a John or Jane Doe.

But of course, she didn't need a name by the door. As soon as she approached the room Corvin was in, she felt a flood of warmth and there was a certain electricity in the air. She didn't even have to peek inside to ensure that it was Corvin. She just marched through the door and looked for him.

There was the familiar strong jaw defined by a short dark beard, his glimmering eyes, and wavy hair a little tousled with sleep. There was a slight bulge under his hospital johnny where his chest was heavily bandaged. Corvin lay on his back, his arms beside him, fingers tapping in irritation. There was a television screen on the wall opposite the bed, but he seemed to be annoyed by it rather than entertained, as if it were playing a children's cartoon instead of something that he would be interested in. What *was* Corvin interested in? Did he even watch TV when he was at home alone? Usually, when Reg connected with him, either by phone or just by reaching out her thoughts to see what he was doing, he was studying or chopping herbs or some other warlocky activity. She wasn't sure he even owned a television.

Corvin turned his head as Reg walked into the room. The anxious look on his face melted away, and he smiled at her warmly, sending out waves of heat and the heady rose smell of his pheromones.

"Regina," he said in a low, throbbing voice.

Reg tried to breathe shallowly to avoid being affected by him. She approached his bed and sat down on a hard visitor chair a few feet away.

"You'd better lay off the charms, or I'm not going to be able to stay here."

"You look lovely."

Reg studied his face. His expression was open, adoring, and he seemed like he was far away. She looked at the bag of clear fluid in the IV bag that hung from a pole beside him and wondered what they had given him.

"You're high," she informed him, shaking her head. "I assume they're keeping you comfortable."

"Very comfortable, now that you're here," he assured her. "Will you stay with me?"

Reg laughed. "I will visit with you for a little while. But you have to back off on the pheromones, or I will be just as drunk as you are."

"That would be charming," he told her, still in that low, throaty voice.

Reg tried to find a comfortable position in the hard chair and redirected the conversation. "Jessup said that you were attacked last night. What happened?"

"Marta was here," he remembered.

"Yes. I imagine she was. She said that you couldn't describe the person who had attacked you, though."

Corvin raised his hands and rubbed at his eyes with the heels of his hands. "No." His brows drew down. "Why would anyone attack me? In the middle of the night? It doesn't make any sense."

"Well... if they wanted to kill you, it's best to do it while there aren't a bunch of eyewitnesses around," Reg pointed out.

"Why would anyone want to kill me?"

"I would guess that it's because of the election. Someone in your coven doesn't want you to take up leadership of the group."

"No... that's not it."

Reg shook her head. "Why not?"

"There isn't that much opposition to me being elected. And if there is, people can vote against it. There wouldn't be any reason to... assassinate me."

"But the neophytes, the young men in the coven, they can't vote against you. It's up to just your core group. And it doesn't have to be unanimous. You only need six people voting for you. Everybody else could be against it, as long as you had six votes."

"Why would anyone kill me for that? Like Davyn told you before, it isn't a position of power. It is about spiritual leadership. If someone doesn't think I'm providing what they need... they can go to another coven. Or wait until someone else takes over after me. Or get a mentor. There are many different ways for them to find a spiritual leader other than me if they don't feel comfortable coming to me or don't like my philosophy or ideas."

Reg shrugged. But she was pretty sure that it was just as she had said—he was being targeted because he was trying to take over the coven and someone didn't like it. Maybe it was someone who thought that they should be elected—only no one other than Corvin and Davyn had thrown their hats into the ring, so Reg didn't think it was that. Maybe it was someone who was afraid of Corvin and his abilities and didn't think that he should be allowed to be elected. Until recent changes had been made to the group's rules, someone with Corvin's gift or affliction could not lead a coven. A lot of people had been against someone so predatory being in a position of trust and authority over the group. Even if Davyn and Corvin did say that it was actually an opportunity for service.

Destine had certainly thought that it was a position of power. And he had shared Corvin's brain.

Reg watched Corvin for a minute, considering his aura and the feelings she was getting from him. He had apparently been able to pull back on his charms despite being medicated, and the smell of roses had slowly faded. She studied the bump under his robe. The left side of his chest. As Jessup had said, someone had been committed to killing him. It wasn't just a half-hearted attempt. The stab wound had not been deep enough, or maybe had glanced off of his ribs. Maybe he had woken up and moved as the attempt was made.

Corvin was watching Reg.

"How do you feel?" Reg asked. "Is it painful?"

"Not bad. But I don't know how much medication they have me on. It feels… like it's bruised. But also like it's very deep. I've had superficial cuts before, but nothing that has felt like it went right down into my middle."

"Does it hurt to breathe?"

"Everything hurts right now. But not unbearable. And they keep telling me that I'm not allowed to sit up or get out of bed. I guess they're afraid I'm going to tear out the stitches or do something too strenuous before my body is ready." He rubbed his forehead. "I would rather be at home in bed. I would be much more comfortable there."

"But you'd have to get up to do that. If it's that dangerous to be up and around, you can't go home."

"*You* could take me home."

"Not if you can't sit or stand," Reg pointed out.

"Yes, you could."

"Oh." Of course, Corvin was right. She was still a beginner, but she had learned how to *call* someone to her or *port* herself or someone else to another location. She could *probably* transport Corvin from the hospital bed to his own bed without his having to sit or stand. But she couldn't be sure. She hadn't worked on that kind of specificity, and sometimes the people she called seemed to just fall out of the sky into a random location nearby. It wouldn't do Corvin much good if, instead of transporting him safely to his bed, she dumped him unceremoniously in the middle of his floor. "Well... I might miss. You wouldn't like it if I dropped you."

"You seem to have pretty good control if you are holding on to someone." He gave her a slow, languorous look. "You could come with me to my bed."

Reg laughed briefly. "You think it is going to be that easy to get me into your bed?"

He chuckled, then held his hand over his chest, wincing. "I'm not sure I could actually do anything right now. It might be the safest time for you to end up there."

But she was sure it wouldn't take much effort for him to overwhelm her with pheromones and to convince her to give up her powers yet again.

If she let down her guard.

But she wasn't going to let that happen.

She frowned, thinking about his house. Would she be able to transport into his house? She had been there before, and she assumed that if she were porting there with Corvin's permission, she wouldn't have any problems with whatever wards and spells he had safeguarding his home. But if she didn't have his permission, she wouldn't be able to get past them, would she?

And yet... someone had.

CHAPTER EIGHT

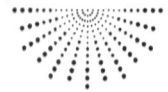

*H*ow did they get into your house?" she asked Corvin.
"Broke in."

"But how? You must have wards to protect yourself."

Corvin nodded, scowling. "Yes. I'm not sure how someone could get past them. That is a problem."

"There can't be that many people who are more powerful than you. Not at this point."

"No." Corvin considered Reg, studying her closely. "You might rival me. But not very many others would."

"Me? I'm not that strong. Not when you have the Witch Doctor's powers."

"I am not able to fully access them yet. More and more, but not everything. And you... who knows how many of Weston's powers you may have inherited?"

Reg didn't like to think of the possibility that Weston was her father and that she had inherited anything from the powerful immortal. Reg had grown up without biological parents, at least after her mother had been killed. Even when her mother had been alive, Norma Jean had done little to support and provide for Reg. Having grown up without them in her life, Reg didn't like the idea of having a father. Especially one who knew who she was. She didn't want anything from him. Not his protection or his powers or anything else she might have inherited from him. The gifts she had could be attributed to her mother, Norma Jean. Weston didn't have to figure into it. In mythology, immortals created or begat progeny through other means, not always reproducing in the way humans did. He might not have been in a human form when he had formed Reg. She might not carry any of his genes. If immortals had genes.

She pushed this to the side and focused on what she had come there for. Not to talk about her heritage, but to see how Corvin was and find out about the attack. The police were already investigating, but they were, for the most part, non-practitioners, and they wouldn't consider things like how Corvin's magical wards had been defeated. They would look for fingerprints on whatever door or window had been broken into or for a knife of a particular shape. That was not going to lead them to Corvin's potential killer. Any half-intelligent human would have thought to wear gloves and dispose of the weapon after it was used.

"Do you have any enemies?"

"There are people who don't like me or don't approve of me," Corvin admitted with a shrug. "My kind has always been discriminated against because of our affliction."

"And there are all of the people you have taken the powers from until now."

Corvin shrugged as if there were no point in even considering this possibility. "Those people would not be able to make it past my wards," he pointed out, raising his eyebrows. "They don't have any powers."

"Oh. Well, yeah, there's that."

"And if they don't like me being here in Black Sands… then why come here? I have lived here for many years. They can buy a house or rent somewhere else. They don't have to move into my neighborhood."

"What about the other members of your coven?"

"This was not done by someone in my coven."

"How do you know that? You didn't recognize them."

"Exactly. If it had been someone from my coven, I would have recognized him."

"Even though you were woken up in the middle of the night from a sound sleep, and the room was dark."

"Yes," Corvin insisted. "I know the other warlocks in the coven. Whether I saw them or not, I would have known who it was. I can feel them. I know… their powers, their auras. Their minds."

"I thought you weren't supposed to read people or intrude on their minds without their permission."

"Of course not." He tried for an innocent look, but he just looked sly. "I can't help it if people are open to me. And when you practice the craft with people… they have to be open. By following these rituals together, we make ourselves vulnerable. We open ourselves up to each other. I can't help reading people when they offer themselves up to me."

Reg tried, but failed, to suppress a shudder. The thought of Corvin being able to enter the minds of each of the warlocks in his coven at a whim was more than disturbing. How was anyone going to be able to prevent him from being elected to the leadership of the coven when their intentions were all open to him?

That was just the trouble. They weren't going to keep him from anything.

And maybe that was why the only feasible recourse had been to kill him.

But if the intended killer was a member of Corvin's coven, why hadn't he recognized them when they attacked him?

Or maybe he had. Maybe Corvin was lying to Jessup and lying to Reg. Maybe he knew very well who it was that had attacked him and was just biding his time until he was able to be released from the hospital and take his revenge on the attacker.

A nurse bustled into the room, smiling in Corvin's direction. When she saw Reg visiting him, the smile was quickly replaced by a scowl.

"I didn't see you come in here," she said accusingly. "Mr. Hunter needs his rest. You should go."

Reg looked at Corvin. "He's been just fine. It is visiting hours, isn't it?"

"He has suffered a very traumatic injury. He needs plenty of rest if he is going to recover from it. You've been in here for long enough."

The nurse didn't even know how long Reg had been in there before she had come in. Reg rolled her eyes. "Okay. I'll leave in a minute. Do you mind giving me a minute of privacy to say goodbye?"

She looked like she would argue, but couldn't come up with a good reason not to let Reg have a private moment with Corvin before leaving. "I'll be right back," she said, her mouth a thin, straight line. "So please be quick about it."

"I will."

The nurse reluctantly left again. Corvin turned his gaze from her to Reg.

"A minute of privacy?" he repeated dryly. "Do I dare hope that you are finally succumbing to my charms?"

"Not a chance," Reg said brusquely. "But I thought if I have tired you out..." She reached both hands toward Corvin's bandaged chest and held them over him, close to the surface but not touching. She focused on pushing warmth into him. She wasn't a healer by nature, but Davyn had shown her that she could help someone recover faster if she transferred some of her energy and the heat from her fire into them. She had helped Starlight that way when he had been sick. And she had helped to heal Calliopia, once they were able to remove the impediment to her recovery. It was becoming easier for her, just as handling and controlling her fire during her mentoring sessions with Davyn was.

Corvin closed his eyes, making a comfortable, murmuring sound. The process certainly wasn't hurting him.

Reg guarded her powers carefully, making sure that he couldn't take hold of the energy she was transferring to him and take more than she intended to give him. Corvin's body relaxed.

"Have a good sleep," Reg told him. "You'll be out of here in no time. They'll be amazed at your quick recovery."

Corvin made a noise of agreement and didn't open his eyes. Reg withdrew her hands and left before the nurse could return and ask what she thought she was doing.

CHAPTER NINE

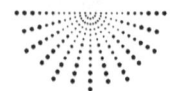

*R*eg was a little tired going home, having given a good amount of her strength to Corvin in the heat transfer. She stopped at the cafeteria before leaving the hospital and purchased a bottle of water to help to replenish herself. Even though she hadn't used her fire directly, Davyn had drilled into her always to keep herself hydrated when she was using her firecaster powers, or she would end up with something akin to heat exhaustion. She didn't want to end up unable to meet with her clients or reach the spirits.

It seemed like a good time to sit beside the pond, drinking her water and refreshing her mood.

There seemed to be unfamiliar sounds in the garden today. Rustling in the undergrowth. Or maybe it was just that the birds were not singing as much and she could hear more from the other creatures that lived in the garden, hiding from human sight. She knew about the elves and had met some of them, but she knew there were other creatures in the garden too. Forst didn't seem inclined to tell her much about the creatures she was too blind to see. In her mind, she saw the sad shake of Ruan's head as he called her, "oh, blind one."

Reg found herself spending more and more time there. It seemed to help her to stay focused and centered. Not something that she had ever worried about before coming to Black Sands. Her concerns had always been with filling her physical needs then. It was hard to think about her mental health if she didn't have enough to eat or somewhere safe to spend the night. She had ignored the voices in her head and the emotions and concerns of everyone around her and had just focused on survival.

Is Reg Rawlins sleeping?

Reg opened her eyes to look at the gnome who had spoken to her in her mind. *Forst, it's nice to see you,* she replied in kind.

He gave a slight bow. While gnomes were not eloquent when forced to use their "outside words" to talk with humans, they were much more communicative when they could rely on their "inside words," the telepathy that they used when communicating with each other.

And nice to see you, Reg Rawlins.

I wasn't sleeping. Reg paused to take a sip of her water, though it occurred to her that the rules about not talking with her mouth full probably did not apply when communicating by telepathy. *I was just thinking. Enjoying this beautiful garden that you've created.*

He smiled, his cheeks growing rosier. He took out the curvy pipe he kept in his pocket, filled it, and lit it. *Forst did not create the garden. A gardener merely helps guide the living things and gives them what they need to grow.*

Well, you do it very well. I've never enjoyed a garden so much before. I never knew how… soothing and restful it could be.

Forst nodded cheerfully. *Humankind do not spend enough time with the living.*

I guess not. We've forgotten our roots.

And your stems and leaves, Forst replied, chuckling aloud.

Reg laughed and watched him blow smoke rings. *Gnomes—gnomen,* she corrected, remembering to use their own designation, *haven't forgotten. They have the right idea.*

Forst nodded. *Gnomen know what is important.*

Reg turned her head at the sound of footsteps on the garden path. Jessup rounded the corner of the cottage, neck stretched out as she peered around the side to see if Reg was around the back. "Oh, there you are!"

"Oh, hi. Have you met—" Reg turned to introduce Forst and Jessup, but Forst was gone, disappearing into the lush growth of the garden. It was hard to believe that he could hide himself so well despite the bright red cap, but it happened often enough that Reg wasn't exactly surprised. "Whoops. He's gone."

Jessup's brows went up as she approached Reg. "Who is gone?"

"Forst. You met Fir before. Forst is his twin."

"Oh, the garden gnomes?"

"Yes." Reg gestured around her. "This is his garden. Or Sarah's garden, I guess, but he is the gardener that tends it, which kind of makes it his."

Jessup nodded. She motioned to the bench. "Do you want to visit out here? Or go inside?"

Reg studied her. "What kind of a visit is this? The kind where I need a lawyer?"

"No!" Jessup laughed and shook her head. "Nothing like that. I just thought... I'd see how you were doing and if you had, uh, talked to Hunter."

"Did I say I was going to visit Corvin?"

"No, but you did go to see him, right?"

Reg nodded.

"Did he tell you anything? Does he suspect anyone in particular of the attack?"

"Why don't you ask him?"

"I would, but he wasn't in that great of shape when I saw him. He said that he didn't know who it was, but I think he might be lying about that. And I couldn't question him for very long. They had to take him in to surgery."

"He's doing okay now. Looking pretty good. It's obvious that he's being medicated, but he seemed pretty strong. Not like he'd lost a whole bunch of blood. The pain was controlled."

"That's good." Jessup nodded. "I've talked to his doctor but haven't made it over there to talk to him again. And I figured things would go better for your visit if I wasn't there at the same time trying to get information out of him. He isn't always the most cooperative person."

Reg snorted. "I don't think Corvin knows the meaning of the word cooperative."

"So, did he give you any information, or even any impressions, about who it might have been? A known enemy? Someone who has sent him threats?"

"No. I thought maybe it was someone from the coven who doesn't want him to be elected leader. Maybe one of the neophytes who doesn't have any say in how the voting goes."

Jessup nodded. She pulled out her notepad and jotted a few things down. "And what did he have to say about that?"

Reg shrugged. "He said no. That he would have recognized the aura of another warlock from his coven, even if he didn't see them."

"And do you think he was telling the truth?"

Reg hesitated. "I don't really know. I think he was telling the truth as much as he knows it, but maybe he doesn't realize how upset some of the warlocks are about him running for leadership. And maybe it isn't a warlock that he has had a lot to do with. I can understand him being able to recognize the people he's with a lot. But if it is someone who is fairly new and who has held back when they were doing their rituals, whatever they are, maybe he wouldn't. I don't know. I'm not any kind of an expert."

"Yeah. We should probably still explore that possibility."

"Good luck with that." Reg thought about the members of the coven she had met while Davyn was missing. They hadn't been particularly helpful. She paused. "It was the younger members that I felt objected to Corvin becoming leader of the coven. I had thought that it would be the older warlocks, the old guard, because they would be set in their traditional ways and not want anything to change. Especially something like that. Changing major rules that were there for the protection of the coven." Reg shook her head. "I still can't understand why they would do that."

Davyn had suggested that it might be greed. The opportunity for the coven to share in the gifts that Corvin had. It was one thing to have him in their coven, but if he were the warlock they looked to for spiritual advice and support, they would be able to directly access him and his powers.

Jessup's phone rang. She pulled it partway out of her shirt pocket to look at it, then slid it back into place. "Sorry about that."

Reg had a sudden wave of vertigo that nearly made her fall off the bench. She grabbed at the bench and at Jessup to keep herself upright, trying to steady herself.

"Whoa, are you okay? What's wrong?"

Reg winced at the clamor of voices suddenly shouting in her head. "You should answer that." She gasped for breath, trying to get her equilibrium back. "It's important."

Jessup shook her head. "It's my dad. He knows that if I don't answer the phone, I'm working. I'll call him back when I get home."

Reg couldn't control her own body and voice. She struggled to push out the new spirit who had decided that it had the right to channel through Reg's body, but it was too strong and had taken her off guard. It had been a long time since she had been taken unaware like that. She could feel her face changing, morphing under the ghost's control. Her mouth opened.

"Marta Angelica Jessup, you answer that phone now!"

Jessup stared at Reg, her jaw hanging open and eyes popping. "What?"

"Don't you ignore your father when he's trying to get ahold of you. You need to answer that call now!"

Jessup pulled the phone out of her pocket and swiped to accept the call, her eyes still fixed on Reg. "Dad?"

The voice on the other end of the phone was loud, as if Jessup had put him on speakerphone, but she had not. Reg had experienced hyperacute hearing before, and it wasn't fun. It was like there was suddenly someone with a loudspeaker talking in her ear.

"Marta." The man's voice was hoarse and broken. "Marta, I've been trying to get you."

"What's wrong? Dad? What's going on?"

"She's gone, honey. Your mom. She's... she's passed away."

"What?" Jessup's voice rose in shock and disbelief. "Are you kidding me? How could mom be dead?"

"I'm sorry, sweetie. It happened last night. That's... when we found her." Reg's sense of the man on the other end of the phone was so clear that she could see the horror and grief on his face. "She…" the words clogged his throat and he was unable to finish the sentence. Jessup waited for him to explain what had happened.

"Where are you?" Jessup demanded. "I'll come to you."

"We're here in town, Marta. At the old house. We were looking at selling it. We were here to clear up some of the things that were still there. Get it ready. I guess… it was too much for her, being back here."

Jessup looked at her watch. "I'll be there in a few minutes. Stay there."

Reg highly doubted that Jessup's father was going to go anywhere. He sounded utterly broken.

Jessup hung up. She looked at Reg, her eyes still comically wide, as they had been when Reg had channeled the spirit. "What just happened?"

Reg motioned toward Jessup's phone. "Your dad…"

"I know what he said. But what… what was it you just did?"

"We'll talk about it later. You need to go to him now. Don't worry about me."

Jessup stood up from the bench. "Are you sure you're okay? I thought you were going to pass out for a minute there. Do you want me to walk you into the cottage?"

"Well…" Reg didn't want to make Jessup take any longer to get to her father. But she wasn't sure she would be able to make it on her own either. "Umm… just to the door. I'll be fine once I'm inside."

Jessup studied her carefully for a moment. She held out her hand and helped Reg to stand, then put her arm around Reg's shoulders and walked her slowly down the path, around the corner, to the front door. It was unlocked. Or at least, it unlocked when Reg put her hand on the doorknob.

"Are you sure? You'll be okay? I can walk you to your bed or couch, or get Sarah to help out?"

"No. Go to your dad. That's where you need to be right now."

CHAPTER TEN

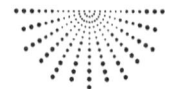

*R*eg was relieved when Jessup was gone. Some of the anger and disappointment Reg had felt went with her. But she could still feel the ghost of Jessup's mother with her, hear her voice as she tried to figure out what was going on. Reg staggered a little in her walk over to the couch.

"Starlight, come here," she called.

Normally, she would have told Starlight what she wanted to make sure that he would agree with her chosen course of action and hopefully help throw his psychic strength in with hers to help her do whatever she had to do. But she didn't have the words today. It was all she could do to get to the couch and sit down.

Starlight apparently sensed the urgency in her voice or could feel that something was wrong. Instead of being stubborn and needing to be called several times or coaxed, she heard him immediately jump down from the bed or windowsill in the bedroom. He marched up to her, meowing several times in query.

"Come here." Reg patted her lap.

He jumped up. Reg combed her fingers through his fur, needing his sense of calm and confidence that everything would work out just as it was supposed to.

"This is all a bit much," Reg whispered to him, breathing in deeply, holding her breath for a few seconds, and then breathing out again. "I need your help. Jessup's mother… it has thrown me all off-balance."

Maybe it was hearing someone else's mother giving orders, when usually she just had to deal with her own mother, Norma Jean. Maybe it was just that the spirit was so strong, so green, having only passed over the night before.

Reg should have found out her name before she had made Jessup leave. But then, maybe she didn't want to call the ghost by her name, which would serve to strengthen her and her connection to Reg.

"We need to calm her down. Do you think you can help me with this?"

Starlight purred. Reg felt comforted, despite the heebie-jeebies she was getting from the anxious ghost. She continued to rub and scratch Starlight, making sure that he was relaxed and comfortable and that their connection was as strong as possible.

She had left her crystal ball on the coffee table the last time she had used it rather than putting it back in its place on the shelf so, luckily, she didn't have to get up to get it. She didn't need the crystal to communicate with the ghost, but sometimes it was better to have a strong visual connection. Ghosts weren't always very good at expressing what it was they wanted. Language and emotions got garbled. Confused ghosts most often reverted to anger and trying to affect things in their physical environment, which could be very dangerous with one as strong as Jessup's mother.

Reg stared into the crystal. "Jessup's mother," she said in a calm, low voice. "Marta's mother, I mean. I am here. I am listening."

Trying to keep her attention focused on the mother's ghost was like trying to follow the path of a ball in a pinball machine as it bounced from one obstruction to another, filling the room with noises and flashes of light.

"Calm down. I'm here. I can hear you. Tell me what's going on."

That didn't seem to be what the ghost needed to hear.

"Or tell me what you need to know," Reg tried. "Do you have questions?"

Where is he? The discordant voice came to her as if blasted into her ear. *He must pay for what he has done. For what has happened to all of us over the past thirty years.*

"I'll help if I can," Reg assured her. "Who is it? What did he do to you?"

He ruined our lives. Everything was fine until he came around. Then... he ruined everything. I tried for decades to try to overcome the damage he did.

"And now, you've come to me," Reg said. "What can I do for you? Who is it you are seeking?"

There were flashes of memories, the images moving too quickly and too fractured for Reg to be able to make any sense of them. She tried to keep herself separate from them. Not to be drawn into them.

"Can you slow down? Calm down. I'm listening."

There was little she could make out from the memories, other than a deep sense of dread in the pit of her stomach. There was something terrifying out there. Something dark and predatory that had affected Mrs. Jessup's life for so many years.

Reg's first thought was the sense of dark foreboding she had experienced when the Witch Doctor had moved into town and started raising draugrs, a sort of a zombie creature, from the dead. Was it a draugr that had frightened Mrs. Jessup? Or one of the immortals? Reg had no idea what the immortals she knew had been doing around that time. It would have been while Reg was very young, maybe when Weston had hidden himself away so the other immortals could not find him and punish him for having brought Reg into being. It had been long before the Witch Doctor started operating in Black Sands. Who knew where he had been or what he had been doing then. Harrison had been protecting Reg at least part of the time, trying to keep her from any harm.

It *might* have been one of the immortals. Or someone else who had raised a draugr. Either one would explain Mrs. Jessup's terror and how the experience had continued to affect her for so long.

"Was it this?" Reg tried to build a vivid picture of the draugrs she had seen, both visual and reflecting the sense of dread that they had caused in her.

There was a crash as several objects went flying off of Reg's shelves. Actually, they weren't Reg's things, but Sarah's. Reg had never bought very much by way of decorating the cottage. She rented it furnished and had not seen the need to buy a bunch of knickknacks to express her own personality. Reg tried to focus on the ghost again, but Mrs. Jessup seemed to have withdrawn from her. Reg didn't know whether that meant the answer to her question was a no or a yes.

CHAPTER ELEVEN

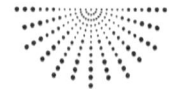

*E*ven though Reg knew she had clients coming later in the evening, she decided she'd better call Jessup and see if everything was okay. Or at least as okay as it could be. She felt the need to apologize for channeling Jessup's mother, even though it had been beyond her control. And she worried that Mrs. Jessup's spirit had gone on to torment her daughter after leaving Reg. Jessup could probably handle a few paranormal phenomena. Even though she was not very gifted herself, she had grown up in a practicing household, so she'd undoubtedly seen the unexpected before. She certainly had during the times she had been with Reg and hadn't expressed shock or horror in those instances. But a raging ghost could be pretty scary for anyone, even someone like Reg, who was used to dealing with restless spirits on a daily basis.

The phone only rang a couple of times before Jessup answered it. Her voice was low and sounded strange. Maybe she had a hand cupped around her mouth and the phone to muffle her voice from whoever was around her. "Reg? Hi, what's up?"

"Nothing from me," Reg assured her. "I just wanted to see how you were doing. Are you okay? Do you need company?"

"Oh." Jessup let out a sigh. "Thanks, that's nice of you. Things have been kind of disrupted here. Word gets around a community like this fast and, even though my family hasn't lived here for a few years, people have been dropping by to offer their condolences. And casseroles. I'm just... I guess I haven't quite taken it all in yet. I'm playing the gracious hostess and telling people how kind they are, and inside, I haven't really processed the fact that she is gone. It's just so unbelievable."

And it would be harder for Jessup to believe if her mother's spirit were still hanging around. She probably wouldn't feel that sense of loss if Mrs. Jessup were nearby, even if Jessup couldn't see or sense her consciously.

"Sorry. Your mom... was she sick? Did something happen? I didn't ask before you left, but I figured you might not know, and it wasn't the time..."

Some of the background noise faded and Jessup's voice became clearer. "Well... Mom hasn't been well for a long time. She's always been fragile, has dealt with a lot of depression. Sometimes serious enough that she had to be hospitalized."

"Oh. That must have been tough."

"It was. As a kid, I couldn't really rely on her being there, and she wasn't the kind of parent who would help with homework or go to parent-teacher interviews. I was kind of on my own. But I have my dad and my older brother, and they did what they could to help and make things easier on me."

"And... was it the depression? Or did something happen?"

"Yeah. She overdosed on pills. By the time anyone found her... it was too late."

"I'm so sorry." Reg had her own experiences with an overdosing mother. Not the same kind of drugs, she assumed. Jessup's mother had probably used prescription drugs, while Reg's had OD'd on street drugs. That was in the other timeline, yet Reg could still remember it. That was the childhood she remembered. Not the one where Norma Jean had survived, but where Reg had been taken from her and put into foster care because Norma Jean was not capable of providing the necessities of life.

Jessup took a deep breath in. Reg expected to hear a sniffle or two, but Jessup had already said she wasn't really feeling the loss yet.

She didn't cry, just breathed and didn't say anything for a long moment.

"Thanks. I appreciate that. I don't know what we're going to do. I guess we'll have to wait until the medical examiner is done with the body and then make arrangements for a funeral or memorial. I don't know whether it will be here or in Miami or if they'll do something in both places. I don't know what she would have wanted. I haven't had much to do with the family since I became a cop and they moved away. I guess Mom and Dad figured that they'd done their duty; I was a grown-up, and they could move on."

"Do you know what it was that happened to your mom to make her like that?"

"Happened?" Jessup's voice was a little surprised. "Nothing. Just one of those things. Some people are more susceptible to mental illness. Genes and all of that."

So Jessup did not know about whatever it was that had happened to her mother that had traumatized her so deeply. She thought it was just brain chemicals. The same as the doctors who had treated Reg had always believed that the voices were hallucinations or psychosis. But hadn't Jessup's family had the benefit of a magical community? People around them who would understand how something paranormal could have affected someone and had lasting effects? Hadn't she had a spiritual leader who could help her understand and deal with what she had gone through? Friends who could reassure her that she wasn't alone?

"But didn't something happen to her when she was younger? Like... thirty years ago?"

"No. Other than me being born. And then my younger brother, William."

"And nothing else that you know of? Some kind of violent attack or traumatic paranormal experience?"

"Uh... no. What are you talking about? Why would you even ask that?"

"Just because... well... I was talking to your mom. After you left. And she was talking about someone she wanted to get back at, and when I tried to find out who or what she was talking about... the images were just too confused. But it seemed like she was attacked at some point or started having nightmares or premonitions..."

"You talked to my mother." Jessup's voice was flat and disbelieving. "How exactly did you talk to my mother?"

"She was there. You know she was there because I channeled her. That wasn't my idea, by the way. I'm sorry about that. I couldn't stop her. New ghosts can be very powerful sometimes. They can do things that ghosts that have been around for longer aren't capable of. And so... after you left to meet with your dad like she told you to, she was really angry. Having a bit of a temper tantrum. And I tried to help her, to find out what was wrong and calm her down."

"I know that you make a lot of money off people who believe in that kind of thing, Reg... but it isn't my thing. I don't believe in ghosts. When people are gone, they're gone."

"You believe in ghosts. You know that I speak with spirits."

"I know that you make money pretending to talk to spirits. But that's not the same thing."

"You were raised in a practicing household," Reg said in disbelief. "How can you not believe in spirits?"

"There's a difference between believing that things can be accomplished through magical or non-traditional means and believing in disembodied spirits. Yes, I know that some people have gifts or powers that others don't have or that mainstream society doesn't accept. But that doesn't mean I have to believe in ghosts or spirits."

Reg was stumped. "But... you took me to the morgue to talk to Nagendra's spirit after he died."

Jessup cleared her throat. "I did that because it was the only thing I could think of that we could do but hadn't. I was willing to... suspend belief to see whether you could gain any new information that way. But I don't think the insight you got was from a spirit. It might have been some kind of metaphysical impression left on the body after death, maybe something that was still stored in his brain, that stays after a person dies that you could still sense. But ghosts? I can't explain everything I've seen, but that doesn't mean I have to accept that ghosts exist. When a person dies, Reg, they die. That's the end of it."

It was an incredibly depressing thought. Reg couldn't imagine living with that kind of outlook on life. That people were just born, lived their lives, and died, and it was over. She had always talked with ghosts and had to deal with the constant voices in her head. She'd had rich encounters with the dead, and it baffled her that anyone could believe they didn't exist.

Did Jessup think that Reg was just a con artist? That she just made everything up?

"Okay... but what about me channeling your mom when your dad called?"

"You just had an impression I should answer the phone. Maybe you could sense my dad's frustration at not being able to get me. So you did what you could to get me to answer it and come deal with him. Anyone could call me by my full name and tell me to answer the phone. Just use a good stern voice." Jessup cleared her throat again. "Most people will obey if you use a commanding voice. Cops do that all the time."

"But I don't know your full name. You never told me your middle name."

"I'm sure we talked about it at some point. It stuck in your brain or came back to you for some reason. That doesn't mean you were channeling my mom's spirit. Just that you knew I should answer the phone. Maybe you sensed my doubts about why he had called several times instead of just waiting for me to call him after work. I was getting worried, so you pushed me to find out why he kept calling."

Reg didn't know what else to say. She just shook her head. "Okay... well... maybe something happened to your mom that you didn't know about. Back around the time you were born, or before that. No one ever told you anything...?"

"No." Jessup sighed. "She was that way as long as I can remember. Mental illness doesn't usually just appear out of the blue. Not in your twenties. Usually, when you are a teenager or even younger. I know that it can happen... people get schizophrenia or have their first depressive episode in their twenties... but usually, there are signs earlier than that."

Jessup had probably read up on it a lot, trying to understand her mother and what was going on with her. Kids did that. Felt guilty for their parents' problems. Tried to figure out how to fix them, even when it wasn't their fault and wasn't fixable.

"What was it like, growing up like that? It must have been hard."

"As I said, Dad and my brother Harker did what they could to help. I had all of the parents I could handle. They were good, but they kind of… smothered me. Didn't want me to take risks. Or grow up. They were never happy about my decision to go into law enforcement. None of them."

"Why?" Reg could understand such a sentiment if Jessup had come from a family of criminals, but it didn't sound like it. Reg thought she had grown up in a pretty normal suburban family.

"There isn't a lot of trust between the magical community and law enforcement," Jessup explained, although Reg had already seen this demonstrated and shouldn't have needed to be told. "Law enforcement thinks that the practitioners are cranks, and the practitioners know that law enforcement won't believe them and that they are just as likely to end up in jail or on a 72-hour hold at some mental institution as they are to get help."

Reg grunted at this. That had certainly been her experience. It was strange to think that it was a common experience among practitioners. She had always seen herself as alone, an outlier—someone without a tribe.

"Were they afraid that you would think your family was crazy? Or that the other cops would think that you were crazy?"

"Neither one, I don't think. Not consciously. There's just this divide between the police and the magical community. They didn't like me crossing that line. I've heard the same thing from others who are practitioners or from practicing families who are drawn into law enforcement. It's a hard thing. It alienates you from your own community."

Reg had heard the same thing from other minorities. Someone would join the police force, hoping to make things better for their own race or culture, only to be considered a traitor by the community they were trying to help.

"And your parents moved after you joined the police? You've been living here on your own ever since?"

"Yep."

"Didn't they want you to stay in their house? If they didn't sell it, I would have thought that they would have wanted someone they knew living in it."

"No… they never asked me to. They've rented it out until now. Then I guess they decided to sell it. Rental properties can be a pain, you know, always having to deal with the upkeep and complaining tenants. When they first moved, I wasn't making very much money and wouldn't have been able to afford the rent that they charged. And they had to charge that to cover the mortgage. Even then, it was a bit of a money pit over the years. I don't know how bad; they didn't share that with me. I just knew that they were often paying more to keep it up than they were getting out of it."

There was a knock on Reg's door. She looked at the time on the phone. "Oh… I've got a client. Sorry. Can we talk more tomorrow?"

"Sure," Jessup agreed. "Thanks for checking on me. That was really nice of you."

CHAPTER TWELVE

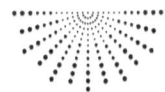

*R*eg hurried to answer the door, but tried to give the impression that she had been waiting for the client rather than talking on the phone right up to the point that they had knocked on the door.

It was a woman in a long skirt. Not someone that Reg remembered doing a reading for before. It was easy to lose track sometimes. Especially when Sarah was adding appointments into her book; people that Sarah knew or had talked to at the store who were in need of a psychic. It could get a little confusing.

"Hi, come in. I'm so glad to see you," Reg greeted, smiling as if the woman were an old friend. "Come and sit down in the living room, and I'll just get us some tea."

"Just… maybe just water for me," the woman protested.

"Sure, of course, whatever you like."

Reg made sure that she was comfortable in the living room, then went to the kitchen area to start the water heating for her own tea. She looked down at her appointment book. Sarah's neat printing—she had learned by now not to use her old style script or Reg couldn't read it—indicated that the woman's name was Mariah Broadbottom. Reg tried to suppress a smile at the unusual name while she went about preparing their beverages.

She carried the tea tray over to the living room and put it down on the coffee table.

"Mariah, here you go." She folded herself onto the couch. Mariah had taken one of the wicker chairs. "Why don't you tell me about yourself and why you're here today?"

"Well, okay." Mariah sipped the water, looking slightly uncomfortable. People often felt awkward for the first few minutes. They were walking into the unknown. Sometimes, into something that they had considered taboo before coming. "I guess I'm just looking for direction. Here I am, a grown-up woman, and I thought that when I got to be this age, I would have some idea of what I want out of life. I would have some direction... but I still feel like a kid. Like I'm just faking it and everyone else knows what they are doing."

Reg nodded and rolled her eyes. "I feel the same way. You're not alone in that. Who knew that being an adult would be almost as hard as being a kid."

"I thought that when I was grown up I could do whatever I wanted to and make whatever decisions I wanted to about my life. But those things were just like... being able to eat ice cream for dinner or choosing my own bedtime. I never thought about the other decisions I would have to make and how they would affect my life. I wish someone would just tell me what the best course of action is, where I am supposed to go with my life. Every decision has consequences, and I really don't want to have to weigh them all out and make all of these decisions for myself."

"Is there a particular spirit you are looking for guidance from? Someone on the other side that you feel helped you out when they were alive?"

"Funny you should ask that! I was just thinking of my grandmother and how she was so wise. I don't know how she got to be that way. With all of the muddle I'm making out of life, I don't think I'll ever have the wisdom that she did. And she died when she was sixty. That used to be really old, but now I feel like... I'm going to get to be that old and will still be trying to decide what career to pursue."

Reg smiled. "What was her name?"

"Oma." Mariah giggled. "Desiree Broadbottom."

"Okay. And how do you want me to do this? Do you want me to look in the crystal? Hold your hands? Say a few words together? There are lots of ways to do this."

"Uh…" Mariah's eyes went around the room as she considered this. "I guess… your crystal ball would be good." She nodded to it. Reg understood that Mariah didn't want Reg to touch her. That would be too intimate. People were different. Some liked the close contact and feeling like they were participating and providing energy to the reading, and others didn't want any kind of physical contact. Some enjoyed talking directly to a spirit and some preferred tea leaves or palmistry.

Reg prepared herself, putting the crystal ball where she could see into it properly and moving anything else away from it so that it had its own physical and psychic space. Starlight came over to her without being asked and jumped into her lap.

"Oh, you have a cat," Mariah's voice was high. "How nice!"

Reg nodded. "You're not allergic to cats, are you? If you don't like cats, I can ask him to go to the other room."

"Oh, no. I like cats." Mariah reached out a tentative finger for Starlight to sniff, and after he did so, petted the soft fur on the top of his head very gently and rubbed around the base of his ears. "What's his name?"

"Starlight."

"Oh, because of the star on his forehead?" Mariah looked at the white spot, but didn't touch it, which was a wise choice.

"Yes, exactly."

"Does he help with the reading?"

"He's actually very powerful. It helps me to combine his psychic abilities and mine. It produces a clearer image and better results."

Mariah nodded, her eyes wide.

Reg rubbed her fingertips into Starlight's fur, preparing herself. She closed her eyes and breathed deeply in and out, slowing her heart rate and opening herself up to the influence of the spirits.

That instantly made her job more difficult because not only would she hear anything Mariah's Oma had to say, she would also have to hear all of the other ghosts and filter their voices out.

There was a raucous crowd in her head today. Reg suspected it was because of Mrs. Jessup, who immediately pushed front and center, demanding to be heard.

I demand retribution. I demand justice!

Reg breathed slowly, trying to push the woman's ghost away by ignoring her. But that didn't work. Jessup's mother was insistent. Reg opened her eyes again, focusing on the outer surface of the crystal ball. She saw the ghost reflected there.

"What is your name?" she asked aloud.

Lily. Lily Lee Jessup.

"I am looking for Desiree Broadbottom," Reg said, reaching out with her senses and trying to tell whether Mariah's Oma was there. "I have Mariah Broadbottom, and she is looking for the spirit of her grandmother."

Listen to me! Lily insisted. *I demand vengeance!*

Reg gave a slight nod. "We'll see what we can do for you later. But right now, I need Desiree Broadbottom."

Different faces were reflected on the outside of the crystal ball, sliding in and out of view like a very bad horror movie.

"Desiree Broadbottom," Reg repeated. Invoking the grandmother's spirit three times should do something. If she were still reachable, she should respond.

Lily, on the other hand, needed to take the hint and leave, coming back another time when Reg could deal with her.

Mariah? Another ghost's soft voice brushed at the edges of Reg's consciousness. *Is that my grandbaby Mariah?*

"Mariah is here," Reg confirmed. "Come and speak with her."

Reg allowed the spirit entrance into her mind, gently encouraging her. After hearing Mariah's description of her Oma, she should have known that this woman would be very tentative, not wanting to interfere with the normal workings of the earthbound.

"Oma?" Mariah asked, her face partway between joy and anxiety. "Is she really here? Can you hear her?"

Not answering, Reg waited for Desiree to take her place and speak to her granddaughter. It was easiest if Reg channeled the spirit.

Better than if she tried to interpret or summarize, which was always prone to error or misunderstanding.

"Mariah," Reg breathed, and looked around herself in wonder. "It's been so long."

Mariah was still exactly as she had expected her to be. A few lines of experience but, overall, still a young, earnest woman, looking for direction.

"Oma?" Mariah's voice cracked. "I needed so badly to talk to you. I miss you so much!"

"I miss you too, sweetie. It's hard being separated from you."

"Are you happy?" Mariah asked worriedly. "Aren't you with Opa and the others? The babies you lost, your parents, the whole family?"

"They aren't here. They have gone on in their journeys. But you still needed me."

Mariah nodded, her eyes flooding with tears. "Yes. I do."

"No!" Reg felt as if she had been wrenched to the side. "I must have vengeance!"

Oma Broadbottom was gone, and Mariah sat there gaping at Reg's face, trying to understand what had happened and respond to the raging ghost.

"It's okay," Reg tried to force the words out, past the ghost's consciousness, demanding to re-take control of her own body. "We'll get her back again. This other ghost is just very *insistent!*"

Mariah stared at her, wide-eyed. Reg couldn't worry about her. She had to keep her focus on Lily and on Mariah's Oma, if she was still there.

"Lily," she said in a firm voice. "Out!"

But Lily resisted. Reg's mouth became a grimace, showing threatening teeth, gnashing and fighting against Reg for control.

"If you want to talk to your daughter," Reg said, "you need to leave now. I'm not going to be your conduit if you keep trying to hijack me."

There was a stillness. Lily considered this offer and threat.

"You will let me speak to Marta?"

"If you behave yourself."

Everything went black.

Reg was disoriented for a moment, and then her vision reasserted itself and she was looking out at the room with her own eyes rather than sharing with Lily or Oma Broadbottom. Mariah was looking very shell-shocked, not sure what to do.

"Sorry," Reg told her. "A friend of mine recently lost her mother... and she's hanging around here. I'm sure in a few days, she will fade but, right now, she is very strong and she interfered with your grandmother's appearance. I'm sorry. Do you want to reschedule for next week? I won't charge you for today."

"Um." Mariah stood up. "No. I don't think so. That was fine. I have some ideas now. Some things to think about."

She made her exit very quickly. Reg sat there with Starlight in her lap, shaking her head.

CHAPTER THIRTEEN

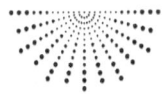

*R*eg awoke to the phone ringing. Normally, people didn't call her that early in the morning. And she usually turned off her ringer or put her phone into "do not disturb" mode so that if people did call her, they wouldn't wake her up. But really, people should know that a psychic performing seances regularly at midnight would not be up at six o'clock in the morning. Like doctors, mediums didn't exactly work bankers' hours.

Not that it was only six o'clock, but close enough.

She ignored it at first, waiting for it to go quiet so that she could go back to sleep. But whoever it was called several times in a row. Maybe she had remembered to put it on do not disturb. The same number calling repeatedly was enough to break through the electronic gatekeeper. Because what if it was an emergency? People needed to be able to reach each other in the event of an emergency.

Finally, Reg opened her eyes a crack to orient herself in her room, then reached across the bed to the side table and picked up the phone. She looked at the screen before swiping to answer it.

"What is it?"

"Reg? I'm sorry to wake you up." Jessup didn't sound very sorry. She sounded more like she thought Reg should have been up already, regardless of her nightly schedule.

"Yeah? So what do you want?"

"I did wait," Jessup pointed out, still sounding perturbed. "It's ten-thirty."

"I'm going to hang up now," Reg threatened.

"No, don't hang up. I'm sorry. I just don't like being put off."

"Put off? Who put you off? We didn't make arrangements to call or meet at any particular time."

"Never mind." Jessup sighed in exasperation. Reg waited, considering whether to hit the disconnect button. "Okay. I just wanted to let you know that Hunter has been released from the hospital. It's a courtesy call."

It would be nice if she actually showed some courtesy.

"Okay," Reg said. "Thanks."

She hung up.

Jessup tried to call her back again, but Reg rejected the call to voicemail and then held the power button until the phone's face went black. There was more than one way to put her phone into "do not disturb" mode.

* * *

Unfortunately, once Reg had been awakened by the phone, it was impossible to sleep again. She tried, figuring she'd be able to get another hour in so that she'd be awake and alert the rest of the day. But it didn't work. Her body was too itchy and restless. The sun was too bright. The room was too hot. She could hear Starlight wandering around, playing and waiting for her to get up. It wouldn't be long before he was in her room yowling loudly for his breakfast. There was dry kibble in his dish, but His Majesty preferred fresh or canned fish.

With a groan, Reg pushed her feet off the edge of the bed and got to her feet. After splashing water on her face in the bathroom, she was more alert. Coffee would take her the rest of the way.

At first, she couldn't even remember what the call had been about. Something to do with Jessup's mother's death?

Lily Jessup had been hanging around ever since the failed reading. She had shown up at the seance, not allowing her clients to make contact with the spirits they had come to see, no matter how much Reg begged and cajoled. She wanted to see and talk to her daughter. And Jessup had already said that she didn't believe in spirits. Maybe Reg shouldn't have promised Lily that she would be able to talk to Jessup, but it had seemed like the best way to get her attention and make her listen. Now Reg was stuck with a promise made to a ghost, and she knew what her life would be like until she followed through and gave Lily what she wanted.

Corvin was out of the hospital. That's what Jessup had called to tell her.

Reg was glad that he had recovered so quickly. Hopefully, some of it was to do with the strength she had given him at the end of their visit. It was good that he hadn't been killed or injured more seriously.

But it also meant that he could drop by her house any time he pleased, and Reg had not done what Sarah had told her to and strengthened the wards against Corvin or other intruders. She was supposed to do it daily to make sure that they were as strong as possible.

She wandered out the door and into the backyard with her first cup of coffee in her hand. The sun seemed extra bright and Reg felt like she was baking in the unseasonably warm weather.

Reg tried to ignore the angry face of the sun as she moved around the yard and paused at each of the wards Sarah had set, trying to pour her good intentions into them and give them a portion of her strength. It was too early to be doing such a thing.

The ward she was focusing her attention on suddenly burst into flame. Reg swore under her breath. She didn't do anything at first, letting it burn while she took another sip of her coffee to help her to wake up properly. Maybe she shouldn't have tried to do it as soon as she had gotten out of bed. After having a calming swallow of the scalding hot coffee, she put out the fire. She glanced at the big house to make sure that Sarah wasn't watching out one of the windows. She would not be happy with Reg starting a fire in the yard.

That was the kind of thing that she was supposed to be avoiding with her training with Davyn.

But it hadn't been intentional—just one of those things that sometimes happened when she was stressed out or agitated about something.

It wouldn't happen again. Now that she was aware of it, she could control it.

Reg continued to walk around the yard, going from one ward to another and doing her best to strengthen them without igniting them. Most of the time, she succeeded in not setting them aflame. Though she wasn't sure how much strength she had been able to put into them. Davyn would have to tutor her on the difference between transferring power and transferring heat.

It was a good thing she hadn't set fire to Corvin when she had given him extra healing power at the hospital.

Reg sat down on the bench to relax and drink the remainder of her coffee. Then she would go back into the cottage and get herself another coffee. And then maybe around lunchtime, she would get herself breakfast.

As she sat contemplating the bubbling pond and singing birds and the sun streaming down on her, its light filtered by the leaves of the tree that spread out overhead, she became aware of a noise.

Several noises, in fact, but they all seemed to be coming from the same direction.

A sort of a tuneless humming sound, low and throbbing. And a scratching, scraping sound. Some animal or creature was there behind the bench, hidden in the undergrowth. Reg tried several times to get a look at it, standing up for a moment, kneeling on the bench, draping herself over the back of the bench. But she couldn't see whatever it was.

It would be embarrassing if it were just Forst, humming to himself while he dug holes to drop some new seeds or bulbs into. But she'd never heard him hum like that before, so she didn't think that was what it was. Reg crept around the bench and pushed aside branches from bushes and smaller trees, sweeping her foot in front of her to move aside the long grasses and wildflowers. She usually kept to the little pathways of paving stones that ran through the garden, but this time she did not. She plowed through all of Forst's living, growing things, her eyes sharp for the sight of what kind of animal was making the noise. It couldn't be an alligator. Sarah had assured her of that. But still… Reg was braced for something that might startle or chase her. Just because Sarah said that nothing that was harmful to Reg could get into the yard…

Reg pushed aside a branch laden with blushing pink blossoms and caught sight of it for just an instant before it saw her and bolted farther into the undergrowth. She made a loud squawk, but managed to stifle a full-on scream. The undergrowth was too thick for Reg to pursue the creature. And she wasn't sure that she wanted to anyway. What was that thing? She had expected it to be something that she could at least put a name to, but she was stumped. She hadn't seen it clearly enough. It had run away before she could make a proper identification.

But she was kind of scared by what she had seen.

CHAPTER FOURTEEN

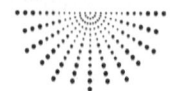

*R*eg decided it was a good time to visit Sarah in the big house.

Sarah would know what was going on and could reassure Reg that what she had seen in the dimness of the undergrowth had either been a figment of her imagination or had been something normal and harmless.

She would settle for just harmless.

She went to the back door and knocked before entering. "Sarah? Are you home?"

She could sense that Sarah was there, somewhere in the house. Sarah called back, her voice muffled, and it was a few minutes before she entered the kitchen, smiling sunnily at Reg.

"Reg, it's been forever since you've come over for a visit. Shall we have tea?"

Reg had nearly finished her coffee and was ready for another one. But tea would do. She could always have more coffee—or a stiffer drink—when she returned to the guest cottage. "Sure, that would be nice."

Sarah put the kettle on and bustled around the kitchen getting things ready. She put both sachets of her own tea blends on the table as well as some commercial teabags. Reg wasn't enamored with Sarah's medicinal teas and was not sure how her regular drinking teas would be, so she stuck to the big names she knew from the store and selected English breakfast. It was breakfast, after all, so it seemed appropriate.

"How are you doing?" Sarah asked after pouring boiling water into both of their mugs and sitting down. Reg added copious amounts of sugar to hers.

"Me? I'm fine. Can't complain. I did my best to strengthen the wards in the backyard today… maybe you could take a look at them later."

Sarah cocked an eyebrow. "Oh?"

"I'm not sure how good of a job I did. And… I might have burnt a couple of them."

"You burned them?"

Reg nodded. "Sorry. I didn't mean to. I was just trying to strengthen them like you said, and… poof!"

Sarah chuckled. "I see. I didn't think about what could happen having a firecaster strengthen them. I suppose it was inevitable. Everything is okay, though?" Sarah looked out the kitchen window into the yard. "You put them all out, and you're sure there weren't any sparks or glowing embers…?"

"Yeah. I was careful. No sparks."

"Good. After all of the work we have put into the yard and the garden, it would be tragic if there was a fire."

Reg nodded. "Right. I know. Of course."

"And the house…" Sarah looked around her fondly. "I don't know what I would ever do if a fire destroyed the house."

Reg shuddered at the thought. Not only would Sarah lose everything she'd spent a lifetime—several lifetimes, by Reg's measure—accumulating, but it would also be the end of Reg's comfortable circumstances. Sarah would definitely not want to keep her around after something like that. She would be out on her ear and would have to find another living situation. At least she had money in the bank now. That was more than she could say for any other time of her life.

"I'm always careful," she assured Sarah. "I wouldn't let anything happen to your yard or house."

"Of course not." Sarah gave a smile. "I know that."

Reg sipped her tea, thinking, trying to find a way to bring up what she had seen in the garden.

"What is it, dear?" Sarah asked. "Something is on your mind. Is it Corvin? I heard about his accident."

"It wasn't an accident. He was stabbed."

"Yes, well, *someone* made a mistake."

"In trying to kill him, or in failing?"

Sarah just raised her brows thoughtfully.

"It isn't about Corvin," Reg told her. "And before you ask—I didn't have anything to do with Corvin. Or know who did."

"Probably just one of these random things," Sarah assured her. "Maybe gang violence."

How would a gang have broken into Corvin's house to kill him? And why would they? That didn't make any sense.

"An initiation," Sarah suggested. "They do that, you know, kill people they don't even know in order to get into the gang."

"I know that. But a guy sleeping in his house? That doesn't fit. I don't think it was anything to do with a gang."

"Oh, well. We'll leave it to the police to figure out. In the meantime… what is it you are worried about?"

"I guess I just wondered… about… animals in your garden."

"Did you see a cat?" Sarah put down her mug and looked at Reg, her forehead lined with worry.

"No. Not a cat. You know, when Orri was here, he said to protect the creatures in the garden. What do you think he meant? Do you think there is something in the garden that is… rare? Or in danger?"

"Harbinger elves are notoriously difficult to understand." Sarah picked up her tea and had another sip. "They can be very cryptic. And even when you think you understand what they are talking about, it could be something completely different, and you don't know until after the dust has settled what they were trying to tell you in the first place."

"I don't think he was trying to give me a warning," Reg clarified.

"He wasn't using his big 'portentous' voice. Just talking to me normally, before he left again."

"Well…" Sarah met Reg's eyes. "What do you think he was trying to tell you?"

Reg shifted uncomfortably. "I don't know… I think just that it is a beautiful garden, and we should take good care of it. And make sure that… any creatures living there are protected. From… outside dangers."

"That seems fairly clear."

"Exactly," Reg agreed. "I'm just wondering if you know if you have anything living back there that is rare… or endangered."

"The way Forst has been working on the garden, it could be practically anything, couldn't it? We already know about the elves. And you have undoubtedly seen the many different birds that come to the feeders and birdbath."

Birds were Sarah's particular affinity. She had an African gray parrot for her familiar. And heaven help any cat who hunted in her garden.

Maybe it was the cats that needed to be protected.

"I suppose it could be a particular bird or variety of bird that comes here," Reg agreed. "I just wondered if there might be something that was a little less *ordinary*."

"Like what?"

"I don't know." Reg took a long swallow of her tea and tried to think of the best way to describe what she had seen. "I was out there just now, sitting on the bench, enjoying the garden. And I heard something in the bushes."

"Maybe it was just Forst?"

"I looked for him, but I couldn't find him. I think maybe he is out, picking up supplies, or maybe he went home to see his family. It seems like he's always in the garden, but he isn't there now."

"Or maybe he doesn't want to be disturbed. He might just need time to himself. Garden gnomes are very reclusive, you know. They don't want a lot to do with the outside world."

Reg thought that was more the result of their difficulty speaking out loud to humans than that they just didn't want to go out. Forst had always been quite friendly with her. And so were the other gnomen she had met personally.

"It wasn't Forst I heard. I followed the noise, tried to see what it was…"

"And what was it?" Sarah looked suddenly concerned. "Was it a rat? Do I need to get an exterminator out there? We keep the garbage covered. I don't know what a rat would be eating in the garden."

"No. It was bigger than a rat. And… not furry."

"Oh. Some kind of lizard, maybe? I only kept out venomous snakes, you know. Only things that could actually harm you."

"No, it was kind of round, not long like a lizard or snake. At least, not all of it was skinny. It had a round belly in the middle. And a long tail. And its face…"

Sarah leaned forward, interested in the description. "Yes?"

"I don't know… I only caught a glimpse of it. It was sort of a long, narrow face. But it disappeared again so quickly…"

Sarah frowned, wrinkling her forehead again as she thought about Reg's description. Then she started smiling merrily. "Oh. I'll bet I know what it was."

"What?"

"An armadillo. You wouldn't be used to seeing them, coming from the north, but they are pretty common in these parts."

"Oh!" Reg let out a puff of breath, relieved. Just an armadillo. Very common in Florida. And they were cute; Reg had seen pictures of them. She thought about the thing she had seen. The scaly skin a pink-gray color. Just an armadillo. She had scared herself over nothing. It was just a common armadillo—nothing to be concerned about.

"They're not endangered, are they?" she checked.

"Not the nine-banded armadillo. There are other kinds in other parts of the world that might be endangered. But here, no. We only get the one species, and they are thriving."

"Oh. Okay. Well, that's good, then. Nothing to be worried about."

"They are good for pests," Sarah contributed. "They eat insects and grubs that could be harmful to the plants. They can make a bit of a mess digging around sometimes, but they aren't a danger themselves. They will just run away if they see you coming."

That was probably what had made the strange scratches that Reg had seen before too. It all made sense.

"Good. I was afraid it was some kind of… monster. I don't know. Something weird that could be dangerous. Since it ran away from me, I guess I should have known that it wasn't anything that would be a danger."

"Many animals can be dangerous if cornered. But I can't say I have ever heard about an armadillo harming anyone. You are quite safe. The wards are holding, and nothing should be able to get in that would do you any kind of harm."

CHAPTER FIFTEEN

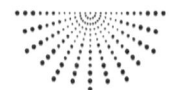

*R*eg returned to the yard, relieved by her conversation with Sarah. She was being silly, jumping at shadows. There wasn't anything at all to be worried about. She went back to the bench and looked around, wondering if she would be able to catch another glimpse of the little creature. She had always liked the idea of an armadillo. In cartoons, they could curl up into a roly-poly little ball. Reg didn't know if they could do that in real life. Maybe she would look it up later.

She closed her eyes and reached out, trying to make contact with the little armadillo. She'd never had any trouble connecting with a cat, but she didn't know what other animals she could or couldn't communicate with. Armadillos seemed so foreign to her. Maybe their brains were constructed differently and she wouldn't be able to interface with it.

When she reached out, all different areas of her brain lit up immediately. The garden was full of life. Far more than she could see or ever would have guessed. She liked to be out there sitting on the bench because it was quiet and peaceful and she could be alone there. But she could see, when she reached out, that she was far from being alone. Maybe when she thought she was feeling better because she was alone with her own thoughts, she actually felt better because of the company. Perhaps she liked being surrounded by life rather than separate from it.

Reg tried to catalog the various forms of life as she examined them. Lots of birds, Sarah's pride and joy. Plenty of insects, crawling and flying and burrowing, moving together in an intricate web of relationships and dependencies. The tinkling, blinking lights that she associated with the elves.

There were other things there. Things that Reg could not identify. Because they were things she didn't know of? Things that wanted to stay hidden? Or maybe things that were too hard for her to understand and communicate with, like tree spirits?

Reg found the armadillo. She tried to stay perfectly still as she observed it in her mind. She could find it again if she wanted to. She could follow it to its hiding place by following the psychic imprint. But she didn't want to scare it again, especially if Sarah was wrong and it was something that could do her harm. Maybe not kill her, but bite or claw her. The claw marks in the garden had seemed to indicate claws that were pretty sharp and long. It stayed in one place, hiding, not curled up into itself, but scared and uncertain, watching and listening to everything to learn about the world around it.

It didn't seem to be a danger or to have any malevolent feelings toward her or humans in general. It just wanted to be left alone to scavenge for food and go back to its burrow to sleep.

* * *

Reg liked it when she and Davyn went to the forest, where she could play with her fire, trying more and more challenging exercises, becoming a more and more accomplished firecaster. At least, she hoped she was becoming more accomplished. Maybe she was still a toddler as far as firecasting went. Davyn had never told her what level she was at. He just praised her when she did well and corrected her mistakes, and didn't say whether she was a novice or an expert.

They met at an abandoned house. Grey, with all of the paint that had once adorned it peeling off in long flakes. A sagging roof that looked like it might fall in at any moment. Davyn tried not to take her to the same places too often, as they might be noticed. And Reg might get overconfident about her knowledge of their setting and not take all of the risks into account. She had to treat every situation as if it were something new, making no assumptions and always being on the alert for people who might observe her or dangers that she had not encountered before.

Davyn got out of his car and approached Reg, his black cloak billowing out behind him in the breeze. He looked good. Reg was glad that he was feeling okay after being kidnapped and held hostage for a few days. But looking at his handsome, clean-shaven face, she never would have guessed that he had been through anything out of the ordinary. He had bounced back from it remarkably quickly and fallen back into his usual schedule. What had he told the people at work who had reported him missing? Had he told them that he'd been abducted and rescued? Or had he lied and said that he had been sick, or had to leave town to visit a sick relative and the message he had left for his boss had been lost? Reg was never sure how the magical world and the non-practitioners interfaced in Black Sands.

He smiled and nodded at her. "Reg. Good to see you. Eager to get started, I see!"

Reg nodded. She was full of energy and anticipation. Firecasting was one of her favorite times of the week. Maybe *the* favorite.

Davyn looked around at their surroundings. "We'll go around behind the house. There is a clearing."

Reg nodded, and they walked side by side. Davyn cocked his head. His nostrils flared.

"You smell like smoke."

Reg didn't think that was possible. The only fires that she had been around were the wards that she had accidentally lit on fire, but those had been so small and she had smothered them quickly. It wasn't enough to leave the smell of smoke on her clothing. She lifted the edge of her shirt to her nose and sniffed.

Her nose tickled. There was an acrid scent. Not precisely like woodsmoke, but Davyn was right. She smelled like she had been near a fire. Maybe lighting a fire.

"I was... I wasn't playing around," she told Davyn quickly. "And I don't know how smoke would have gotten into my clothes because it wasn't that big and was only for a few seconds."

"As firecasters, we are very sensitive to the smells of fire and smoke. You don't smell that smoky. But... hot. Sharp."

Reg scratched the back of her neck, embarrassed. "Well... I was strengthening the protective wards in the backyard today. Sarah said that I need to work on strengthening them every day to keep Corvin from coming back into the yard. Because he is getting so powerful now."

Davyn nodded his understanding. Reg went on, still stilted, embarrassed at having to explain.

"I was just trying to make them stronger. But a couple of times, they burst into flames." Reg's face got hot. "I put them out right away, but... do you think that was enough to make me smell like this?"

She tried again to smell herself, to reassure herself that the smell was very faint. Only another firecaster would have been able to smell it. Or maybe a cat.

"Hm. I wouldn't expect it to. You haven't made any other fires since we last met? Even candles or a campfire?"

"No. I follow the rules. You said I'm not allowed to play with fire when I'm by myself or I could hurt someone else... so I don't."

Davyn studied her closely, his eyes sharp to catch any deception. He wasn't a diviner like Damon, at least as far as she knew, but he was still good at being able to tell when she was covering something up.

"I saw Corvin at the hospital," Reg offered. "I tried pushing warmth into him, for healing, like you showed me. I didn't light *him* on fire!"

"I probably would have heard about it if you had. All right. We'll just assume that it was one of those things. But you make sure that you are not practicing without someone to back you up if things get out of hand. You know that sometimes your fire gets out of your control."

"Yes," Reg admitted, though she was ashamed to have to confirm it. She should be able to control herself. To maintain her focus. She should be able to get it right every time, not to have to have someone there to clean up after her mistakes. Reg had been raised to always clean up after her own mistakes. And others' too, of course. Whether it was because she had been accused of something she hadn't done and had to take the rap for it or because her caregiver couldn't take care of herself, let alone the foster kids in her care.

"Okay. On to work. Let's get started."

CHAPTER SIXTEEN

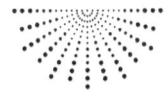

*R*eg breathed out in relief. She wasn't going to get a big lecture or have to do something to make up for her mistake. They would just continue with the training as usual.

Davyn began to spin a ball of fire between his palms, cupping the glowing light between them. Reg immediately mimicked what he was doing, feeling that rush as she was allowed to bring her fire into existence and manipulate it. Like a dog who hadn't been out for a walk in a week, her fire was eager to get going. She let it warm her palms and relaxed all of her muscles. Handling fire was what she was meant to do.

Unless she got her feet wet, then swimming and being one with the water was what she was meant to do. She wondered what would happen if she tried to handle fire while she was stepping into water. Would the whole world explode?

Her fire was dampened slightly by her thoughts about water, so Reg encouraged it, letting it grow larger and get hotter. She smiled proudly, enjoying the flickering warmth and the look of approval on Davyn's face.

"So, you saw Corvin?" Davyn asked.

"Yes. I went to the hospital to see him."

She gave him a look. Davyn frequently criticized her for having anything to do with Corvin. Davyn couldn't understand why, after all that she had suffered at his hands, Reg would keep seeing him. If it were only chance meetings, or always initiated by him, that would be one thing. But that wasn't the case. Sometimes, like this time, Reg would initiate contact herself. And it was too difficult to explain to other people why she would do this.

Someone who wasn't connected to Corvin like she was couldn't understand what it was like. It wasn't the classic abuse-apology cycle. For one thing, Corvin rarely apologized for what it was he did. It was natural. Instinctual. So why should he apologize? And it wasn't because she liked to flirt with danger. She needed to see him and know that he was okay. Part of her was in him and part of him was in her. They were something like family, only, of course, she would never feel about a family member the way she felt toward Corvin when he was trying to charm her. That would be gross.

But for once, Davyn didn't criticize her for going to see Corvin. Maybe it was okay because someone had made an attempt on Corvin's life and the social norms changed a little when there was a murder attempt. Or maybe it would have been okay if he had the flu or another virus.

Or maybe Davyn was just getting tired of telling her the same thing over and over and over again.

"How was he doing?"

Reg shrugged. "He was doing pretty well. A little weak, maybe. The doctors wanted to make sure that he didn't try to do too much while he was still recovering."

"He's been released already."

"Yeah. I heard. I guess maybe the heat I gave him helped?"

"Maybe," Davyn agreed with a nod. "Have you had enough to drink today? With both giving strength to Corvin yesterday and lighting and putting out these fires today?"

"Oh yeah. I'm fine. Neither one felt like any effort."

"Good." Davyn nodded toward the dilapidated house. "We're going to talk about house fires today."

Reg grinned. "Accidental house fires or intentional ones?"

"Both. I know that you have put out your small fires and helped with a building fire once when some people were trapped. Without any training."

Reg shrugged uncomfortably and focused on her fire, making it get bigger and smaller to distract her from the conversation. "I know. It was stupid. But I had to help."

"Of course you did. But today, you're going to get a little more training about what to do in that kind of circumstance, because you will likely be caught in one again."

Reg felt her eyes widen. "Because you think I would light a building on fire?"

"No. Because as a firecaster, it is something that is going to happen around you and you have a responsibility to know how to help instead of making it worse."

Reg thought about this. "Why is it going to happen around me? You're *not* saying that I'm going to light one accidentally, but…?"

He nodded. "Look to your past. There have been fires in your past, right?"

"Well, yeah. But you said that I probably lit them and just didn't realize it."

"Some of them. But in some cases, it was probably just… attraction. Fire attracts fire."

Reg rolled her ball of fire between her hands. It was true; she had felt that tug many times since discovering her firecasting gift. It had been very strong at the forge in the dwarf mountain. And there had been other times, it was true. She felt pulled toward fire.

"So let's go start a house fire," Davyn suggested.

Reg grinned at him. "Okay!"

They entered the house. The door was not locked. Reg glanced around the abandoned house. It was empty. No furniture. No sign that anyone else had been inside in years. Lots of dust, grime streaking the windows, cobwebs. Everything seemed just a little bit blurry.

"Do you know whose house this is?" she asked Davyn. "Is it… are we allowed to be here, or is this *covert*?"

"I know the person who owns it. They're fine with it being

burned to the ground. In a controlled way, of course. Cheaper than paying a wrecking crew."

"Okay." Reg wasn't sure if she was reassured or disappointed by this. It was exciting to think that they were doing something illicit. But she would rather not go to prison for arson if she could help it.

CHAPTER SEVENTEEN

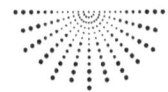

*R*eg always had a happy, satisfied feeling when she finished her session with Davyn. She waited all week to be able to use her fire, and each time she got to learn a little bit more about what she could do and how to control it. She wanted to use fire all the time, but it was probably a good thing that she was not allowed to. That was an obsession that could quickly go wrong.

She was surprised, when she pulled up in front of the house, to see Corvin's car parked there. Was he inside visiting with Sarah? Despite all of the things Sarah said about Corvin, they had an amicable relationship. Corvin flattered and charmed her and had helped her when she was at death's door. Reg had thought at one time that he had designs on her, but it seemed she was just an old friend he was looking out for. The relationship was probably more complex than that, but Reg didn't want to dig too deeply.

But when she cast her mind toward the house to see if Corvin were meeting with Sarah inside, she could sense that he was not in the house, but still in his car. She watched for a moment, then got out of her car and walked up to his driver's side. He buzzed down the window.

"Regina."

"Corvin. I'm glad to see that you're back on your feet. The doctors were pleased with your healing?"

"Very pleased. In fact, the doctor who examined me today is sure that mistakes were made on my chart. That I couldn't have been as badly hurt as the records of the attack indicate." Corvin smiled. "So yes, it would seem that your efforts did pay off."

"Good. Well…" Reg made a motion to the sidewalk that led to the backyard. "I'm heading for home."

"How about dinner?"

"I've got stuff in the fridge."

Corvin snorted. "Food in the fridge. Probably all fast food. How about you join me tonight? Let me repay you for giving me strength by providing for your needs. There's a certain symmetry. Healing and feeding."

"I don't think I want to go to a restaurant tonight. I've just been out and I need a break."

"Ah, the club, then. It is always quiet there. Private. We could even get a private room if you don't want to be in the dining room."

Reg had eaten at Corvin's private club a few times. Not in one of the private rooms. She knew better than to let herself be alone with him.

But the food was good.

And it was quiet.

"Come on, Regina. What's the harm?" he asked encouragingly. She could smell roses, a sure sign he was charming her. But she wasn't in the enclosed space with him, so it couldn't do much other than make her lightheaded. Sort of buzzed. A nice feeling that she didn't have to use any legal or illegal substances to obtain.

"I suppose," Reg finally agreed.

Corvin reached across the seat to open the opposite car door.

"I'll take my own car," Reg objected.

"That's twice the gas."

"I'm okay with that. I don't want to be stuck in a vehicle with you without an escape."

Corvin smiled, showing all of his teeth. A bit too hungry. Had his injury and recovery sapped his strength so much that he needed to feed again? She couldn't understand why he was still hunting after having imbibed in the Witch Doctor's powers, Kareem's, and those preserved in any artifacts he had held recently. All of those powers should have filled him and kept him from hunting for a while, shouldn't they?

Maybe she should not have agreed to a meal with him.

"Do you know the way?" Corvin asked. "I'll follow you to make sure you don't take any wrong turns."

"Wouldn't it make more sense for you to lead?"

Maybe he thought that she would change her mind and return home instead of following him there. If she drove ahead of him, he could at least keep an eye on her.

"Stick close, then," Corvin advised. He put his hand on his gearshift as if he were ready to pull out immediately.

Reg returned to her car. It would be nice to have dinner at the club. The food was always good there, and Corvin was interesting company. It was not the sort of place she would go to unescorted. She had run into trouble there once before. While it gave the air of a gentlemen's club, some of the men were not so gentlemanly. She knew that predators of Corvin's ilk were rare, but there were plenty of other kinds of predators around.

She pondered this thought and remembered how uncomfortable she always was around the hostesses with their very revealing dresses. What else went on in the club that she would rather not know about? She had a feeling that there were other kinds of transactions being negotiated behind the rich draperies and heavy, inlaid doors. And she'd always wondered what part Corvin played in those transactions. Was he provided with girls with powers?

Reg turned her mind away from these thoughts. She probably didn't want to know the answer. She shouldn't even pose the question in her mind, so close to Corvin that he could probably read it.

* * *

Reg followed Corvin to his club and into the underground parking. He joined her as she slid out of her car and they walked together to the ornate door, where they didn't have to ring a bell or knock, as the door was immediately opened by one of the hostesses, clad in a clingy red dress with a plunging neckline and no back.

Reg couldn't picture herself ever wearing anything like that. Even at a fancy ball or dinner, she preferred something more substantial. And besides, where were the pockets? Reg wore long, brightly colored skirts most of the time, and they all had several pockets sewn into them, some looking like the standard skirt pockets and some hidden in places she could stash items without their being noticeable.

"A private room?" the hostess suggested, looking at Corvin and completely ignoring Reg.

"No, dining room this time," Corvin said with a sigh. "And if it could be… perhaps… off to the side."

Reg had previously insisted on being seated near the kitchen, where she could see several escape routes and they were in full view of other guests. But she had gotten more accustomed to eating with Corvin, and with her burgeoning siren powers, she was more complacent about it than she had been before.

Maybe one day soon, she would be open to eating with Corvin alone in one of the private dining rooms.

Reg glared at Corvin, knowing that this last thought had not come from her own brain, but had been planted there by him. He gave her a bland look as if he had no idea what she might have to be angry about.

"I am not going to eat with you in one of the private dining rooms," Reg told him.

"No. Didn't I just say that?"

Reg looked at him and at the hostess, momentarily confused. She shook her head. "Whatever. We want the dining room. The main dining room where everyone else eats."

"*Everyone* else does *not* eat in the main dining room," Corvin pointed out pedantically.

The reply that Reg shot back to him mentally was not very lady-like and would have earned her a mouth full of soap at more than one of her foster homes. Corvin just chuckled.

CHAPTER EIGHTEEN

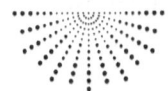

*T*he hostess ignored the conversation between them and led them to the dining room, though Corvin knew the way and even Reg figured she could have found it on her own. The woman let Corvin pick his own table. Reg sat down with him, taking a quick glance around to make sure that they were in sight of others, then put it out of her mind. She would be perfectly safe there with him, just as she had been before. And at the end of the night, she had her car there, so she didn't have to be enclosed in a vehicle with him.

"Relax, Regina," Corvin suggested. "We're all friends here."

Reg looked at the retreating figure of the hostess and the similarly dressed waitress who was approaching them, her eyes bright and interested. "A little too friendly, if you ask me."

"Are you *jealous?*"

"No. I'm concerned about how you could hurt these women, not whether they have any interest in you. All women are interested in you, but that's nothing to do with your personality. It's just pheromones and good looks. Magical charms. Don't you ever wish that they cared about who you are instead of just succumbing to natural attraction?"

Corvin frowned at this. But by the time the waitress reached the table, he was smiling again. He turned his smile on the waitress and she looked like a deer caught in the headlights. Wide eyes, stunned, powerless to get out of the way of the handsome predator. She seemed to have lost the power of speech and just stood gazing at him raptly. Corvin's revenge for Reg saying that she wasn't jealous. Showing her just how powerful his charms were. How he could have any woman he wanted.

Except for her. That was up to Reg, not up to Corvin.

Reg looked away, pretending to be uninterested in Corvin or his games. There were pictures on the wall, and she studied them as closely as if they were works of art in a museum. Some Picasso or Monet that people would swoon over.

"A bottle of wine," Corvin requested and, after looking briefly at the wine list, told the waitress what vintage he wanted.

"And a Coke," Reg said. She knew better than to split a bottle of wine with him. Maybe she would have a sip or two, just to enjoy what was bound to be an excellent vintage. But she had to keep her wits about her. She would succumb to Corvin's charms too easily if she let herself get tipsy.

Corvin flashed her a look of disappointment, as she knew he would. She actually enjoyed getting under his skin. It was almost a game with him. Like a tennis game, each of them batting barbs and charms back and forth, seeing how it would affect the other.

"So," Corvin turned his gaze on her once the waitress retreated, staggering slightly on shaky legs. "How did your session with Davyn go today?"

"How did you know I was with Davyn?"

"Your schedule with him doesn't change much. Davyn is a man who values predictability. And it is pretty obvious when you have been playing with fire." His eyes glittered as he examined her face more closely. "You have a certain... spark. Flushed cheeks. Bright eyes. I would think you enjoyed being with me if I didn't know better."

Reg bit her tongue to avoid retorting that she was enjoying being with him. That was the kind of boost his ego did not need. "My session with Davyn went fine," she said, calmly answering his question instead. "I got to burn down a house."

Corvin chuckled. "He's turned you into an arsonist now, has he? Or were you already one?"

"Fire is a tool," Reg told him archly. "This was a service to the owner. Cheaper way of taking the house down than hiring a wrecking crew."

"And you got to play with fire. I imagine that was very satisfying."

Reg couldn't help grinning in response, still high on the experience. "Oh, yeah."

He laughed again. "What would you say to a bonfire later?"

Reg shook her head and tried to mask the smile. "I don't think that would be advisable. I'm not supposed to use my fire except under supervision. I'm still a newbie."

"Are you sure Davyn isn't holding you back?"

"Of course he's holding me back. To make sure that I'm properly trained and can control my fire. And be able to respond to problems."

"You know your catechism, anyway."

Reg was irritated by the remark. She knew that Davyn was right and she couldn't be allowed free rein. But she also thought she should be able to do more than he allowed her to. Why not light candles at the cottage? Why not have a few exercises she could practice during the week, between their mentoring sessions? Could it really go that wrong? She had much better control than she'd had before she started the sessions with him, and she'd gotten through childhood without burning the house down.

"I have to protect others," she snapped at Corvin. "Something you wouldn't understand."

"Ooh, *burn*." Corvin shook his head. "I thought you weren't supposed to be flaming anyone."

"You're looking pretty good," Reg observed, changing the topic to get control over the conversation. "I wouldn't guess that you were stabbed a couple of days ago."

"No." Corvin touched his chest where the bandages had been the last time she had seen him with light fingers. "I'm doing remarkably well. The result of your healing touch."

"I'm sure you have plenty of healing powers yourself." Reg shrugged it off. "You probably would have been out of there today anyway."

"I don't know. It never hurts to have a red-headed little firecracker —I mean firecaster—on your side."

"Have you had any more thoughts on who your attacker might have been?" Reg stayed focused on the topic of his stabbing, not letting him turn the conversation back to her firecasting or his attraction to her. "I know plenty of people probably want to kill you, but there can't be that many who would actually attempt this."

"Yes... it is disturbing. As is the fact that they managed to get into my house. A man should be safe in his own castle."

"Yeah."

The waitress returned to their table, presenting Corvin with the bottle of wine and putting Reg's drink down in front of her so hard that it sloshed over the edge. The waitress didn't apologize or make any attempt to clean it up. There was another drink on her tray that she placed in front of Corvin. He looked at it in surprise.

"I didn't order..."

"It's on the house," she told him, smiling, her cheeks flushed pink.

"There's no need..."

"It's poured. It's yours."

Corvin shrugged, accepting it. They gave her their dinner orders, and she moved away from them. Corvin lifted the tumbler with two fingers of amber liquid in it, toasting Reg.

"It's poured, so I may as well drink!"

Reg shrugged. She raised her glass of Coke, returning the toast.

Corvin tossed back the drink, swallowing it all in one go. He put his hand to his throat, eyes watering. "That's got quite a burn."

Reg opened her mouth to respond, but didn't get the chance. Corvin appeared to be choking. He coughed, holding his hand over his chest, pressing harder. He picked up his fabric napkin with the other hand and pressed it to his mouth, trying to politely cover a cough, but the choking, rasping sound that came from him attracted the attention of every person in the room.

Reg reached across the table and touched his arm, concerned. An electrical charge tingled under her fingers, as it always did when they touched. "Corvin?"

He tried to say something, but couldn't get anything out.

CHAPTER NINETEEN

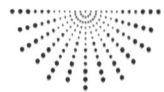

*R*eg stood up, trying to figure out what to do, who to call for help. She looked around her frantically. Where was the waitress? One of the hostesses? Someone who knew what emergency supplies and services the club offered.

"Help! Can someone help me?"

One of the hostesses appeared at Reg's side and pushed close to Corvin to see what was happening. "Is he choking?"

"I don't know. He just had a drink, and then he started coughing and… I don't know if he's choking. He didn't have anything to eat yet, just to drink. You can't choke on a liquid, can you?"

The hostess looked at the empty tumbler on the table. She seemed competent, pushing Corvin's hands away from his chest, throat, and face to assess what was going on, speaking to him in a firm, crisp voice.

"Mr. Hunter. Can you tell me what's going on? Are you allergic to anything? Are you choking?"

Corvin kept shaking his head. The woman turned to look at Reg.

"Do you know if he's allergic to anything? Does he have an auto-injector?"

"No. Nothing that I know of. This has never happened before. He never mentioned being allergic to anything, and I've never seen him with an EpiPen or any kind of needle or drugs." Reg shook her head adamantly. "Nothing like that."

The hostess motioned to a waiter standing back out of the way, looking like he didn't want to be involved. "Abe. Come over here. Right now."

He didn't argue with her, but hurried forward to see what she wanted.

"Call 9-1-1. Tell them we need an ambulance right away. A man is choking or having an allergic reaction. They need to get here right away. You know the address, right?"

The man looked blank for a moment, then he nodded, apparently remembering it.

"Good. Then call guest services and tell them to expect the ambulance and bring the paramedics directly up here. See if there is a doctor in attendance today. Any kind of medical doctor, just get them in here."

The man nodded again, looking more sure of himself.

"Do it," the hostess said curtly and turned her attention back to Corvin.

He was turning an alarming shade of red as if all of the blood in his body had rushed to his head. He tugged at his collar. The hostess pushed his hands away and unbuttoned it for him, pulling it away from his throat. Corvin seemed to want to take off his suit jacket, so she helped him with that. Reg watched, horrified, at a loss as to what to do. She wanted to help, but she wasn't trained in emergency medicine and the hostess seemed to know something about what she was doing. Reg would just have been in the way.

Corvin was wearing a short-sleeved shirt rather than long sleeves with cuff links and, when they had the jacket off, Reg could see red welts appearing on his arms.

"He *must* be allergic!"

The hostess looked at the marks and nodded. "Maybe. Does anyone here have an EpiPen? Antihistamines?"

Everyone just sat and stood around them, staring as if they were watching a theater production.

There was a burst of noise from the dining room doorway, several people running in from another part of the building. Maybe the medical doctor Abe had been told to ask for?

"Is it an allergy?" one man demanded, waving a large tube with a yellow cap. "I have epinephrine."

The hostess didn't look at him, but at one of the men coming in behind him. "Dr. Hood. Am I glad to see you. Can you please have a look? See what we can do while we're waiting for an ambulance?"

Corvin was listing to the side, supported by the hostess now, his coughs and noises weaker than they had been.

"Let's get him down on the floor where I can examine him," said the man who was apparently Dr. Hood, wearing a white shirt, suit jacket, and black cloak, like most of the other patrons. "Best if he's already down in case we have to start CPR."

He and the hostess lowered Corvin to the carpet and the doctor began an exam. "Tell me what happened."

"He had a drink," Reg croaked. "He started coughing and choking. He has hives or something on his arm."

The doctor looked at them. He asked Corvin if he had any allergies, but Corvin seemed past being able to make any coherent response.

"Give that to me," Dr. Hood ordered the man with the EpiPen, and snatched it from him when he got close enough to reach it. He popped the yellow top and slid out the auto-injector, blue at one end and orange at the other. "Blue to the sky and orange to the thigh," Hood told Reg. "You should know how to do this."

She wasn't sure why he picked her out as the person who should know. Maybe he thought that Corvin was her partner, and she might, at some point in the future, have to head off another anaphylactic reaction. He pulled off the blue end, then stabbed the orange end against Corvin's thigh, making him jump and groan. Hood held it there for a few seconds before pulling it out. He rubbed the injection site, watching Corvin's face for any changes.

"He said it burned his throat," Reg remembered. "Is that an allergy? Or do you think it was something else?" She looked at the glass, wondering if she should grab it and make sure that no one could clear it away and clean it, destroying whatever evidence might remain inside.

"Can't tell one way or the other," Hood said. He held Corvin's wrist pinched between his fingers, monitoring his pulse. "Whatever it was, he's had a very bad reaction. Did anyone else drink from this glass? Where is the bottle it was poured from?"

Reg shook her head, indicating that no one else had drunk it and that she had no idea where the bottle it was poured from was. The hostess, crouched next to Corvin and the doctor in a way that Reg would never have dared to do with such a short skirt, said that she would find out. She walked briskly toward the kitchen, demanding to know which staff member had served Corvin the drink and what bottle it had been poured from. What if the whole thing was poisoned and they suddenly had patrons all over the club dropping like flies?

Reg shifted, trying to see past the doctor to get a good look at Corvin's face. His expression was flat, no longer in a grimace of pain, no longer coughing, and Reg wondered whether he had passed out. He looked older, gray and pasty, his skin slack. She looked around the dining room, straining her ears for the sound of an ambulance siren. Where were they? How long would they take to get there? She had heard before of ambulances taking inordinate lengths of time to respond to calls, leaving seriously ill or injured patients in desperate situations. But a little town like Black Sands wouldn't have that problem, would they? They couldn't have that many emergency calls going on at the same time.

As she was starting to worry about whether the ambulance would ever get there, a man and a woman in dark blue uniforms hurried in through the dining room doorway with a gurney, accompanied by a hostess. Reg hadn't heard the siren at all.

The two paramedics moved in beside Dr. Hood, asking questions and getting a rundown of what he had already done, which pretty much amounted to getting him down on the floor, giving him a dose of epinephrine, and monitoring him.

"He's still breathing, but you might want to get a tube down his airway before it swells shut."

They talked back and forth, reporting Corvin's vital signs and what each of them was doing. Reg was dizzy watching them, but still wanted them to go faster. She wanted to know that he was out of danger. As much as she feared and disliked Corvin for what he could do, she had gotten used to having him around and didn't want him to die right in front of her eyes.

Eventually, the paramedics strapped him into the gurney and took him out the door. Reg didn't know what to do. Stay there? Follow the ambulance to the hospital?

The hostess looked around at all of the spectators. "I would like everybody to stay where they are, please. There may be questions to be answered."

The other patrons murmured back and forth among themselves. Reg imagined a number of them were objecting, saying that they didn't need to stay and they didn't know anything about what had happened. Their doubts, irritation, and anger ate at Reg, their own emotions being added to hers and stirred around, sure to produce something explosive. She wouldn't be able to stay around them for long.

"Have a seat, miss," the hostess told her, motioning Reg to her chair.

Reg wasn't sure at what point she had stood up. Had she been on her feet throughout the whole scene?

"Can I get you a drink?" the woman offered. "I see you already have a Coke, but maybe something stronger?"

Did she think that Reg would actually drink anything out of the kitchen? Reg just shook her head silently.

The hostess gave her a stern look. "Please just stay here. In case there are questions."

"I don't know anything."

"You were the one dining with him. You'll be needed to at least explain what you saw." She avoided saying that it was the police who would be asking the questions and wanting to know what had happened. But of course, Reg and everyone else in the room knew. No one was shocked when a couple of uniformed officers appeared in the doorway and seemed to be guarding against anyone entering or leaving the room. They didn't ask anyone any questions.

It was a while before the police detectives arrived, not wearing uniforms. Looking like they were just regular people when Reg knew they were wolves in sheep's clothing. There was some talk back and forth, the patrol officers, club staff, and detectives making motions toward the table where Reg still sat. They eyed her and spoke too quietly for her to tell what they were saying, and Reg didn't feel like listening in telepathically. She didn't want to know what they thought of her or of what had happened to Corvin.

Was he still alive? Had he made it to the hospital okay? Were they treating him now, making sure that everything was fine, or were they baffled, trying to figure out what was going on?

Eventually, a woman made her way across the room to Reg. Not one of the sexily clad hostesses, but a figure Reg knew well.

Detective Jessup.

CHAPTER TWENTY

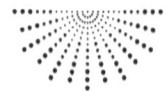

*R*eg, are you okay?"

Reg looked for some escape but, of course, there was nowhere to go. Even if she teleported herself out of there, it wasn't like Jessup wouldn't know where to look for her. Reg couldn't just pull up stakes as she had in the past. She had a cat. Responsibilities. And she really didn't want to leave this place where she had finally found her tribe. She didn't want to leave her new friends and her new life.

Jessup pulled up a chair to sit close to Reg without disturbing the chair that Corvin had sat in or any evidence that might still be there on the carpet where he had lain. Reg closed her eyes, a wave of dizziness cutting through her. She had watched Corvin collapse to the floor. Watched him lie there, maybe breathing his last breaths. How could the world have been turned on its head so abruptly?

"Reg." Jessup took her hand. Reg pulled back but, when Jessup held on, she gave in and let Jessup hold it.

"I'm fine," Reg said. "Corvin is the one you need to be concerned about."

"Believe me, we are. It will be a while before the hospital can tell us anything, so we will talk to everyone we can and get the story and any evidence while we can." Jessup gave her hand one last squeeze and then withdrew it.

She had probably been taught in cop school that she couldn't touch a suspect during an interview.

Reg waited for the questions. Jessup waited for her. Maybe she figured that if she were quiet for long enough, Reg would just start talking and would maybe implicate herself or give Jessup some vital clue. But Reg wasn't going to spill anything. She knew to watch everything she said. And she knew that Jessup was there as a detective, not a friend. They had been on opposite sides of the table enough times before.

"So, you and Corvin got together for dinner," Jessup suggested, starting out gently.

"Yes."

"His idea, I assume?" Jessup gave her a wry smile.

"Of course."

"Was this something you set up when he was in the hospital or did you talk earlier today?"

"He was waiting for me at home when I got back from my meeting with Davyn."

"At home?" Jessup repeated, looking surprised.

"On the street. Not in the house."

"Oh." Jessup nodded quickly. "Of course. He wouldn't be able to get into your yard or house."

Reg considered that, not confirming or denying. Jessup had pulled out a notepad. She looked at Reg as she flipped to find a fresh page.

"Right?"

"He did get into the yard the other day. Sarah said… he is growing in power and maybe she is waning, so he was able to break through the wards. But if I strengthen the wards each day, we should still be able to keep him out." Reg stared across the room, not meeting Jessup's eyes or watching her expression. "For a while, anyway. He still isn't accessing all of the powers he took from the Witch Doctor, so I don't know… That's more power than I have.

More power than Sarah and I together. An immortal. We can't match that."

"You don't know that Hunter will ever be able to access all of those powers. It may be too much for a mortal to handle. It could actually be detrimental to him. You don't know how holding powers like that might twist him."

Reg had seen how Kareem had been after holding just a fraction of those powers. But what had he been like before that? He must have been susceptible to the evil of the Witch Doctor.

And Corvin wasn't?

He was already a predator by nature. Add incomprehensible powers to that, and…

"We don't know," Jessup repeated. "Don't bother trying to predict the future."

Reg couldn't help letting out a laugh at that. Jessup stared at her for a moment, then a smile crossed her face.

"Yes, I'm telling a fortune-teller not to try to predict the future," she admitted. "I've probably done stupider things, but that one's gotta be up there."

Reg shrugged. Fortune tellers were notoriously bad at reading their own futures. Maybe there was something about knowing her own future that was against the laws of the universe.

"Sorry. Let's get back on track," Jessup apologized. "So Corvin was at your house when you got home today. Not inside the yard this time, but waiting for you out front. Because…?"

"He wanted to go out to dinner."

"Did he say why?"

"He always wants to. He said it was to thank me for helping to strengthen him, so he could heal quickly enough to already be released from the hospital. But he didn't really need an excuse."

"Right." Jessup nodded. She made a notation in her notepad, but Reg didn't know what that would be about. She hadn't said anything that Jessup didn't already know. And there was only so much that she could pass on to her nonmagical colleagues and bosses. Nothing about wards or other spells.

"So you agreed and came here together."

"Came separately. Met here."

Jessup nodded again. "Great. And once you were here..." Jessup glanced over the table. "You ordered drinks. But meals had not arrived yet."

"We just ordered before... he had the drink he reacted to."

Jessup's eyes went from the bottle of wine to Reg's Coke, to the empty tumbler in front of Corvin's seat.

"He ordered wine and the two of you ordered other drinks as well? The wine to go with the meal, I suppose?"

"I wasn't going to have any wine. Or maybe just a sip or two. He was going to have it. But the waitress brought him another drink. Whiskey, I assume. But he didn't tell me what it was. I don't know if he even knew. He just accepted it and tossed it back..."

"And did he react right away? Or was there a delay?"

"Right away. He said it burned. Then he started choking and coughing. He couldn't say anything after that."

"Who brought him the drink?"

"The waitress brought it. I'm sure she's still around here some-where. She said it was on the house. He said no, but she said it was already poured, so he might as well have it. I guess they would have just dumped it down the drain if he didn't. I figured... you know how women react around him. I thought that the waitress had poured it for him personally, to impress him."

"I'll have a chat with her."

"You don't think it was on purpose, do you? That he reacted like that? She must have just given him something that he was allergic to by accident, right?"

"There's no telling right now whether it was accidental or on purpose. I don't know of any allergies that Hunter has, do you? You've probably eaten with him more times than I have."

"No, he's never said anything. He never asked about the ingredi-ents in an order or told the server that he was allergic to anything. I don't think he was. Or, he didn't know if he was. Sometimes people just develop allergies out of nowhere."

"Sometimes," Jessup agreed curtly. She leaned toward Corvin's glass and took a loud sniff. She sat up straight again. "It just smells like whiskey."

"Would you be able to tell if there was anything else in it?" Reg asked skeptically. Her foster sister, Erin Price, could smell a tea or some other food and tell most of the ingredients in it. But most people did not have her sensitivity. It made for a good parlor trick but had never made Erin any money.

"No. Probably not. Cyanides leave an almond smell, but I don't smell anything like that. I don't know if I actually can. Some people have the ability to smell cyanide and others don't. Who knows what someone might have put in the drink that would make him that sick."

"Cyanide? You think it was poisoning? That someone did this intentionally?"

Jessup stared at her for a minute, then finally shrugged. "He *was* recently the victim of a murder attempt."

Reg felt as if she were choking. She had told herself that she wasn't going to drink anything that had come from the club's kitchen, but she felt like her throat was closing up. She needed a drink to wash down that lump in her throat so she could breathe properly again. She took a few swallows of the Coke, hoping it would calm down the wild beating of her heart.

Corvin had been *poisoned?*

"Let's put that aside right now," Jessup said, as if it were something that Reg could forget about. Something of little concern. "Can you walk me through what happened after Hunter had the drink and started choking? What he looked like, who said what, what first aid he was given before the paramedics got here...?"

"I suppose." Reg took a couple of deep breaths and then tried to give Jessup the whole story at once, without having to go back over anything she had already said. It was harder than it sounded. She forgot interim steps or what order things had happened in. It wasn't that she was stupid or hadn't been paying attention. It was just confusing. She had been in a panic herself, and that had colored everything.

"Do you mind staying here for a bit longer?" Jessup asked, when she had finished. "I want to talk to the staff before they start going their different directions. They've already been talking to each other, so their testimonies will be tainted. The sooner I can find out what went on behind the scenes, the better. But I'd still like to talk to you afterward. And the techs will be coming to collect evidence. I don't know if they'll need your fingerprints or any kind of swabs to confirm that you weren't contaminated with something. So can you stay?"

"I... I guess so. You don't think that it was something infectious, do you? Like I could have SARS or something?"

"No. I don't think it was infectious, and I don't think you were contaminated with whatever was in that drink. But it's best to be sure."

Reg looked down at her hands. Her fingertips started to tingle and it was suddenly getting hard to breathe.

CHAPTER TWENTY-ONE

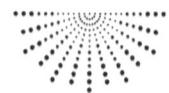

*R*eg sat and stared at her glass of Coke and tried to pretend that she wasn't aware of everyone else watching her and the suspicion that hung in the air. She wasn't the one who had poisoned Corvin. She hadn't done anything to hurt him. She had helped to heal him! Why would she then turn around and try to kill him?

If she wanted to kill him, she could easily have used her siren wiles, which she knew he was susceptible to, and drowned him as she pleased. That was what sirens did, after all. But she didn't. She let him live even though he had harmed her in the past and she knew how dangerous he could be. They were alike in some ways, both sort of outsiders because of their parentage, living on the borders of the magical community. Participating wherever they could, but still kept out of some circles. Still, a low level of suspicion followed them around wherever they went.

She sipped her Coke slowly, watching the time on her phone and only allowing herself to take a sip every five minutes, trying to draw it out so that it would last until Jessup got back from her interviews with the staff. However long that would take. It could be half the night. Police interviews weren't quick. If there were any legitimate leads to follow, Jessup might chase after those and leave Reg in the lurch for hours.

The forensic science people took possession of Corvin's glass. They didn't ask Reg for her fingerprints or any DNA or other evidence. They wanted to take her glass too, but she refused. She was perfectly healthy. They didn't need to test her glass for anything. They didn't find anything on the carpet where Corvin had lain. After futzing around for a while, they left again.

Reg didn't *have* to stay. Jessup had asked her to, but that didn't mean she had to. If Jessup took too long, Reg could just go home. She could say that she had appointments to deal with, which she did. She really didn't want to have to call and cancel on people. She liked the idea of being reliable, of being there when she said she would be. That was good for business. It built trust.

Her glass was almost drained, and Reg considered starting on the bottle of wine. As long as she drank it slowly, she wouldn't be too impaired to drive. She would hold herself to just one glass.

It seemed like the club staff had forgotten about her dinner order. Or maybe they had decided she would be too upset by the events of the day to eat it. That she wouldn't want to touch any food from the kitchen after what had happened to Corvin. And she had felt that way initially, but she was pretty hungry now and it would be nice to have something to nibble on. Maybe the police had shut down the kitchen, deciding it was too risky to allow them to continue to serve food until it had been determined what had ailed Corvin.

Maybe it was food poisoning.

Maybe it was nothing to do with the drink and was the result of something that had happened earlier in the day. Maybe it was something to do with his injury—what did she know about things like that? It could have been a poison-tipped weapon. Or enchanted in some way. Intended to make him think that he had escaped being killed, only to have it hit him later.

Maybe it was something in the air.

Or a candy that he had sucked on before arriving at the club so that his breath would be minty fresh.

Reg drained the last of her Coke and put the glass down. She decided to head home. Jessup knew where to find her once she was finished talking to everyone else and was ready to speak to Reg further.

Of course, it was just at that instant, when she pressed her hand to the top of the table to rise to her feet, that Jessup returned. Reg slumped back in her seat. *Really?*

"Hey, Reg, sorry to be so long." Jessup sat back down in the chair that she had vacated earlier. She glanced around and saw that Corvin's glass had been taken and gave a slight nod. "Trying to talk to people about something like this… they all just want to sweep it under the rug. Say that it was just an allergic reaction and Mr. Hunter will need to be more careful in the future."

"But…?"

"I can't really tell you anything about it," Jessup reminded her.

"Who poured Corvin's drink? Who wanted it given to him?"

Jessup leaned in. "I don't know who ordered the drink or had it sent to Corvin. It's all a little vague. I'm not sure *they* know who it was."

"Somebody had to pay for it."

Jessup nodded. "What they generally do here, is that members charge the meals and drinks to their account and then pay their account once a month. They each have a membership number, and they write that on a chit, and sign it, and the server adds anything that they order to that paper. The chits are all entered into the computer system, and a monthly invoice goes out to each member."

Reg nodded. She had seen Corvin scribble his signature or initials onto a small piece of paper. He never pulled out a credit card at the table like he would at a restaurant.

"So there must be a piece of paper for the drink. It wasn't on Corvin's account. He's not the one who ordered it. Or if it was the waitress herself, she would have to cover it, wouldn't she?"

"She didn't know who it was from. She was able to produce the chit that the man who sent the drink had signed."

"Then whose account was it?"

"The number was for an old member who isn't here anymore. The account has been closed for years."

"Oh. Someone just picked a random number and pretended to be a member? Don't the staff know the members personally? They always call Corvin by name."

"If they come regularly. But there are some people who are members who only come once or twice a year, or whose memberships are still active, but who don't live in town anymore. If someone knows their number and writes it on the chit, the server assumes they are a legitimate member."

"How did they sign? Maybe they accidentally wrote the wrong number?"

"If you were going to poison someone, would you use your own membership number?"

"No, of course not," Reg agreed.

Jessup glanced around to make sure that no one was sitting too close and might be listening to them. "The chit was signed 'Justice.'"

CHAPTER TWENTY-TWO

*R*eg frowned, thinking this through. All sorts of random thoughts pinballed through her head as she looked at it from different angles. "So... do you think that is a person's name or the reason they are trying to kill Corvin?"

Jessup nodded. "I'm having them check their records for anyone who might have the name Justice or who might be a judge or something like that. But I think it's a clue as to who is doing this. And that means that it wasn't an accident or an allergy—or if it was an allergy, it was one that someone else knew about and used against him. That means that it was planned. And they're not going to give up after one attempt. The stabbing failed, so then they moved to poisoning."

"And then...?"

"Exactly. Then what? We can't protect Corvin. If this was a TV show, we'd have a guard inside and outside his room and following him around when he was released, doing drive-bys past his house. But in real life...? A real police force can't afford to do those kinds of things. We don't have the money or the manpower. He has to be responsible for his own safety. And so far..."

"This person has attacked him while he was sleeping in his bed and eating in his private club. How is he supposed to guard against anything while he is sleeping? And what place is more secure than his home or club?"

"He'll have to set up some wards," Jessup said. "He can protect himself that way."

"He already *has* wards at his house. We talked about that. Someone more powerful than him must have defeated them."

Jessup's eyes got big and round. "Someone more powerful than him? Like who? Zeus himself?"

"I don't know. I have no idea who would have more power than he does. He says he's not using all of the powers he got from the Witch Doctor and Kareem, but he's still pretty strong."

"I don't know how you can put yourself in this kind of position," Jessup said, indicating the table where Corvin and Reg had sat down to eat together. "Knowing how powerful he is."

"*You're* not afraid of him."

"I don't have enough powers for him to be interested in me. If I work hard, I can do a few minor spells. Very minor. Not enough for Hunter to care about. And even if he did, it wouldn't change my life if he broke the rules and took them. Not like with you."

Reg remembered the empty, bereft feeling. The hollowness of being the only person in her head. No more voices. No more old friends. No thoughts coming to her from the people around her. Like being in a big, echoing gymnasium all by herself.

And that had been before she had understood anything about her powers. Before she knew how to use fire or properly do a *seek* or *call* spell.

"I just know... what to do if he tries to charm me now. He can't fool me and I have my own ways to fight back against him."

Jessup looked doubtful about this but wisely kept her opinion to herself.

"So... did the waitress say whether it was a woman or a man who sent the drink to Corvin?" Reg asked, "Someone wants justice... but it can't be a woman whose powers he stole."

"Why not?"

"Because..." Reg thought about it. What had happened during

the two attacks that would indicate it was someone who possessed powers? "They got past Corvin's wards."

"Right." Jessup nodded slowly. "Yeah. I guess someone without powers probably couldn't do that. But we should investigate further to find out how the wards were defeated. That might be important."

"We?"

"Well, me," Jessup laughed. "You wouldn't be involved in it. I meant 'we' as in the investigative team. But since the rest of them are not practitioners, it's something I will have to follow up on by myself. I don't know a lot of magical lore about wards, so it might take some research."

"I'm sure Corvin would be happy to lecture you on it. If he's..." Reg trailed off, afraid to say what she was thinking or to ask.

"He's okay," Jessup assured her. "He's holding his own at the hospital. They said they're not sure what the drink was contaminated with, but he got help in time and probably won't have any lasting effects. Except maybe he won't be quite as quick to accept a drink he didn't order."

Reg turned her thoughts to this. "How did someone get something into his drink? Even if someone else ordered it, it would still have been poured by the staff and delivered by that waitress. Who else would have had a chance to touch it?"

"Maybe he's allergic to an ingredient that is already in it. Then no one would have to contaminate it. But... they don't have a lot of security measures inside the club. There is security to get in but, once you are in, everyone is just expected to behave. There isn't anyone enforcing it. The man who ordered the drink ordered it for himself. But after it was brought to him, he asked another waitress to give it to Hunter."

"Why would they do that? Haven't they ever heard of date rape?"

Jessup shrugged and rolled her eyes. "You know how this bunch is. They're pretty medieval in their views. Date rape is probably not in their vocabulary. And who would think that a man would send a drugged drink to another man?"

Reg remembered the uncomfortable feelings she'd had previously visiting the club with Corvin. She knew that there was unsavory stuff going on there. She didn't need to be told or to actually see it for herself. It was in the atmosphere. She had seen and heard enough to fill in the blanks.

"Corvin should sue them. That's ridiculous."

Who was trying to kill him for the sake of justice? What had Corvin done to deserve extermination? Who had he harmed? Was it that person who was seeking justice or a friend or family member seeking retribution?

"What about Julian?" Reg suggested.

"Julian? Your 'friend' from Magical Investigations? What about what?"

"He could be trying to get retribution for Davyn being kidnapped."

Jessup knew from the kidnapping investigation that Julian and Davyn were romantically engaged. She chewed over this suggestion for a while. "I don't know. Murder to avenge kidnapping? Maybe if Davyn had been killed in the process, but he's back well and strong now, so why would Julian go after a person who was only *partially* involved in the kidnapping? Especially since Hunter wasn't necessarily responsible for what he did."

"You don't know Julian. He's volatile. Hot-headed and explosive. He's violent and he does things without thinking. Breaks the rules. He pulled a wand on me and threatened me *in public.* When we were kids, he used to torture me whenever he could. Whenever the parents weren't home, sometimes if they were, but just happened to be in a separate room. He can't be trusted."

"I can't see him *killing.* He doesn't seem like the type."

"It wouldn't be the first time. He tried to drown me once. Who knows what else he might have done. I don't know how he ever managed to get into Magical Investigations in the first place. Don't they have some kind of psychological testing? Certifying that he's not a crazy serial killer?"

"I don't know what their testing process is." Jessup considered this further. "You really think that it could be him? Trying to kill Hunter?"

"It makes sense. I get that it's an overreaction to kidnapping when

Davyn is home alive and well, but you can't expect someone as crazy as—who is crazy—to be logical and carefully weigh whether the punishment fits the crime."

"I'll look into it. See whether he has an alibi. Maybe check in with Davyn. Why is Davyn friends with him if he is so unbalanced?"

"I have no idea. I can't understand it. I tried to warn Davyn about Julian, but he thinks that... I don't know what he thinks. Julian must hold things together when he is with Davyn. He *can* fool people. He can look normal for a while. But eventually, he breaks his cover. He can't keep it up forever."

"I'll check it out. He doesn't still bother you, does he? When he comes to Black Sands to visit Davyn, he doesn't get in your way? Try to bully you?"

"No." Reg rolled her eyes. She picked up her glass, looking at the wine bottle. But she didn't want to drink a full bottle and Jessup wouldn't drink with her while on duty. The staff would end up just pouring it down the drain if she only had a glass or two.

"What?" Jessup asked, sensing that there was more to Reg's answer than the simple "no."

"He... you know that he's involved in endangered creatures for his job. He was investigating the death of a swamp goblin. But when he found out I am part siren... that ended it. He didn't need to investigate me further because *I* am an endangered creature. So now when he's around me, he doesn't bully me and act threatening; he acts all starstruck and lovey-dovey like he just wants to take care of me." Reg shook her head in irritation. "I am not his *pet.*"

Jessup chuckled. "I could just see that. I bet he drives you bonkers."

"Yeah, he does."

Jessup made some notes in her notepad. She looked back at Reg, frowning, her head cocked slightly. "Does he know that Hunter is... what he is?"

Reg flashed back to a conversation she'd had with Julian the last time he'd been in town, when they had been trying to track down Davyn. "Uh... yes, he does now."

"Then would he be likely to try to kill him? If he is committed to protecting endangered creatures, then won't Hunter fall under that classification too? Or is he too human?"

"I'm human, and he thinks it's his job to protect me. He made a big deal of the fact that Corvin and I were both rare and that we had found each other."

"Then he wouldn't want to kill Hunter even if he thinks he was complicit in Davyn's kidnapping. Right?"

"I don't know. Who knows how twisted his thinking is. I've been inside his head once, and that was enough. His thought processes are very…" Reg thought back, trying to find a word for the state she had found Julian's brain in. He had allowed her to share his memories and, in trying to access them, Reg had found a disorganized, fractured mess. "They're broken. I don't know what else to call them. There's something wrong with him."

"What?"

Reg took a deep breath in and let it back out. "I don't know why he was in foster care. A lot of kids end up in care because of some pretty horrific abuse and neglect. I imagine whatever he went through in his natural family left him all twisted up and damaged. It may not be his fault, but he's still not someone I would want as my friend."

CHAPTER TWENTY-THREE

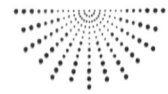

*I*t had been a long night with the investigation into the second attack on Corvin. Reg felt not just tired, but completely wrung out after the adrenaline burst during his attack, the anxiety of sitting there in the dining room waiting for Jessup to complete her questions, and the long night of batting ideas back and forth with Jessup as if she were a police consultant instead of a suspect.

And Reg knew she was a suspect. Jessup knew Reg's history with Corvin. He had attacked her more than once and was still determined that he would somehow charm her powers from her. And even if Jessup's superiors didn't know about all of the magical stuff, they still knew that Reg had been a person of interest in more than one case, including a murder. As far as cops were concerned, "where there's smoke, there's fire," so Reg was still a suspicious person even if they'd never been able to charge her with anything. It was just a matter of time until they could make something stick.

Even if Jessup assured her colleagues and boss that she hadn't had anything to do with the attacks on Corvin, they were bound to overrule her and tell her that Reg was a suspect who had to be investigated. Or maybe they would kick her off the case. Reg wouldn't be able to defend herself against accusations by another cop who didn't understand the magical aspects of a case. He would see Reg's long history of petty crimes and being a con artist, and be sure that she had just taken it to the next level and was trying to murder Corvin for his money or to get him out of the way because of the things he had done to her in the past, even if he thought her reasons were nuts.

Jessup assured Reg that she would follow up with Julian and find out whether he had a reliable alibi for the times of the two attacks. And she would continue to follow up with the club however she could, talking to staff members, trying to find out if they had video of who had been at the club that evening or any other chits or credit card charges that had been made. The kind of routine police work that would hopefully turn up something useful.

Reg had her own ideas about what direction the investigation should take.

She had a long drink before bed. Probably too much and too fast. But she didn't want to stay up and take it slow. She wanted just enough alcohol to anesthetize her anxiety and then she climbed into bed.

Starlight had seen to it that she didn't forget her duties to feed him and change his water before she went to bed. But he seemed to sense that something had happened and she was too tired to play or have to put up with any kitty cat nonsense. He was quiet and just curled up beside her on the bed when she settled in.

"You're a good boy," Reg told him, scratching his ears. "You know that? A really good boy."

He purred loudly. The best, most comforting sound in the world. Reg closed her eyes and just mentally focused on the star on his forehead. He transmitted comforting feelings over their psychic connection and the sound of his purr and, almost before she knew it, Reg drifted off to sleep.

She didn't usually go to sleep so quickly when she was upset or anxious. She would toss and turn half the night and not be able to get to sleep until it was practically time to get up again. So when she woke up in the night, she was surprised she'd gotten to sleep so quickly. She tried to downplay her own surprise and just accept it rather than getting excited and waking herself up even more. She got up to use the bathroom and then climbed back into bed, closed her eyes, and relaxed her body, hoping to slide right back into that sound, comfortable sleep.

But instead of the lovely, undisturbed peace she'd had the rest of the night, she was seized with nightmares. All the anxiety and dread over what had happened to Corvin, over his red face as he coughed and choked, and her concern that in a third attempt, the killer might just get lucky—all of that darkness rolled up into a ball and she found herself at the center of a terrible storm.

There was lightning and thunder. Between the flashes of lightning, Reg was caught in darkness so palpable she could feel it. She knew where she was. She was in the void. She had been there before, and she would never forget it. And at the center of the void, if she could find it in the vast emptiness, fire glowed.

Her own fire. Reg could feel it but not see it. She built it up, worried that it wouldn't be enough. In order for her to be able to keep the piece of the Witch Doctor trapped in the void, she needed to keep her fire burning there. Not just a little fire like anyone would be able to make. It needed to be a big, hot fire that would keep burning forever and *never* let him out.

But she didn't know if that was even possible. Even Francesca's binding spell, designed to last a thousand years, was already unraveling. How could Reg do anything that would last forever?

Reg poured her fire into the void, making her fire burn brightly enough to see it from where she was.

Starlight yowled somewhere close by, and Reg awoke with a start, her whole body tensed with effort. She had that sinking feeling that she used to have when, as a child, she would wake from a dream of needing to go to the bathroom and then discover that not only was that part true, but she hadn't woken herself up in time to take care of it and was lying in a wet bed.

But she hadn't been dreaming about relieving a full bladder this time. She'd been dreaming about lighting a fire.

Starlight was perched on the windowsill watching Reg, his green and blue eyes narrow. He yowled again, a mournful call Reg hadn't heard him make before. She sat up, clutching her stomach.

"What's wrong? Are you okay? Are you sick?"

Reg moved toward him, but he hissed at her so fiercely that Reg took a step back. Her head was still fuzzy with sleep but, when he hissed, his connection with her became more clear and she knew there was trouble. She hurried out of the bedroom and glanced around the kitchen and then the living room.

The end of the wicker sofa was on fire. Not a big, raging fire like in Reg's dream; just a little one, but Reg nearly lost her head. She had lit a fire in the cottage? She had assured Sarah repeatedly that she would never light any fires in the cottage, not even candles, until Davyn said that she had progressed enough that she wouldn't be a danger to anyone else.

She swore and reached out with her mind to gather the little fire in. She didn't behave like a non-firecaster, rushing over and beating it to death, but she pulled it to her, away from the flammable furniture, and formed it into a ball between her hands. She handled it like she would in one of her training sessions with Davyn. It wasn't danger-ous. It was just a part of her. A little part that had escaped while she was still sleeping. She handled it for a few minutes until her breathing was back to normal and her pounding heart had slowed down signifi-cantly. Then she absorbed it and took a few deep breaths.

She walked over to the couch and looked with dismay at the scorch marks on the arm. Sarah was sure to notice them the instant she walked into the cottage.

Reg looked around the room, thinking quickly. She went back to the bedroom and rifled through her closet, eventually pulling out a couple of large scarves. They were more wraps than scarves, big pieces of colorful fabric that could be pulled together and knotted into a scarf, a baby sling, a sari, or another configuration. They were very versatile. Reg took them out to the living room and draped one artis-tically over the arm of the couch to cover the scorch mark and the other over the back of one of the chairs to balance it out. The splashes of color looked nice, like an interior decorator had added them for a photoshoot. Not really practical, just a bit of eye candy to brighten the room up and give it some personality. Reg liked the look.

She turned around to go back to the bedroom. Starlight was sitting in the middle of the floor looking at her, his eyes accusing.

"It's not my fault," Reg protested. "I was asleep. I didn't *try* to do this, you know."

She still got waves of disapproval off of him.

But it wasn't her fault. She couldn't help having fire dreams any more than she could help having dreams about needing to go to the bathroom or about feeling excited about a handsome stranger. Nightmare or fantasy, she wasn't in control of what her brain did after she fell asleep.

"Are you going to come with me?" she asked Starlight, walking back toward the bedroom. "You helped me to go to sleep earlier."

He did not appear to be interested in joining her a second time. He stayed glued to the floor, watching her owlishly. When Reg looked back at him one more time before going back to bed, he had started to bathe.

CHAPTER TWENTY-FOUR

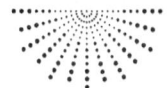

*W*hen she awoke in the morning, Reg felt awful. She could tell that she was dehydrated, whether from the alcohol she had consumed or from firecasting in her sleep, she wasn't sure. Probably a combination of both. She forced down a glass of water before doing anything else, and then had a long, hot shower, soaking under the spray until Starlight started to complain about her not feeding him.

Starlight was so powerful, he should be able to feed himself. If he was that hungry, why didn't he just move the food from the cupboard or fridge to his bowl with telekinesis instead of complaining to her about it?

But, she knew he wouldn't, so Reg turned the shower off and forced herself to get ready for the day. She had work to do.

* * *

Reg met Davyn at his house, which was on the edge of the city and sat on a big, wild property with dense woods that opened up into a clearing with an altar and a number of other amenities that apparently made it a good place for his coven to meet on occasion. Reg had hoped to get there before anyone else so she could ask Davyn a few casual, well-placed questions but, by the time she dragged herself out of her car, looking like a cat that had been through the washing machine, a number of the coven were already assembled. Reg looked around at them, matching up names where she could. She didn't know them well, but had met with them a couple of times when Davyn had disappeared.

Wilf Martin, a warlock with a white handlebar mustache and red face, had been the one who had acted as leader or spokesperson of the coven the last time Reg had been there, when both Davyn and Corvin were away from the group. He would be the first she would suspect of trying to get Corvin out of the way. He hadn't joined the leadership race for the coven—only Davyn and Corvin had thrown their hats into the ring—but he had implied that if there had been no one else running against Corvin, he would have stepped up so that there would be a choice. Was he hoping to get Corvin out of the way through other means and then to run against Davyn? Or maybe he expected that Davyn would bow out once Corvin was gone. Davyn was tired and ready to turn the responsibility over to someone else, but he couldn't just turn the leadership over to Corvin by default. The members of the coven had to know that they had other choices. If Corvin were going to lead the coven, it would be by majority vote, not default.

Wilf stood talking with a couple of the other warlocks. He looked at Reg and raised his brows, but didn't launch into a tirade about her being there. Davyn's coven was, of course, restricted to warlocks. It was not open to witches or psychics.

One of the young warlocks was watching Reg with great intensity. She looked back at him, uncowed, holding his gaze until he finally looked away, laughing and saying something to his companion. Reg remembered him. John Saunders had not been impressed with her. He had questioned her abilities as a practitioner and had not been terribly helpful in her investigation into Davyn's disappearance. But he had been vocal about his opinions against Corvin leading the coven. But he was just a young pup and not one of the voting members of the coven so, while his opinion could be heard, it didn't carry any weight.

Davyn nodded to Reg as she approached and addressed the men who were gathered so far. "Some of you already met Reg Rawlins when she was trying to find out what had happened to me and then to return me to this plane," he told them, reminding them that Reg had been of service to them in the past and that Davyn owed her a debt of gratitude. Reg hoped it would help the warlocks to feel well-disposed to her. But she didn't suppose it would make a lot of difference.

"Hi," Reg greeted nervously. "I'm sorry to be bothering you, but I'm sure that you're all just as concerned about Corvin as I am. Probably more so. I don't have to work with him, but you expect to be able to have his guidance and the strength of his gifts as part of this coven…"

They looked at her balefully, waiting for the punchline. There were a couple of small nods of agreement, but no smiles or amens.

Reg cleared her throat and shifted her weight from one foot to the other as she tried to find a way past their resistance. She could tell that they didn't want her there. Even if she hadn't been the least bit psychic, that much would have been easy to read on their faces.

"So…" Reg drew the word out, "I was hoping that some of you here might have some insight or knowledge to share. About why someone would be trying to kill him? Maybe there are rumors about who it is?"

They looked at each other, closing ranks.

"Did you hear that he is back in the hospital?" Reg asked.

There were a couple of nods, but most of the warlocks looked surprised to hear this news.

"I *thought* they released him too soon," Wilf offered. "When a man gets stabbed in the chest like that, narrowly escapes being killed, they shouldn't be releasing him the next day. That was a mistake."

"Actually, that's not why. It's because someone tried to poison him last night."

A murmur ran through the coven. Reg had already told Davyn everything she could about what had happened the night before, so he nodded his confirmation that it was true.

"They tried to poison him?" John Saunders scoffed. "Why would someone go from stabbing to poison? That's going in the wrong direction. People work their way up from poison to more direct violence."

"Maybe because stabbing him didn't work?" Reg suggested.

A ripple of laughter went around the group. They were beginning to assemble into a large circle. Reg looked around at them. She was pretty good with faces, and there were a few that she didn't know.

"We have a few visitors today," Davyn said. "If everyone could make room in the circle for the newcomers. As you know, we sometimes have the opportunity to welcome out-of-town guests to our group, which makes things more interesting for us and allows those from other covens the opportunity to still practice and participate with others while they are away from home."

Everybody jostled, making adjustments to what was probably their traditional arrangement. Like families always sitting on the same pews at church getting disrupted by a new family choosing to sit in the wrong place. Reg could feel the annoyance of the regular members at having to give up their usual order.

The three strangers seemed to be together. One, a white-haired man with a large beak of a nose, dressed like a farmer or casual laborer in a flannel shirt and khaki pants, one Asian man in a business suit, and a brown-haired, shy-looking man, younger than the other two, in blue jeans and a t-shirt. A dark pall hung over the three of them. Reg could see the darkness that surrounded them. Something had happened to them recently—some terrible shared experience.

The white-haired man looked around at the other warlocks, a frown on his face. Pronounced lines were drawn downward from his eyes and the sides of his nose.

"My name is Arthur Jessup," he told the coven. "And these are my sons, Harker and William."

CHAPTER TWENTY-FIVE

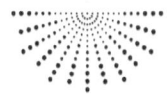

*H*arker was the Asian-looking man and William the youngest, the baby of the family. Reg couldn't see a big resemblance between any of the men and Detective Marta Jessup. Marta shared Harker's golden-brown skin. But she didn't look as obviously Asian as Harker did. Reg had often wondered about Jessup's racial heritage, but had never been brave enough to ask. Her mother had said that her name was Lily Lee. So Reg assumed that she was Chinese. Arthur was clearly not. William had inherited more of his father's skin tone. Arthur had probably had brown hair earlier in life.

"You're Jessup's—I mean Marta's family." Reg fumbled to find the right words. "I'm so sorry to hear about the loss of your wife. Mother. About Lily."

They looked at her with varying reactions. Arthur looked suspicious and irritated, as if no one was supposed to know about Lily's death outside the family. Jessup hadn't given any indication that it was something she wanted to have kept quiet. Reg couldn't have known, if that were the case. Harker looked angry. William looked sad. His eyes were far away, as if considering something in his past. Memories of happier days. While Jessup had said that her mother had suffered from depression, Reg assumed that she'd still had good days.

Days when she had been able to provide her children with the love and encouragement they needed. Times when she had been able to put her pain aside to give them a happy experience. Going to the park or zoo or shopping in Miami.

"I'm so sorry," Reg repeated, not getting an actual answer from any of them.

William nodded in response, with an automatic "Thank you. You're very kind."

"The Jessups have returned to Black Sands to take care of some family business," Davyn informed the group. "I'm not sure how long they will be in town—but you're welcome to join us in any of our activities." Davyn addressed the family directly with this last comment.

There were grudging nods from others in the circle.

Reg watched them for a moment with interest. She had never pictured what Jessup's family would be like, but she hadn't expected this.

"We should get started," Wilf said gruffly. "I don't suppose Corvin will be joining us today, and we don't want to waste all of our time answering useless questions."

Useless?

Wilf clearly expected Davyn to dismiss Reg at that point. He shook his head like an irritated bull trying to escape the pesky flies. Reg didn't have any place with the coven. She should leave.

"I wondered if there is anyone you know of who had a grudge against Corvin," she pressed. "Maybe someone who didn't like the idea of him running for the leadership of the coven?"

"You expect us to put ourselves forward as suspects?" John Saunders demanded, giving a wild laugh. "If we did have something against Hunter or didn't want him to lead the coven, don't you think there are other ways to prevent that from happening?" He shook his head. "You think I would break into his house and stab him in his sleep?"

There were nods and grunts of affirmation around the circle.

"Someone did," Reg pointed out.

"Not someone from the coven."

"You don't know that. It could be. I don't expect you to rat on each other. I'm just wondering what the group consensus is, and if there is anyone outside of the group you know who might take things to extremes."

"The coven is fine with Corvin becoming the leader of the group. We wouldn't have passed the changes to the coven rules otherwise. It's time to get with the times and let go of old prejudices."

Despite his words, Reg knew that wasn't how he really felt. It might be the official consensus of the coven, but it wasn't Saunders's opinion, and many others around the circle didn't hold with it either. Saunders was, in fact, quite angry about it. He would probably be much happier if the killer had succeeded.

"Old prejudices?" Reg repeated.

"You haven't been around here very long. Maybe you don't know anything about Corvin Hunter or his kind. People don't like to talk about it, which is stupid."

"Yes, it is," Reg agreed evenly. This was a beef she had with the magical community as well. "Exactly how is a person supposed to know what he is and what he can do if no one will talk about it? It's too rude? Rude is letting a woman be taken advantage of, to have her powers stripped away, just because you don't want to talk about something uncomfortable."

Saunders nodded his eager agreement. "We should be open about predators like Hunter and what they can do." He didn't go as far as to say that they should not be allowed to be members of the coven or their leaders, but such a comment would be unwelcome in the gathering.

"John," Davyn reproved quietly.

Saunders pressed his lips together and shook his head.

"How *can* you let someone like him be a member of your group?" Harker demanded. "He should be outlawed. He shouldn't be able to participate in polite society. Send him… away. To live like a hermit. Away from anyone he could hurt."

"We are here today to perform sacred rites," Davyn said. "Nothing but good, peaceful feelings should exist in this circle."

Harker looked at his father, his face tight with anger. Arthur looked back at him impassively, as if he couldn't see or feel his son's anger or the reason for it. He just gave his head a slight shake.

Harker seethed, but he kept his mouth shut and didn't make any accusations.

How would he have behaved if Corvin had been there? It might have been different if they were actually face to face. It was easy to disparage someone he couldn't see or know personally. If Corvin were there with him, exuding his charms and good manners and acting as if he were a perfect gentleman rather than the predator that he was, Harker probably would have reacted differently.

He would forget his outrage at a power drinker like Corvin being allowed membership in a coven and would have nothing but happy, comfortable feelings around him. Corvin might not affect men as strongly as he affected women, but he could still calm and seduce them if he wanted to. And he himself had said how the warlocks performing a ritual together opened themselves up to each other, making it that much easier for him to affect the men in the circle.

With warlocks like Corvin being elected, Reg figured it was only a matter of time before one of them lost control and attacked a member of their coven. The shock waves would be felt worldwide, and practitioners everywhere would be asking why they were never warned such a thing could happen.

"Has Corvin mentioned any trouble he's had with anyone outside the coven?" Reg tried. "Phone calls? Threats? Confrontations?"

They looked around at each other but were clearly not interested in answering Reg's questions.

"You'd have to ask Corvin that," Wilf said, shrugging.

"I will. But if he had said anything to any of you, that would help. Because he might not want to share that kind of thing with me. Men get so... macho, you know?" She was asking a group of warlocks this? "He'll think that confessing to me that someone has been harassing him would display weakness—when I couldn't care less about his machismo. I just want to figure out who is trying to kill him and to put a stop to it."

"I am not aware of any trouble he has had," Wilf said stiffly.

"Nor have I," Davyn agreed. "Although, as with you... I'm not sure that he would say anything to me even if there were. I'm sure he's faced a certain level of animosity over the years and has learned to live with it."

Reg looked around at the circle of warlocks, waiting not-so-patiently for her to leave so they could continue with their ritual. They were not going to give her anything of value. She nodded. "Do you mind if I hang around your house?" Reg asked Davyn, "so I can talk to you when you're free?"

He nodded. "Of course."

A murmur of protest went up from several of the warlocks around the circle. Davyn turned back to them.

"I am Reg's mentor," he pointed out to them. "It is entirely appropriate that I meet with her after we are done. We are not *spying* on the coven."

Those who had protested avoided his and Reg's gazes.

"Reg is not sneaking around trying to get dirt on everyone. She came to us openly asking for help. Maybe you don't know anything that would be helpful to her. But if you do… I hope you will get in touch with her. Everyone may not like Corvin… but I don't think that any of us are hoping he gets killed."

He looked around at the group. They were mostly looking at their feet. Davyn shrugged at Reg. "I'll see you at the house after. We should be done here in about an hour."

CHAPTER TWENTY-SIX

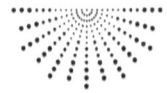

*D*avyn looked a little tired when he got back from the coven. He nodded to Reg, sitting at his kitchen table scrolling on her phone.

"Well, that's done. Sorry to keep you waiting."

"It's okay. I had stuff to do."

Reg did not confess that she had been sleeping on his couch most of the time. She'd set an alarm for an hour so that she would be awake when he got back, and had actually had a pretty good nap. His couch was comfortable.

"So, how can I help?" Davyn sat down at the table with her. His nostrils flared and he looked at her curiously. "Any more trouble with lighting your wards on fire?"

Reg shook her head. "I've been really careful. No more fires."

He nodded. Reg thought about her couch catching fire in the middle of the night and tried to mask her expression to keep him from figuring out that there was anything else to be worried about. The fire had been so small. It probably would have just burned itself out on its own. And she didn't know that it had anything to do with her or her dream. Yes, she had been dreaming about a fire, but that was probably because she had smelled the smoke and knew there was a fire nearby, rather than her actually lighting it herself. It could have been from… an electrical short. She couldn't blame it on candles, since she hadn't lit any, or on the stove, which had not been turned on. She couldn't think of any other reason for a fire to spontaneously ignite in her living room. She knew that things like gasoline or painting supplies sometimes ignited when they were too hot. And there was always the problem with cell phones melting or bursting into flames. But her phone had been beside the bed, where it always was.

"Reg?"

"Sorry. I didn't get as much sleep as I should have. So… I'm not saying it was, but if the person trying to kill Corvin was someone in the coven, who would you suspect? Who would have a problem with Corvin that was big enough for him to want to kill him? And who could get past the wards?"

"The second question is the one that is probably the most constructive. It's impossible to know who has been slighted or harmed by Corvin in the past and thinks that they have a reason to kill him. Sometimes people's reasons are very petty. But who *could* kill him… that's a whole different story."

Reg nodded. "If anyone in your coven was that strong, you would know about it, wouldn't you? If someone could break through Corvin's wards, then he must be powerful, and you would have seen that."

"On the surface, yes. Digging down a bit deeper… I'm afraid not. While I can guess at whether any of the established members are strong enough to take on Corvin's protections, the neophytes are all wild cards. If someone is new, I wouldn't necessarily have had a chance to see their gifts in action. People don't always show you all of their gifts, of course; some of them we keep pretty close to the chest. I know what to expect from the warlocks that I have been meeting with for years. Even if I don't know all of their gifts."

"But a neophyte wouldn't be very strong, would they? I mean, by definition, they haven't been practicing for very long."

"They haven't been meeting with the coven for very long. They might have been practicing for years."

"Oh." Reg realized that she had assumed that all of the neophytes were young men looking to join a coven for the first time. But of course, they might have been in another coven somewhere else. They might have just moved there or have had a reason to leave their last coven. Maybe they would disclose that fact, and maybe they would keep it a secret.

"And even if they haven't been practicing for very long, even if it has only been a few months or a year since they started practicing, a neophyte can still be very powerful. And dangerous, because they don't know how to control their gifts yet."

"Like with you teaching me how to handle fire safely."

"Yes. You can see, of course, how unwittingly starting a fire that you can't put out could be an issue."

"Yeah."

"Other gifts could be similarly destructive."

"Fairies are like that too," Reg remembered. "Like Calliopia when she first came into her own. Adolescent fairies can be dangerous and unpredictable because they are still learning how to harness their powers."

Davyn nodded. "Exactly."

"But would somebody like that, someone who doesn't know their own strength—would they be able to defeat Corvin's wards? Wouldn't they be... clumsy? Maybe not know how to do it? Or would they just know, instinctively?"

"There's no telling. A phenom or savant can sometimes accomplish something that someone who has years of experience and knowledge can't."

"Beginner's luck."

He nodded. "Something like that. Don't tell someone they can't do something they are already doing."

Reg laughed. "And you wouldn't know if you had someone like that in your group?"

"Maybe I would. Maybe I wouldn't. I wish I could say one way or the other, but I can't."

"And do any of the neophytes have anything against Corvin? That you know of. I know you can't read their minds..."

"No. I'm not aware of anything. I assume that if they had a

problem with Corvin, they wouldn't want to come to his coven. They would select another coven. Or remain on their own. Not all practitioners choose to do things in a group. Some people are very introverted. They don't desire that fellowship and would prefer to work on their own."

"And I was wondering about… Julian."

Davyn had been looking away from Reg, staring out the window as they talked, but his gaze snapped back to her. "Julian? What about Julian?"

"Do you think he could be the one trying to kill Corvin?"

Davyn shook his head, frowning. "Why would he want to kill Corvin? No, I don't think Julian has anything against him. The opposite, in fact, I would think that Julian would want to preserve him. To keep him from any harm. Besides, he hasn't been in town this week. I don't think you need to worry about him."

"Well… that's good. I don't want it to be someone I know. But Julian can be quite violent…" She trailed off and ventured a look back at Davyn. How would he take that revelation?

But Davyn appeared unaffected by this accusation. "He had a very difficult childhood. I can understand where that anger comes from."

Reg didn't know a lot about Julian's history. She couldn't assume that because she'd also had a difficult childhood that she understood where he was coming from. Their experiences would have been very different. She remembered that when they had been in the same foster home, Julian had been able to remember his family. He had been much older when he was put into care. The home he had grown up in had been magical so, unlike her, he had been aware of his gifts and how to use them. He had been a bully, cruel and cunning, which she assumed meant that someone had been cruel to him, too.

A pretty fair guess for a child in foster care.

Reg's phone rang. She looked down at it and saw Jessup's name. For a moment, she was confused, remembering the three Jessup men she had just met and wondering which of them it was. Why would one of them be calling her? Then she realized that of course it was

Marta Jessup, wanting to know if Reg had found anything or calling to say what she had discovered.

"Do you mind if I take this?" Reg motioned to it.

"Is that everything you wanted from me?"

"Yeah. I guess so."

She knew that she should talk to him about the fire dream she'd had and the fire on the couch when she had woken up. She should confess what was going on and see if there were a cure or a spell for fire dreams so that she wouldn't burn the place down around her as she slept.

But she'd lived that long without ever burning the house down, so what were the chances she would now, when she was getting control of her powers? It should have been more likely when she was younger and didn't know her powers.

Davyn was still looking at her questioningly. Reg nodded that she had said everything she needed to and reached for her phone. Davyn got up from the table and went to do something else while she took the call.

CHAPTER TWENTY-SEVEN

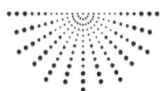

*H*ello."

"Oh, Reg. I thought it was going to go through to voicemail. You're up."

Reg looked at the time on the screen. "I've been up for hours. I'm at Davyn's. I was talking to his coven."

"You're always surprising me. Well, you'll be interested in my news. I was calling to tell you about the preliminary testing done on the glass collected at the club last night and the testing done on the residue of the alcohol."

Reg braced herself. What was it? Strychnine? Peanut oil? What nefarious poison had the killer tried to use to kill Corvin? "Okay, what did you find?"

"Nothing."

"What?"

"Whiskey. No noxious substances that they've been able to find. There wasn't very much to work with, so they ran a gas chromatograph profile, or whatever they call it. They've been looking for any common poisons or allergens. And nothing."

"So it was a rare poison or allergen?"

"I guess so. They can't test for everything. They have to be looking for something in particular. The techies say it looks like a regular alcohol profile, with no unusual spikes. But they've still been looking for some poison that might have been there in very small amounts. Something that is just really potent."

"But nothing."

"Nothing," Jessup agreed. "Was… it wasn't out of your sight at any time, right? No one could have swapped it out while you weren't looking?"

"Well, I wasn't exactly looking while Corvin was having his reaction. I was pretty distracted. Someone could have swapped it out, if they were smooth."

"Maybe that's what happened, then," Jessup said thoughtfully. "That would make more sense. Someone swapped a 'clean' glass that had just had whiskey in it for whatever had been in the one that Corvin drank."

"Are his fingerprints on the glass?"

"Yes." Jessup swore explosively. "Then that's not what happened. How could they get his fingerprints on a dummy glass? You were watching Corvin the whole time. No one was putting a glass into his hands to get his fingerprints on it."

"No," Reg agreed. So they were back to the fact that the glass Corvin had drunk out of did not have anything in it but whiskey, apparently unadulterated. "How is he today? Have you talked to him?"

"He's out of the woods. It was a bad reaction, but he's recovered. Sore throat for a few days. I suspect they'll release him today."

"And maybe he'd better stay home under lock and key and avoid any situation where someone might try to harm him again."

"Except that's exactly where he was the first time."

"Oh. Right." Reg shook her head. "What exactly is going on here? Who could be trying to kill him?"

"I don't know. You would think that suspects would be coming out of the woodwork, considering the kind of warlock he is. I thought we would have too many suspects. But everybody seems to be keeping quiet about him. No one is pointing any fingers at anyone else."

Reg had the uncomfortable feeling that Jessup was thinking about

Reg. She and Corvin had been enemies. Reg was the only other person who had access to Corvin's glass. Or maybe she hadn't put poison in his glass. Maybe it was something she had transferred to him with a touch or a kiss. Just because he'd had the attack right after he took a drink, that didn't mean that it had definitely been in the drink. In fact, it looked like it had not.

Jessup didn't say so, but Reg knew that meant they would be looking at her all that much harder.

* * *

As she returned to the house, Reg remembered her duty to strengthen each of the wards, which she had not done before leaving the house that morning. She made her way around the backyard, giving attention to each one, being careful not to set them on fire. It had been challenging to keep her fire under control lately. It should be the other way around. She should have been able to control it better the more she learned from Davyn.

She sighed and made her way around the cottage to the garden behind it. Forst was digging with a shovel in one of the beds and smiled when he saw her.

It is good to see Reg Rawlins.

You too, Forst. How are you?

He removed his red cap to wipe his sweaty forehead. *It is good to get hands dirty and to work hard.*

Then this is the right place to be, Reg told him, and laughed.

Forst smiled, nodding, and continued to dig. Reg watched him out of the corner of her eye as she continued to cast her spells to protect the garden. The beautiful gardens needed special care. For Forst and the elves and whatever other creatures lived there.

Oh… I wanted to ask you about something. I saw something in the bushes the other day.

Forst nodded encouragingly. *Yes. There are many things in the garden.*

It was… unusual. Sarah said she thought it might be an armadillo.

131

He smiled, his cheeks getting even redder. He took off his red cap, mopped his face with it, and put it back on. *You have met the hatchling.*

Well, we didn't exactly meet. He took off.

He is still here, Forst assured her. *I am keeping watch.*

He's okay, then.

He is healthy and strong and learning.

And he's not... I mean, he's not a danger to me, or Sarah, or anyone else who comes by.

Forst stroked his white beard thoughtfully. *One should always be cautious in such cases.*

Sarah set these protections, Reg made a motion to indicate the work she had been doing. *They are supposed to keep anything dangerous from entering the garden.*

He nodded his agreement.

So nothing that is poisonous or dangerous to me can get in.

Forst nodded again.

Reg felt like there was something important he was not telling her. But he had agreed that the armadillo was not a danger to her. And Reg knew enough about the animals to know that they did not normally attack people. As long as she left it alone, it would leave her alone too.

So I don't need to worry?

Forst continued to stroke his beard. *Humans should always be careful around creatures. Especially ones they do not know.*

CHAPTER TWENTY-EIGHT

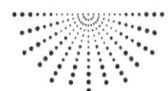

*R*eg had almost forgotten about Lily Lee Jessup.

She had been able to put the ghost out of her mind while she had been pursuing other matters. Maybe Lily was starting to settle down and see that her afterlife wasn't so bad after all. Maybe she'd been distracted by something.

Or maybe it was Reg who had been distracted.

When she walked back into her cottage, it was a mess.

Reg tried to keep things tidy, putting them back where they belonged after use so that she wouldn't have to do any major cleaning up. She wasn't the best example of a good housekeeper, but she did her best and, when things got bad, she buckled down and worked away at it until she could get things back in order again. Having Sarah there as a landlord helped in more ways than one. She knew that she had to keep things reasonably tidy or face Sarah's wrath—or disappointment—over how her tenant was keeping the place. And Sarah still seemed to see it as her job to make sure that the cottage didn't fall into wrack and ruin, so she picked things up and tidied here and there as she saw something that needed to be done.

So it was not normal for the cottage to look like that.

Reg's first thought was that someone had broken in and ransacked the place. It looked like a room that had been "tossed" on a police drama. The type of thing where, as soon as the homeowner or friend stepped into the room, they gasped and asked what had happened. Had someone been looking for something? Valuables? Some kind of written records that they imagined Reg kept? She didn't, of course. She didn't write any more than she absolutely had to and, when she did, it was generally a note typed into or dictated to her phone, not something that would be left lying around the house.

She went to the bedroom and checked the back of the closet for a small wooden chest. She opened it with her heart pounding hard in her chest, afraid it would be empty. But the gems glittered, apparently undisturbed. Reg contemplated them for a few minutes, reaching out with all of her senses. A year ago, she would have laughed at anyone who suggested that an inanimate object like a diamond could have feelings and react to the way that it was treated, but her sensitivity to the stones had been honed over the past months and, like the dwarfs, she saw the gems as having their own personalities, shaped by their histories, each one having different needs and experiences.

But they weren't talking to her about who had been in her cottage throwing everything she owned onto the floor. Reg held her hand over the gems for a moment, sending them positive thoughts and feeling a warm glow in return. She replaced the lid and put the box back in the closet. She knew that she needed to find a better place to store them. Somewhere they would be safer.

But she liked having them near her. She wasn't sure she could stand to put them in a safe deposit box in a bank or some similar situation.

Reg stood up and looked around. "Starlight?"

The cat was nowhere to be seen. Reg gulped, a lump forming in her throat.

"Star? Where are you?"

She walked through the rooms, checking all of Starlight's usual sleeping places. Maybe the cat had just been too deeply asleep to wake up when Reg walked into the house. But he wasn't on any perch or patch of sunlight he usually chose.

"Starlight?" Reg focused on him and reached out for his presence. To her relief, she could sense him there, somewhere close by.

Whoever had broken into her house had not let him out and scared him away.

She backtracked through the cottage to find him and eventually discovered him under her bed, crouched down, his eyes big, looking very disturbed when she tried to get him out.

"Are you sick?" Reg asked worriedly, "or just scared by whatever happened here?"

He stared back at her.

"Just scared?" Reg asked. "Do you want to come out for something to eat?" she tempted.

His ears rotated, listening to her and thinking about it.

"I'll get out some nice tuna. How about that?"

His nose wiggled, sniffing the air around him, wanting to know if Reg actually had fish for him.

"Come on. Out to the kitchen. I'll get you some."

She stood up and headed for the bedroom door. Starlight slithered out from under the bed and followed her.

"You could hear me calling you," Reg told him. "Why didn't you come out when I called you? I was afraid that you got outside."

He did not attempt to excuse himself for his behavior. As he followed her, his ears rotated around and around, his nose and whiskers twitched. He startled at any unexpected sound.

Reg opened a can of tuna rather than rifling through the fridge to see if she already had tuna in another container. It was an emergency. If she ended up with two containers of tuna in the fridge, she would deal with it another time. She put a large spoonful into Starlight's dish, spread it out a bit, then watched him eagerly dive in and start snarfing it down as if he hadn't eaten in days.

"What happened here? Who did this?"

He looked up at her briefly, then went back to eating. Reg took a slower look around, trying to find any patterns and to determine whether anything had been irreparably damaged.

"Who would do something like this?" she demanded aloud. "It couldn't be Corvin; he's still in the hospital. And no one should have been able to get here past the wards. I've been working on them and so has Sarah. No one should have been able to get in here."

There was a rushing noise. A wind seemed to blow through the room, raising goosebumps on Reg's skin. The wind swirled several times, making everything flutter and shiver. Reg held on to the kitchen island, bracing herself. What was going on?

The wind continued to build until it was howling and she could see something emerging from the nothingness, a shape resolving in the air in front of her.

Lily.

"Oh." Reg let out her pent-up breath. "It's you. Did you make this mess?"

It was the kind of thing a ghost might have done. A really angry, strong ghost. With the kind of strength that only a new ghost had.

"Lily. Look at this place. What have you done?"

"Where is my daughter?"

"She is at work. Trying to solve two attempted murders. It's very important work."

"You said I could talk to her!"

"Well, yes," Reg admitted. In the midst of everything else, she had forgotten about her ghost problem. She *had* promised Lily that if she did not channel through Reg in the middle of her consultations, she would make sure Lily got to talk to Jessup. "I just haven't had the chance to set anything up yet. We have been very busy."

"That is not important." If a ghost could stomp its feet, Lily would have. "I need to talk to Marta."

"I'll set something up. I'll make sure that you get the chance."

"Now. Get her now."

"Mrs. Jessup. Lily. You're proud of her for being a cop, aren't you? All of the good that she does? Right now, a man has been the victim of two murder attempts. He was stabbed in the chest—"

"I don't care. I seek vengeance!"

Reg made a calming motion with her hands. "Okay, okay, I hear you. But who are you seeking vengeance on? You killed yourself. No one else did that."

"You don't know!"

"I know what Jessup's father said. You overdosed on pills. What exactly do you want vengeance for?"

"I want my baby. I want my life back. This is wrong! Why won't anyone listen?" Lily shrieked.

"I am listening. And I'll make sure that you get to talk to Marta. It's just that… she doesn't believe in ghosts, so she's really not interested in anything I set up. If I help you communicate with her, she'll think it's just me trying to scam her."

"I will talk to her. She'll know it's me."

Reg shrugged, clenching her teeth. "If you think that I'm going to help you when you're throwing things around the house like this, you'd better think again. What did you do this for?"

Lily looked at her blankly.

"Look around here!" Reg insisted.

Lily wasn't inclined to do anything but glare at Reg with fire in her ghostly eyes but, eventually, she broke her gaze and looked around her. She seemed unmoved by what she saw.

"This is my house," Reg told her sternly. "If you're going to haunt my house, you'd better behave yourself. Or I'll have to get rid of you."

Lily still didn't seem to understand what Reg's problem was. Reg sighed.

"I'll call Jess—Marta back. But only if you stay quiet and don't throw things around anymore. I'll have to spend my time cleaning up instead of making arrangements."

Lily glared at her, gradually turning from a ghostly white to a shadowy smoke color, and finally dissipating. Reg looked at Starlight, whose eyes were big black pools with barely any blue or green around them. She shook her head. "Ghosts!"

CHAPTER TWENTY-NINE

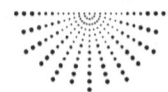

*R*eg wasn't sure what to say to Jessup to get her to agree to come to the house where her mother could try to talk to her. It didn't feel right to tell her that it was about something else and let Lily ambush her. But she already knew that Jessup wouldn't accept that Lily's ghost was there. They'd already been through all of that.

But, as it turned out, she didn't have to lie about it. She waited until later in the day, putting it off as long as she could under the pretense that it was because Jessup would have a better chance of seeing her mother later in the day, but really she was just procrastinating. She tapped Jessup's number on the phone, frowning as she tried to figure out what to say.

"Reg! I'm glad you called!"

"Oh… did you need something?"

"Well… I hate to be a bother, but with this case…" Jessup trailed off.

"What about it?"

"I know that you didn't have anything to do with Corvin's reaction to whatever was in his drink. That's not your style and it doesn't make any sense that you would do something like that in front of an audience."

"Uh-huh."

"But… my boss, you know. He wants me to pursue it further. To get an official statement, ask you all of the tough questions… I just need to touch all the bases."

"He thinks I did it."

"No… just that you are a strong person of interest. You were there and the two of you have a past. You know. Whatever hurt him was in the drink that the waitress brought him from the mysterious Mr. X. Whoever sent that drink went to a lot of trouble to get in and out of the club without detection, and he signed the chit 'justice,' so clearly this *is* someone who was out to harm Hunter. It isn't a coincidence that someone sent him a drink, putting 'justice' on the form, and he just happened to react to something within seconds of drinking that drink."

Reg nodded her agreement even though Jessup couldn't see her. "It doesn't make sense that it was someone else."

"Right," Jessup agreed. "But I still have to come and talk to you. Just to say that I did, and I'll tell them that I don't think you're the one who did it. It would be great if you had some kind of alibi, but I know you don't, sitting at the same table as Hunter."

"So you want to come here to talk to me about it," Reg said flatly.

"Well, I'd rather you came into the station, actually, to make a formal statement…"

"No. You come here or no deal," Reg insisted. She knew that Jessup would take advantage of the opportunity, and she was right.

"Yes, yes, if you like, I'll come there," she agreed.

"Good. I mean, I guess that would be okay. Are you coming over now?"

"Yes. Unless you're in the middle of making dinner…" Jessup laughed. "Or ordering dinner, since I don't think I've actually seen you make anything yet."

"Dinner would be good," Reg said. She felt like if she ordered in, maybe that would make up for the fact that she knew Jessup would be walking straight into an ambush. Never mind that Reg hadn't invited her over, but had just accepted that Jessup had to come over to interview her. She still felt guilty. "Have you eaten yet? What do you want?"

"You don't have to feed me. Not when I'm imposing on you."

"No, I want to. Nothing to do with the police interview." At least that part was true. "What should I get?"

"I don't know. Whatever you like. How about Spellbinding Pizza?"

Reg had always been hesitant to order anything from a restaurant that had the word spellbinding in the name. Wasn't that for things like books? And if you could bind something to a pizza with a spell, what would it be? She wasn't sure she wanted to eat anything that might have some unknown spell attached to it.

"Is it good?"

"Oh, they're the best. You haven't tried it yet? You really need to. Get a special. You won't regret it."

"What's on a special?"

Reg wasn't picky about food. She would eat pretty much anything. She'd learned to accept whatever was put in front of her in foster care. But that didn't mean that she always enjoyed it. Some places had served her very nasty things in the guise of food. Maybe that was one reason Reg was so anxious about the unnamed spell on the pizzas.

"Veggies, pepperoni, sausage. And their sauce is the most amazing thing. It's sweet and zesty, and it pulls all of the tastes together…"

And binds them together, Reg assumed. She didn't say so to Jessup. If she said that the special at Spellbinding Pizza was the best, then Reg could only assume that it was true and Jessup wasn't trying to fool her. She was going to be eating the pizza too. It wouldn't make sense for her to try to give Reg something that she wasn't willing to eat herself.

"Okay. I'll give it a try. I'll order now, then it should be here pretty soon after you get here."

"That's great!" Jessup sounded pleased. Maybe she was looking forward to her duty now instead of dreading it.

"See you in a bit."

* * *

Reg worked on cleaning up while she waited for the pizza and Jessup to arrive. It was amazing how much stuff a ghost could knock down and throw around with a few hours on its hands. Most ghosts that she had dealt with in the past had not been able to move things around very well. They didn't have much substance, and it was only with very strong emotion, like rage, that they could affect the corporeal world around them. Lily's ghost, being fresh and angry, was much more active than a typical spirit that had been hanging around for a few years.

The place didn't look too bad when there was a knock on the door. Reg tossed the last few items into her spare room, which she still intended to make into an actual office or consultation room one day, but she had not gotten around to it so far. It was hard getting up the motivation to get things done. One day…

Reg opened the door for Jessup. Jessup looked around, then nodded and entered. "This is really nice of you, Reg. Thank you for cooperating. I know it can't be easy for you, and I was not looking forward to calling and asking if you would mind…"

At least Jessup had not switched back to "Miss Rawlins," which was always a red flag that she was going to treat Reg like a suspect instead of a friend. Though Reg had told her how much that irritated her, so maybe Jessup just had the verbal tell under control.

"You can sit down wherever," Reg made a vague gesture to the seating area. "Did you see the pizza delivery guy out there anywhere?"

"No, but it's hard to tell these days, with people using their own vehicles rather than one marked with the restaurant's logo."

Reg waited for a minute at the door to see if the pizza deliveryman would magically show up, but he didn't. She shut the door again.

"Been redecorating?" Jessup asked, looking around.

Everything was picked up, but maybe she noticed how things had been moved around. It wasn't until Reg started picking up stuff off the floor that she realized she didn't know where everything was supposed to go. A lot of it was Sarah's and Reg had never touched it.

"Yeah, I moved some things around," Reg said with a shrug.

"It looks nice."

Reg cast around for a way to start a conversation about Jessup's mother. It wouldn't be easy to convince her to listen to what Reg had to say. Or to what Lily had to say.

"So, how are things going with the arrangements for your mom? I'm really sorry about your loss."

"Thanks. Yeah, we're keeping it all pretty low-key. Just close family friends, and there aren't a lot of them around here now. They've been away for a few years, and people have drifted apart. I'm not sure how close Mom was to anyone. She seemed like kind of a loner to me. But then, you don't see your parents as real people, do you? You have your own impressions about what they are like from inside your family. Maybe she had friends and was just too wrapped up in her family life to keep up with them."

"What was she like?"

"I don't know. Like I told you, she was depressive. Spent a lot of time just in bed or sitting in front of the TV. She wasn't that involved in my life or anything *outside* of herself."

"Did she come from a magical family? I know your mom didn't have any powers, but was that because she came from a regular, non-practicing family? Or just by chance?"

"Her family was practicing too. I knew a lot of them way back when… but I've lost touch with all of the cousins over the years. We just have different interests. The fact that I don't have much by the way of powers, and I'm interested in police work and other kinds of things. Not magic."

"That bothers your dad. Did it ever bother your mom? Or did she not care, because she wasn't magical either?"

Jessup considered this. "She was never keen on any of it, but she said I could do whatever I wanted to. I could choose to be in the police force, to stay in Black Sands when they were ready to leave, whatever. She let me have my independence. My dad never did let me do my own thing. Not without comment, anyway."

"I met him."

"You met him?" Jessup cocked her head to look at Reg. "When?"

"He was at Davyn's coven. I was there to see if I could get any information from them that might help the case. Didn't have any luck."

"Warlocks are pretty private, with outsiders anyway. They gossip like old biddies when they're by themselves, but get an outside party asking them what's what, and… they don't know anything."

Reg pictured Corvin and Davyn sitting around with teacups balanced on their knees, discussing all of the rumors about the other warlocks. She laughed.

Jessup smiled, but didn't look as if she understood what Reg had found funny. "So… what did you think?"

Reg looked at her blankly.

"About my dad. Was he… what you expected?"

"Well, I wouldn't exactly say that." Reg thought about the white-haired man. "You don't look like him."

Jessup snorted. "No!"

"I didn't spend much time with him, just met them. Didn't really have a conversation other than to say sorry about your mother."

"Oh." Jessup nodded. "Yeah. Thanks for that."

"I'm sorry for what you guys are going through. It's obviously affecting them—you a lot." Oddly enough, Marta Jessup did not seem to be affected by her mother's death as deeply as the men were. Reg would have expected the opposite. She would have expected Lily's only daughter to be more upset by it than the others. But maybe the two of them hadn't been close.

Everyone else had moved, leaving Jessup behind. So maybe she had always felt like an outsider. She was neither the most nor least Asian-appearing of all of them, so Reg didn't think it was a racial thing. But maybe it was a family where sons were valued more than daughters. That was true of a number of cultures.

"And they're all practicing other than you?" Reg asked, still having difficulty wrapping her mind around the possibility of not all of the people in a particular family being magical practitioners.

"William doesn't really practice either," Jessup said. "He's more like me. Not as much of a dunce about the magic, maybe, but he still never really took to it. But that doesn't mean he can't go to coven with the others. Not everyone who goes has gifts. Outside of Black Sands, many people who attend covens don't have anything you would recognize as powers."

Reg thought about Erin Price's friend Adele, who was a practicing witch. Reg hadn't seen or sensed anything out of the ordinary about her. She shook her head, no closer to understanding how it all worked than before.

The doorbell rang. Reg got up to get it, just barely remembering to check through the peephole before opening the door to a stranger. She was getting complacent with the wards in the yard. She needed to remember that Corvin had bypassed her wards once before and, any time she opened her door, it could be him.

She took the pizza from the delivery man, smiling and thanking him, then shut the door. She'd check later to ensure she had tipped him in the app.

"Smells good," she offered, smiling an invitation at Jessup. She put the pizza box on the kitchen island and opened it up.

And then Lily made her presence known again.

CHAPTER THIRTY

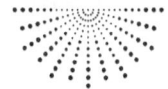

$\mathcal{T}$he pizza bounded out of the box as if it had been spring-loaded. Some of it ended up on the counter or floor, and a good amount of it on Reg's face and clothes.

Reg shrieked as the pizza went everywhere, hot sticky cheese landing on her face. She grabbed a napkin to wipe away the cheese as it started to burn, swearing angrily at the stupid ghost.

"I told you not to throw anything else around!" she shouted at Lily.

Jessup was only partway to the island, her eyes round and face pale. "What happened? You dropped it?"

"Dropped it?" Reg repeated. She indicated her face as she tried to clear the mess away. "Since when does dropping something send it up into your face?"

"Well, if it bounced back..."

"Are you kidding me?" Reg shook her head. "Does this look like I dropped the pizza?" Reg looked exaggeratedly around her at the slices of pizza and globs of cheese and topping everywhere. She looked up and saw one piece stuck to the ceiling. She swore again. How was she going to get that cleaned up before Sarah saw it?

Jessup gaped up at the piece on the ceiling. "You must have thrown it!"

"I didn't throw anything. You saw me set the box down on the counter and open the lid."

"Then… something is wrong. Pizza doesn't just explode like that." Jessup looked around, blinking. But of course she was completely ignoring the other entity in the room, her mother hanging over her shoulder. Literally floating a foot or so above the ground in order to look down at her daughter. "The cheese must have been superheated," Jessup suggested. "So when you opened it, and the colder air hit the pizza, the shock of the hot and cold hitting each other made it explode."

People who didn't believe in ghosts would go to great lengths to explain away any supernatural or paranormal phenomenon they had witnessed.

"It is not superheated cheese," Reg told her. "It is your mother, and it's time you talked to her."

"My mother?" Jessup laughed. "Good grief, Reg. Why would my mother blow up a pizza? This was a completely natural and explainable occurrence. It might seem strange, but it makes perfect sense when you look at it from a purely scientific standpoint."

"It's your mother, and she's mad because she's wanted to talk to you since the day she died, but she hasn't been able to."

Jessup shook her head in irritation. "I told you I don't believe in ghosts."

"Well, one just blew up your pizza, so maybe you should start."

Jessup scooped up a piece of pizza that had landed right side up and was mostly intact on the counter. She took a larger-than-recommended bite and chewed quickly, fanning her face. Obviously, the cheese was still hot enough to make eating it quickly a bad idea.

"You should have some too," Jessup said. "I don't think you're feeling very well."

She was being generous, blaming Reg's words on something other than trying to scam her.

Reg picked up a piece of the pizza as well. She didn't bother putting it on a plate. It wasn't exactly going to make the counter or floor a bigger mess if the sauce or cheese dripped. She took a smaller bite than Jessup had. It was delicious, as Jessup had promised. Whatever magic they were using on it was clearly working.

"I'm sure that if there were ghosts, I would love to speak to my mother," Jessup said in a conciliatory tone. "But since there are not… can we just drop the subject?"

Another piece of pizza rocketed from the counter up to the ceiling and stuck there, making them both jump back, startled. They both stared up at it for a minute.

"Stop doing that," Jessup told Reg in a calm, controlled tone.

"I'm not doing it!" Reg looked over at Lily, who was looking fairly substantial, but not substantial enough yet for Jessup to see her. "And I told *you* to stop. No more throwing things around. If you want your daughter's attention, you get it another way. I'm not spending all day cleaning!"

Though she would be spending several more hours that night scraping up pizza bits and scrubbing every surface of the kitchen from the ceiling to the floor.

"This isn't funny, Reg," Jessup said.

"I'm not playing a joke. I'm trying to get your mother to talk to you instead of having a ghostly temper tantrum. It would help if you talked to her. Even if you don't believe, just say something to acknowledge her."

"I'm not talking to someone who is not there."

Reg was braced against another invasion from Lily, not wanting to channel her like she had the first day when Jessup received her father's phone call notification. But it didn't matter if she was ready for it or how powerful she was. All at once, control was wrestled away from her and she could feel Lily's facial expression taking over from Reg's own.

"Marta Angelica Jessup, you listen to me! Quit being so stubborn! Just because you cannot see the unseen world does not mean that it does not exist. I am here now! I am not a figment of someone's imagination. I am here and I need to talk to you."

Jessup's eyes widened as she saw her mother's face in place of Reg's and heard her mother's strident voice. She took a step toward Reg, and then backward again, shaking her head.

"Mom," she said in dismay. "I don't believe it's you."

"You never would listen to me. But you need to now."

Jessup looked around for some reprieve, but couldn't think of anything. The ghost using Reg's body took a long, deep breath. Everything the ghost had done that day had drained it a little bit more. Throwing things around and talking took energy. A lot of energy. And talking to Jessup seemed to be the biggest strain of all, holding on to possession of Reg despite her struggles to regain control. Reg could feel her energy flagging.

"Your father and your brothers know," Lily said. "You need to talk to them. I will be avenged!"

"Avenged for what? You—she—committed suicide. That wasn't anyone else. There isn't anything for me to do other than to wait for the medical examiner's office to release your—her—body so that we can have a service. And hopefully put your spirit to rest." Jessup rolled her eyes and her mouth twisted into an ugly scowl.

"I couldn't bear it anymore," Lily said. "I couldn't live with it anymore. I did for as long as I could. I thought... maybe I would have grandchildren I would want to see. But I can't wait for that. I couldn't. It was just... too much."

"I'm sure you couldn't wait any longer," Jessup snapped. "And that is my fault, just like everything else, for not going out and getting myself pregnant at the earliest possible date. That isn't what I want out of life."

Reg's hands wiped her eyes and massaged the frown lines across her forehead.

"And you knew I wouldn't live forever."

"Yes. I knew. You—she—told me that plenty of times. Trying to blackmail me into doing things I wasn't ready for so that you could see me do them before you died. Well, I wasn't living my life for you. For *her*."

"I was living mine for you," Lily countered.

She leaned tiredly on the counter, using her elbows to help to support Reg's tiring body. She wouldn't be able to hold on to the body for much longer.

"Reg, are you okay?" Jessup asked in concern.

"Avenge me!" Lily demanded, then finally relinquished her control. Reg tried to hold herself up, weak after how much energy she had used to hold off and fight Lily for control.

"Come here. Lean on me," Jessup directed, taking her back to the couch and helping her to sit down. "Stay here. I'll get you some more pizza. Brain food, right?"

"It's a mess!"

"I know. But there are still some pieces here that are perfectly good." Jessup returned with another slice of pizza. This time served on a dinner plate. "Have some more. You need to build up your energy."

"It *was* your mother," Reg said.

Jessup snorted. "Avenge her? Yeah, okay. That's not something my mother ever said when she was alive. If she was wronged, she should have dealt with it then. She should have stayed alive for however long she needed to in order to take her revenge. Because I'm not up for that. I'm a law enforcement officer. I'm not in the vengeance business."

Reg nibbled at the pizza, unsure whether her stomach was up to it. It tasted just as good as the first bite had. She had a few more bites, thinking about what Lily and Jessup had said.

"You *know* that was your mother," she asserted.

"If my mother wanted to tell me something that was so important, she could have told me while she was alive."

Reg wanted to push it further, but she knew it wouldn't do any good. She wasn't going to force Jessup into believing that the words had come from Lily's ghost. If she wouldn't believe pizza rocketing to the ceiling, then she wasn't going to believe what Lily had channeled through Reg, no matter what her eyes and ears told her. Especially if the words that came out of Reg's mouth didn't match up with what Lily had said and done while still living.

Ghosts could be confused. Reg knew that. She'd seen it happen before. They didn't believe that they were dead and went to great lengths to prove that they were not. They thought that they had been taken before their time and must have been murdered. Like Lily, they might storm up and down, demanding vengeance.

Maybe Lily could not accept that she had ended her own life and was looking for someone else to blame. And if she had committed suicide, what was the benefit in Reg pushing Jessup to listen to her? It was just hurting her.

CHAPTER THIRTY-ONE

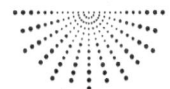

*D*id you and your mom talk a lot?" Reg asked.

"No. When they moved away... it was like they moved out of my life. I might call her on her birthday or at Christmas, but she didn't act like she wanted anything to do with me, so..." Jessup shrugged. "Why push it? It would just make both of us feel bad. I had to accept a long time ago that my mom had other things to worry about. The best thing for me to do was just take care of myself and let my dad take care of her."

"That must have been hard for him if she's had mental health issues for so long."

"Yeah. I think it aged him. A lot of men his age are still active and vital, in their prime. But he's been an old man for a long time. Maybe Mom saw what it was doing to him and decided to give him his life back."

Reg thought about the dark pall surrounding the three Jessup men. Of course, it was too early to tell what kind of a life Arthur Jessup would live now that he didn't have to care for his fragile wife anymore, but if she were to judge by what she had seen so far... he wasn't going to be much happier with her gone than he had been taking care of her.

"But you're close to your brothers. You said that they helped to take care of you growing up. Tried to take over on some of those things that your mom couldn't do."

"Yeah. Harker was like another parent to me. He wasn't that much older, but he was always doing whatever he could to look after his little sister. I don't know that it was very good for him, forcing him to take that responsibility when he was still a kid, but he did what he could, and I don't have any complaints about that."

Reg nodded. She continued to nibble the pizza.

"William was born a few years after me. So he didn't take care of me, but he was always around, and he was fun to be with. We had such a serious family, and he was kind of the class clown. Cracking jokes, trying to entertain me and everyone else. I thought it was so wonderful when I found out that mom was pregnant. I thought it was just what she needed. I guess I bought into all of the crap you see on TV about motherhood being so fulfilling and how much parents loved their children. I thought that she would be happy to have another baby and look forward to holding him and looking after him. All of these families on TV were always so happy when another baby came along. But… she was hospitalized for a lot of the pregnancy. Dad said it was because of complications. She had to be on bed rest and wasn't allowed to have visitors because they might make her too stressed. But I don't think that was actually true. I think it was probably her depression. He just didn't want me to know about it."

"And I don't imagine postpartum was any better."

"No. I don't remember much about what happened during that time. Maybe it was so bad that I've blocked it all out. I remember helping to take care of William. Thinking it was wonderful to play with this living doll. I wanted to take him to school with me, but they wouldn't let me." Jessup laughed at this. "And when he was a toddler or in those early grades, I spent a lot of time playing with and entertaining him. I guess Mom just didn't have the emotional resources…" Jessup wandered back over to the kitchen island and picked at bits of exploded pizza on the counter. "I was lucky, I guess, because I didn't have to look after William the same way as Harker looked after me. Or maybe I just wasn't up to it. I never felt like I was his parent or had to discipline him or make sure he was doing well in school. We just played together. Had fun. Ran a little wild."

There were a lot of complexities in family relationships. Reg had been in all kinds of families and seen all sorts of interactions. Jessup's relationship with William didn't sound too bad. It was good that Jessup hadn't felt like she had to be his parent. The poor kid already had enough to endure with his mother, father, and brother all telling him what to do.

Jessup stretched and arched her back. "It's been a long day. We should probably do what I came here for and talk about what happened at the club."

Reg had almost forgotten that was the reason Jessup had come over. She sighed, not wanting to get into it.

"Is he okay? Corvin?"

"The doctor said he'll make a full recovery. Whatever was in that drink… probably won't have any permanent effects. He's still in the hospital under observation to ensure he doesn't develop any other symptoms. Toxins can cause kidney or liver failure, or some of them can cause heart problems. They're just being careful."

"I'm glad they're keeping him there for a while. Do you have someone guarding him?"

"You really only see that kind of thing on TV. He's on his own. We don't have the resources to provide him with a police guard. He could hire private security if he wanted to. Maybe Damon Knight's company."

"I can't see Corvin doing that."

"No. Me neither, to tell the truth. And not just because he doesn't get along very well with Damon. I think even if they were buddies, or he had some other company that he felt comfortable with… he would probably still be too stubborn or macho to hire someone to protect him. Someone as powerful as he is should be able to protect himself. Whoever it is trying to kill him, they've failed twice already, so they're weak."

"But if they keep at it… sooner or later, they're going to succeed."

"Maybe they'll give up now. Two failed attempts. I wouldn't keep trying and risk getting caught. The first two failures just prove that it's not meant to be."

"Well, hopefully, our killer thinks the same way as you do. I don't want to see Hunter killed, even if he is a pain in the neck."

Corvin seemed to have ways to help the police force. Reg didn't know exactly what kind of consultation service he provided, but Jessup seemed to be able to utilize him fairly often. Reg didn't think that they'd ever had an intimate relationship, but she often wondered what the connection between the two was. They seemed closer than just law enforcement officer and consultant. Like Jessup had some kind of hold over Corvin that she had never disclosed to Reg.

CHAPTER THIRTY-TWO

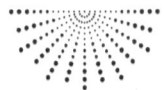

*W*ere you at the table the whole time?"

Reg looked at Jessup, blinking and trying to reorient herself to this line of questioning. "At the club?"

"Yes. Last night at the club. Were you sitting with Hunter at the table the whole time? Or did you get up to go to the bathroom, or he went over to another table to talk to a friend, anything like that?"

Reg thought back. She was sure that they had both been at the table the whole time. But Jessup wasn't asking the question lightly. It deserved some thoughtful consideration. And Reg didn't want to answer too quickly and have Jessup think she was trying to hide something or wasn't taking it seriously.

"No. I was at the table the whole time. We weren't there for that long. We had just ordered our meals. I never did get mine…"

"No, we shut down the kitchen. Couldn't take the chance that there might be some contaminant in the food that could hurt others. That would look really good on the front page of the paper. *Police allow twenty people to be poisoned on their watch.*"

"Yeah, probably not a good idea," Reg admitted. "But like I said… we were both at the table the whole time. Neither of us left it."

"Did anyone come over to your table?"

"Just the waitress. No one else."

"And it was only the one waitress? No one was helping her? Or one of the hostesses? Maybe a friend of Hunter's came over to say hi?"

"No. It was quiet. The waitress that brought over the drinks was the only one."

Jessup nodded. "So no one else could have put anything into his drink."

"No. Just the waitress and whoever had contact with it before that."

And Reg.

Jessup didn't say it out loud, but she was definitely thinking it.

"And how quickly after Corvin drank the whiskey did he have the reaction? Was it right away? Could it have been caused by something else and just *looked* like it was caused by the whiskey?"

"It was right away," Reg confirmed. "The first thing he said was how it burned. And then he started coughing and choking, and when he was on the floor, those welts or hives started popping out. It happened really fast."

"And it looked like an allergic reaction."

"Yeah, I guess. I mean… I haven't seen a lot of allergic reactions or anything, but that's how I imagine a really bad reaction looks."

Jessup nodded.

"Does that mean it *wasn't* an allergic reaction?" Reg asked.

"The doctor said he didn't have elevated histamines or mast cell activation. So… no. Not what we would call an allergic reaction. He does have damage to his throat, like he drank something caustic. But they haven't been able to say what it was, and the lab hasn't been able to identify anything out of the ordinary in the whiskey."

Reg frowned, thinking about this. "That's weird. Could it have been… magic, then? Like it was cursed?"

Jessup shrugged. "Maybe. I can't put that in my reports, of course. If the lab can't find anything, I'll just have to say, 'an unknown substance.' But something isn't right."

"It wasn't just a coincidence, right?" Reg asked. "We're not just seeing it as a second attempt on his life when it was just a random allergic reaction?"

"It wasn't a coincidence," Jessup said firmly. "Somebody sent him that drink anonymously. Trying to mask their identity. And signed their name 'Justice.' There's no way that's a coincidence."

"Unless their name really is Justice."

Jessup glared at her. Reg grinned and shrugged, embarrassed by her own suggestion. "What about at the first murder attempt? There wasn't any note signed 'Justice' there?"

Jessup didn't answer immediately. She considered her answer, pursing her lips. Reg raised her brows. She hadn't expected this to be a difficult question. Jessup started to pick up the rest of the pizza stuck to the counter and to put it into the box where it should have been.

"The police don't release all of the details of a crime like this to the public. They keep a lot of it under their hats. And there may be specific identifying features that they keep quiet so that when they get a legitimate tip, they can recognize it."

"Sure. I've seen that on movies. Is this one of those things? There was a note, but you're not releasing it to the public?"

Jessup shrugged, her focus apparently on cleaning up the pizza. She bent down to pick up the pieces on the floor, putting them into the garbage. Starlight made a *mrrrow* and hurried over to start licking up cheese before Jessup could clean it all up.

"Hey, you shouldn't be eating that!" Reg protested. "Dairy isn't good for cats. It will give you a tummy ache."

Starlight looked up from his feast to glare at Reg, then resumed eating. Reg made a noise of disgust and didn't rush over to stop him. He knew what she had said. If he ended up not feeling well, he would know why. And maybe the next time he wouldn't act like a little pig and eat all of the cheese.

Although, if he threw up all over the house, Reg would be the one suffering for his foolishness.

"Was the note signed 'Justice'?" Reg asked Jessup.

"No."

"Was it signed?"

"No."

"What did it say?"

Jessup gazed up at the pieces of pizza stuck to the ceiling, thinking about it. Reg didn't know how she was supposed to help out if Jessup held things back from her too.

"Death to hunters," Jessup finally said.

Reg thought about that.

It made some sense. Not just because Corvin's last name was Hunter. His name was Hunter because his predecessors had carried the curse that Corvin had, causing them to prey on the powers of others to satisfy their hunger. So "hunters" could refer to Corvin, those of his line, and any who carried the same curse. Death to all of them.

Were there any others like Corvin in the area? And if so, had they been attacked too? Or was it just Corvin?

"Hunters. As in more than one," she said to Jessup.

Jessup nodded. "More than one," she agreed. "But I haven't heard of any more attacks. And I don't know of any others in the area. No one from his family. None that I have heard of from elsewhere, and you would think that I would know if there were any others roaming free in our community."

"Would you?"

"If he tried to satisfy his hunger, yes. I'd hear about it."

CHAPTER THIRTY-THREE

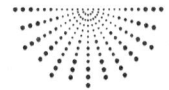

*J*essup had cleaned up much of the pizza. At least what was reachable. Reg was starting to get her strength back. Eating something had helped her recover faster, and Jessup had been right about the pizza being good. Jessup looked around. "I'm not sure how to get the rest. Do you have a ladder?"

"Don't worry about the rest. I'll take care of it. You shouldn't have had to clean up everything you did."

"Well. I did suggest Spellbound Pizza. If there was something wrong with it..." Jessup stared up at the ceiling.

"There wasn't anything wrong with it." But Reg didn't bother to tell her that it had been Lily. Jessup just wasn't ready to hear that, and Reg had to respect that. "Next time, I'll pick the place," she teased.

Jessup smiled. "Good idea. Well, have a good night. We'll get all of this sorted out sooner or later."

* * *

Reg was, once again, dreaming of fire. She ignited and extinguished fires between her hands, in her kitchen, wherever the fancies of the dream took her, whether inside or outside. She handled it confidently and without fear, and none of the fires got out of her control. She felt as if it was all natural, something she had known how to do her whole life, like other dreams where she had been able to breathe underwater. Or to fly. She knew she couldn't do those things, but she did in her dreams and it seemed perfectly normal.

Somewhere outside of her dream, she knew that Starlight was yowling at her urgently. But she knew it wasn't time to get up and feed him. He probably felt sick after eating the pizza cheese when she told him not to.

Then there was an urgent banging, but Reg ignored that too. It was probably just the wind blowing a tree branch against the house.

"Reg! Reg, you need to wake up now! Reg!" Someone shook her by the arm.

Reg swiped to push them away. She didn't want to get up yet. Whoever it was could just go away until she'd finished her dream and had enough sleep. It was rude to wake someone up in the middle of the night when they were sleeping. Even if it wasn't the middle of the night. People who slept during the day on other shifts and schedules deserved the same respect as those who slept "normal" hours.

"Reg!"

Finally, Reg managed to pull herself out of her dreams enough to force her eyes open and look around.

The sun was not yet up, so she had probably only been asleep for a couple of hours. Sarah was still shaking her, staring at her fiercely. Her manner was urgent.

"Reg. Wake up!"

"I'm awake."

"Reg, there's a fire. Get up."

"A fire?"

"Get up." Sarah pulled on her.

Reg slid her feet over the side of the bed and let Sarah pull her out of the bedroom and across to the outside door. She could see flickering flames through the window and Sarah's words were starting to force their way into her consciousness.

A fire? Why was there a fire? Had Reg lit another fire in her sleep? Outside this time? She couldn't do that. She had to find a way to stop herself!

Sarah pulled her out the door in her bare feet. Around the side of the house, looking toward the back, Reg could see the flames in the garden and smell the smoke in the air. Sarah released Reg. She folded her arms, trying to look calm, but Reg could still sense her anxiety.

"You need to put out this fire. Otherwise, I'll have to call the fire department."

Reg looked around at the flames. They pulled at *her* fire, called her to join in and play. But she'd had lots of experience in her sessions with Davyn ignoring that tug and in extinguishing fires. She put out her hands, closed her eyes, and drew in a long, calming breath. The sleep and all of the strange imagery from her dreams cleared from her brain, and she pulled the fire to her, dampening and containing it and teasing it away from the fuel. Within a couple of minutes, she held all of the remaining flames between her hands, where she turned and played with it for a minute before completely extinguishing it. She always felt a little sad when it was time to absorb her fire and end a training session with Davyn, and it was even more poignant putting out the wildfire that had broken free like a little animal and had been frolicking in the yard. She turned to Sarah, forcing a tired smile.

Sarah heaved a huge sigh of relief. "Thank goodness! I'm so glad to have had a firecaster nearby who was skilled enough to take care of that." Sarah walked closer to where the fire had burned. "I suppose I should soak all of this with water to make sure that no embers reignite."

Reg shook her head. "You don't need to. I pulled all of the fire out."

Sarah looked dubious at this. "Even all of the embers? I should probably soak it just to be sure."

Reg rolled her eyes and didn't argue. If Sarah wanted to turn the ashes into sludge, she was welcome to do so.

Sarah looked around at all of the burned bits, shaking her head. "Fire can burn so quickly, even here, where everything is green and damp and shouldn't be easy to burn. Forst is not going to be happy when he sees this."

Reg hadn't thought about the garden gnome. "He doesn't sleep here, does he? We don't need to worry that he might have been hurt by the fire?"

"No, certainly not."

"What about the elves? And other creatures?" Reg reached out immediately, feeling for them. The elves and the birds and the newly hatched armadillo. She didn't sense any pain or injury. Hopefully, that meant that everyone had been able to avoid the fire. Reg could feel the armadillo curled up in a hollow under a tree. He was aware of her, and Reg thought it best not to disturb him. He seemed to be well enough. The fire had not bothered him.

"I guess everything is fine," she told Sarah.

Sarah nodded her agreement. "Well... go on back to bed if you think you'll be able to get back to sleep. We'll deal with Forst and everything else tomorrow."

CHAPTER THIRTY-FOUR

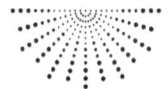

*a*s it turned out, Forst was not concerned about the damage done by the fire. He looked it over and proclaimed it to be minor.

Fire is a new beginning. Helps living things grow, he told Reg.

You're okay with this? It really doesn't bother you?

In a day or two, you will see new growth. A week, and all the burned spots will be covered. No need to feel bad, Reg Rawlins.

It isn't because of me, Reg hastened to tell him. *I put it out, but I was not the one who started it. I wouldn't start a fire in your garden.*

He eyed her speculatively and didn't agree or disagree. Reg couldn't help thinking of the slightly-burned couch in her cottage and the dreams she had been having. She was not the one who had lit the fire outside. She would know if that had been her doing.

* * *

Davyn was another story.

Reg didn't call him to tell him of the fire, but he heard about it anyway, and was at her house early in the afternoon. He didn't throw around any accusations, but he waited for Reg to invite him in and then made himself at home in the living room. He glanced around, and apparently didn't see the faint red tomato sauce stains on the ceiling above the kitchen island. Reg still had to paint over them to cover them up before Sarah saw them. She really didn't want to explain how they had gotten there in the first place.

"So you had some excitement last night," Davyn observed.

"Yes, a little. Lucky Sarah came and got me right away. I was able to contain and extinguish the fire without any problem."

"Yes. Good that you were close by. It was in the garden?"

"Uh-huh."

"Any clue how it might have started?"

Reg shook her head. "Maybe someone walking down the back alley behind the property threw a cigarette over the fence. I don't know. I just know it was starting to burn pretty good when Sarah woke me up."

"She didn't have any idea how it started? She didn't see or hear anyone out there?"

"No, not that she said."

"I'm surprised you had to be woken up. I would have expected you to be aware of the fire before anyone else."

"Oh... I don't know. It had been a pretty long day. I was really tired. Slept soundly."

Davyn nodded. "Soundly?" he repeated.

"Like a baby."

"Waking up every two hours crying?" Davyn suggested dryly.

Reg laughed. "No, I didn't mean that. I meant... I slept well. Sarah had to shake me awake. I was dreaming—" Reg cut herself off before she could tell him any more.

But Davyn was no dummy. He was an experienced firecaster and knew more about the craft than he had been able to teach Reg.

"Dreaming of fire?"

"Umm... well... maybe."

Maybe? Did she think she was being clever by not giving him a straight answer? Did she really think he didn't understand exactly what that meant?

Davyn reached over and pulled aside the scarf draped over the end of the couch, revealing the scorch marks. She'd been impressed before by his ability to smell smoke, reading the signs far better than she could even in conjunction with other clues. He could smell smoke several miles away and tell her which neighbor had lit it, and whether they were burning garbage or wood, even what kind of wood. Reg was far from that kind of expertise, still a novice.

"What's this?" Davyn asked, giving her a hard, steady look that meant she'd better not fudge her answer this time. He wanted all of the details, not Reg being cute about it.

"I... dreamt about fire one other day this week, too. Well, more than once. But one other day when I got up and... Starlight woke me up. And there was a fire here on the couch. Just a little one. I extinguished it. Everything was fine."

"And why didn't you call me?"

"I don't know. I didn't think there was anything you could do about it. You weren't here. I just... I didn't want you thinking that I couldn't control myself or was a danger to anyone. I didn't want you to stop me from using my firecaster skills."

"Is that what I did when you lost control before?"

Reg frowned at him.

"When you were lighting fires at Corvin's tribunal, did I do anything to discipline you? At that point, you didn't even know you were a firecaster. It wouldn't have been fair. And then at Starlight's healing when you lit the box of candles on fire because you weren't following my instructions? When you were pulled in at the forge at the dwarf mountain and lost control. Did I tell you in any of those cases that you had to stop firecasting?"

"No," Reg admitted. "You just... offered to help me. To mentor me. But obviously that's not working, if you think I lit these fires." Reg made a motion to encompass both the couch and the garden.

"No. I didn't say that. You are going to go through different periods of growth and challenges. You don't get better by stopping your training. Or by ignoring that there is a problem. You should have called me. When you started dreaming about firecasting. Or when this happened." Davyn indicated the scorch marks.

"I didn't think it was me. And I was afraid to tell you."

"Don't be afraid. Firecasting is difficult work. We all need training and practice. And when you are going through a stressful period, like when you were at Corvin's tribunal, it can be much harder to control."

Reg remembered how angry she had been at the tribunal. And not just at Corvin. "You're lucky I didn't light *you* on fire during the tribunal."

Davyn looked amused. "What makes you think that you didn't?"

"What? I didn't!"

"I was quick enough to extinguish it whenever you did, before anyone could notice."

"But you didn't when I lit—when Corvin's cloak started on fire."

"No, I didn't," Davyn agreed with a chuckle.

Reg stared at him. She remembered how furious she had been. How sure she was that Davyn had been biased against her. But the tribunal had ruled in her favor, and with a much harsher judgment than people had expected. And Davyn had been able to extinguish the fires that she unintentionally lit in her fury but hadn't? Corvin had made quite the spectacle, ripping off his cloak and jacket to stomp out the fires. While Davyn sat and watched impassively.

She didn't know Davyn nearly as well as she thought she did.

CHAPTER THIRTY-FIVE

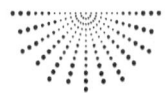

S o... you think that *I* started the fire in the garden?"

"I didn't say that. I'd like to know more about it. But it is certainly a possibility that you ignited it."

"I don't believe I did."

"And this one?" Davyn tapped the back of the couch.

"I don't know. I don't think I did, but..."

"But there's nothing around here that would have been likely to start it," Davyn finished, looking around. "And you were here alone?"

"With Starlight. Yes."

"And no other visitors?"

"No. Not as far as I know. I mean... sometimes Harrison shows up here in the middle of the night and I don't know about it until later. But I didn't see him that night. Or any sign of him."

"And tonight, you *were* dreaming of fire."

"Yes."

He shrugged. "It is possible. Particularly when you are going through stress. You've been involved in the investigation into the attacks on Corvin. I imagine that has caused some discomfort. And sharing the past with Corvin that you do, I imagine there has been a certain amount of suspicion aimed in your direction."

"Some. Jessup hasn't said very much about suspecting me, but she did have to take a formal statement yesterday about what happened when Corvin and I were together for supper when... you know. When he was poisoned."

"But surely they don't think you would do it in such a public way."

"That's what I said."

He nodded. "Are they looking at you seriously? Are you worried about it?"

Reg shrugged uncomfortably. "I don't know. I'm thinking about it... trying to figure out what's going on so that I don't end up getting arrested because they can't find anyone better. I haven't had great luck with the police in the past. But it isn't like they're making accusations right now. Just... looking at me funny."

"Maybe you need to back off a little. If you're trying to solve the case, then your brain is going to be going all the time, focusing on it. If you can just distance yourself from it and focus on your own work..."

Reg grunted. "I don't know if I can. I'll try."

"Good. And you need to let me know when stuff like this is happening. I'm here to be your mentor, not punish you like a child. I want to help you to get through the bumps in the road. Firecasting is not a gift that is easy to control."

"Did anything like this ever happen to you?"

He sighed and shook his head. "Much more than I would like to admit. Without someone to help me along the way, I'm sure I would have either ended up in prison for arson or dead from one of my own fires."

"But... how could you be killed by your own fire?" Reg frowned, trying to understand it. "We can handle fire without it burning us."

"Sure. If you're focused on it and haven't exhausted your strength. But if you start one in your sleep, you're not focused on it. And if you make it too big and get dehydrated and lose control... unfortunately, it isn't uncommon for a firecaster to be badly burned or killed in a fire."

"Oh. I wouldn't have thought that was possible."

"You have been burned before, right?"

"Yeah." Reg remembered Jessup burning herself eating the hot pizza the day before. Reg had burned the roof of her mouth plenty of times. And had scalded herself with hot water or coffee. "But I thought that was because... it was something else hot. Water or food or something, not fire itself."

"You can burn yourself with fire too. If you aren't handling it like you have been trained. You'll be fine as long as you do what you've been trained to do. You managed to extinguish the fire in the yard last night without any assistance?"

"Yeah. It wasn't hard at all. It was just... a friendly little fire. Nothing major. Not like that fire at the conference center."

"I remember that. You remember how tired you were afterward? And a little sunburned?"

Reg nodded. "Yeah. That was a big one. That was really tough."

"Especially when you'd had so little training at that point. You knew that it was too big for you to put out, so you focused on getting people out of the building and getting out yourself. If you had decided to stay and play there, the results would have been different."

"Yeah. I guess so."

"The best thing would be to do what you can to lower the stress in your life right now. Get things off of your plate if they are making you too anxious. Pick and choose what jobs you do. Spend some time meditating."

Reg groaned. "Do I have to meditate? I can't just focus on nothing."

"You don't do too badly when you are working with me."

"I know. But then I can focus on a flame and that's easier."

Davyn contemplated this. "I'm going to let you move up another level in your training," he said finally. He raised both hands to stop Reg from speaking and make her wait and listen. "I will allow you one small flame when meditating on your own. No playing, nothing bigger than a candle flame, but that might act as a release valve, let you bleed off a little energy, and help calm and focus yourself with meditation." He looked around the room, brows drawn together. "Not out here. In the bathroom. A close, confined space with lots of tile and fire-resistant materials. Remove all of the flammable objects you can: curtains, extra towels, wall hangings, whatever. Keep a small fire extinguisher in there. Make sure you are well-hydrated."

Reg was nodding eagerly. Her heart thumped with excitement at finally being able to use fire in her own house without supervision. She could do everything Davyn directed, and she would show him that she was a competent, focused firecaster who could be responsible about using fire on her own.

Davyn returned her smile. "I know you can do this. You have progressed very quickly in your firecasting, and I know I have been holding you back. That has been on purpose, to make sure that you hone the basic skills before moving on to anything complex. This is a simple exercise, but it's important that you follow the rules and stay aware of the flame. You know that sometimes, it can get too big if you get distracted. But you're good about bringing it back down under control, and you demonstrated with your actions last night that you're able to tame a fire that has been burning out of your control."

"Yeah. It wasn't *that* big, though." Reg didn't want him to think she'd done more than she had. She didn't want any misunderstandings between them.

"I looked at the damage done and I talked to Sarah. I have a pretty good understanding of its size and power."

Reg was reassured by this. She smiled again, thinking about being able to finally have a flame in her own house.

"Think about what else I've said," Davyn advised. "Eliminate what stresses you can. We'll get you past this bump in the road."

CHAPTER THIRTY-SIX

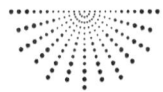

$\mathcal{A}$fter Davyn had gone, Sarah knocked on Reg's door and let herself in. Reg had a pretty good idea that Sarah was the one who had called Davyn in the first place to tell him about the fire and had been watching for Davyn to leave. Now she wanted to know what the verdict was.

"Morning, Reg," she greeted pleasantly. "I wanted to thank you again for helping out with the fire last night. That could have gotten very bad if I didn't have a firecaster here to take care of it."

The fire could have spread to the rest of the garden, the big house where Sarah lived, or neighboring properties. Any of those would have been disastrous. Reg thought that she would have woken up and been able to take care of it if it had spread to the cottage where she was sleeping but, after Davyn's talk about firecasters burning to death, she wasn't quite as confident.

"You're welcome. I'm sorry it was so hard for you to wake me up. I must have been at a deep part of my sleep cycle..."

Sarah nodded, looking unconcerned. "It seemed like a long time, knowing that there was a fire burning outside, but I'm sure it wasn't more than a few seconds."

The older woman puttered around the kitchen, checking the fridge and flipping through Reg's appointment book for any new entries. Reg was sitting on the couch with Starlight purring in her lap, the scarf again draped strategically over the burn mark on the couch. She could tell that Sarah didn't have anything to do there; she just wanted to hear what Davyn had thought of the incident.

"I don't think I had anything to do with the fire starting," Reg told her. "Maybe it was just someone being careless with their cigarette."

"Oh, I never would have assumed..."

"Davyn said I can do some meditation exercises with a flame now. Just in the bathroom, without anything flammable around it. To help me to meditate and relax."

Sarah's brows were down, obviously trying to fathom why Davyn would allow this. "I'm not sure how I feel about that."

"Meditating will help make sure I stay in control," Reg told her, "and to bleed off some stress. He said it will be good for me."

"He's the firecaster, so I guess he knows best. But I would certainly not have suggested it..."

"I know. But I do think it will help. You don't want to be worrying about me getting stressed out."

"No. That's true. Not just because of fire. Stress is very bad for your body."

Reg nodded.

"Hmm." Sarah rubbed the back of her neck, thinking about this. It was probably going to take some time before she was sure that Davyn had made the right decision. But what was Sarah going to do? Tell Reg that she wasn't allowed to have a flame in the cottage, and risk Reg having an accident because she didn't have a way to rid herself of the stress? "Well, that's not why I came down here, actually."

She produced a small bottle filled with a thick, greenish liquid. She held it up to the light for a moment. "I am hoping for your sake the answer is no, but are you planning to see Corvin any time soon? He was in need of an ointment, and I thought that if you are going to see him, you could take it to him and save me the trip." She gave a little shudder. "I do hate hospitals. Of course, modern hospitals are lovely places. Still, I can't help but remember the so-called hospitals of bygone eras, where the unfortunate were sent to die at the hands of some incompetent doctor with a penchant for cutting people open to see how they work. Stinking, sepsis-filled places full of suffering, dying patients."

That really made Reg feel like going to one to see Corvin.

But she had been toying with the idea of going to see him again, despite Davyn's warnings. He *had* said to reduce the stress in her life, and Corvin always made Reg feel warm and relaxed. And she needed to see him and know that he was okay. She couldn't bear the memory of him lying on the floor with the paramedics working over him.

She would feel better once she saw him and knew that he was on the mend. Jessup said he would survive, but Reg needed to see that for herself.

Besides, it was only right that she should help Sarah out by taking her ointment to Corvin. There was no reason the old crone should have to go to the hospital and relive her traumatic memories.

"Sure. I can do that," she agreed.

"Oh, that would be such a big help." Sarah walked across the room and handed the bottle to Reg. "Of course, you are foolish to be seeing him so much voluntarily, but since you are going anyway…"

Reg just smiled. It was nice to help people out.

CHAPTER THIRTY-SEVEN

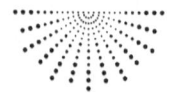

$\mathcal{A}$ t the hospital once more, Reg didn't try to get the staff to tell her where to find Corvin. She just did a quick circuit around the main floor of the small hospital and then followed her instinct as to which elevators to take. As soon as she reached the correct floor, she could feel the tug toward Corvin. She stepped off the elevator to meet nurses with goofy expressions on their faces and knew she was in the right place. It didn't take long to find Corvin in a room slightly too warm and filled with the scent of roses.

"Hi," she greeted, finding Corvin sitting up in bed, scowling at the TV. "Looking for some company?"

"Regina!" He sounded relieved to see her. Because he knew that she had brought the ointment with her or was he happy to see her? There had obviously not been a lack of comely nurses attending to him, but he had told her once before that Reg's powers were one of the most attractive things about her, and the nurses probably did not have the special gifts he craved. "I didn't know if you would come."

"Well, Sarah sent me over with some ointment that she said you needed." Reg kept her voice light and upbeat, trying not to let herself be pulled in by the hoarseness of his voice.

She supposed the raspiness was due to the reaction he'd had to the drink. He had said that it burned, and Jessup mentioned that it had been caustic and damaged his throat. So that was probably why his voice sounded so gravelly.

Taking the time to look him over, she saw the sores that covered his arms, and probably other parts of his body that were not visible to her. They were no longer the weals she had seen popping out, but were open wounds, scabbing over but still painful looking.

"How are you feeling?"

Corvin cleared his throat, wincing as he did so. "It isn't my best day; I'll tell you that. Maybe you could come over here and help me put some of that on these sores."

Reg took a step toward him before deciding that was probably a bad idea. Running her hands over Corvin's skin, even in an attempt to help soothe the pain and itching of those lesions, might be too much for her willpower. She reached toward him, holding the bottle out instead.

"I don't think so. It looks like there are plenty of pretty nurses around here who would be only too happy to help. Get one of them if you can't do it yourself."

He gave her a coy smile. "But I don't want *them*, Regina."

"That's too bad."

Reg put the ointment on the little stand beside his bed and sat down on the visitor chair, ensuring it was not too close. She did not want him reaching out to touch her arm or hold her hand.

"Hopefully, that ointment will help you to recover faster. But the doctor probably won't be too eager to let you go this time. They don't want to see you right back here again."

"They would rather not see me leave in the first place," he agreed. "But I have no intention of staying any longer than necessary. Do you know how hard it is to sleep in a place like this?"

Reg shrugged. "Probably not as hard as in the psych ward."

He raised his brows. "Well… perhaps not."

"Although, they are pretty free with the sleep meds because they don't *want* people to stay awake screaming at the tops of their lungs."

Corvin grunted. "Probably not somewhere I would stay. There *was* some guy down the hall screaming in German most of the night. It's not exactly the Four Seasons."

"But the Four Seasons doesn't have nurses."

"It would if I hired them."

Reg rolled her eyes. "Well, I suppose it would," she agreed. She let a few seconds pass. "So, do you have any idea yet who it is trying to kill you? Or what it was they put in your drink?"

He gazed at her. "Are you working for Marta?"

"Working for her? No. I have talked to her. I'm sure she'd like to know if you have any suspicions. I just wondered…" Reg shrugged, not sure how to put her anxiety into words. "I don't like it. Especially when it happens right in front of me. I felt so helpless yesterday. And I was restless all night. People really should be more considerate; if they're going to kill you, then do it while you're on your own, not when it could traumatize some innocent bystander."

Corvin chuckled, then coughed, putting his hand to his throat in pain. "I'm sure they didn't stop to think about that," he said, after recovering from the cough. "When you find out who it is, you'll have to explain that to them."

Reg nodded her agreement. "Do you not have any idea who it is? You must know if there's someone who wants so badly to kill you."

"You would think so," he rasped. "But… most people who object to my kind simply avoid me. These spurious attacks are extremely annoying."

"I would imagine so. And you don't think that it's someone in your coven? Even one of the neophytes who you wouldn't know as well?"

"I don't think this is the work of a pre-initiate."

"Stabbing you with a knife doesn't exactly require magic."

"Getting past my wards does. Some fairly advanced, complex magic. I think I would recognize anyone with that kind of power who has been around me, attending the coven."

"So you don't think it was anyone with the coven."

"No."

"Are you still going ahead with the election? After all of this."

He stared at her. "Of course."

"Do you think it was the waitress at the club? Or someone else who works there?"

He raised his brows. "Why would they? The club is quite rigorous in its hiring practices. And training people who will be... open and non-judgmental. They need to cater to all kinds. Anyone who showed prejudice against a certain species or gift would not last long there."

"The drink came from someone inside the club. Maybe an insider. If it wasn't the waitress, then maybe someone else who had access to your drink while it was in the kitchen. Just walking by in a moment when the waitress was distracted..."

"Highly unlikely that it would be one of the staff. And most of them are nonmagical. They would not have been able to get past my wards."

"They aren't all practitioners?"

"No, very few of them, in fact."

"Huh." Reg tried to figure it out. There had to be people who hated Corvin for what he did. Not just that disliked his kind out of general principles, but who had suffered at his hand. "What about someone whose powers you stole? There have to be a fair few of them, and they're not going to be happy with you. I know what *that* feels like."

"I don't *steal* powers," Corvin argued. "I am required to get consent from them, to offer something in exchange. Just like I did with you."

"Like you did once," Reg reminded him. "But not every time. And when you did, I had no idea what I was saying yes to. You misled me."

He shrugged. "It was still consent as far as our community is concerned. You have nothing to complain about."

"Whether this community agrees with it or not, it was still an assault. It wasn't informed consent. You know that wasn't what I was agreeing to."

"But it was consent," he maintained stubbornly. "You have no recourse. Besides, your powers were returned to you." He raised his chin slightly. "So you still owe me. We made a bargain and you reneged."

"You conned me and then you chose on your own to return what you had stolen."

They both stared at each other, not backing down. It had been a long time since Reg had discussed this with him last. She had thought that she was over it and was past caring about what he had done since she had gotten her powers back. No lasting damage. But she found that the hurt was still there. She still wanted him to admit that what he had done was wrong and he owed her an apology, at the very least. And if she felt that way, despite the fact that her gifts had been returned to her, then how did a woman who was forced to go through the rest of her life bereft of the powers she had grown up with feel? They had to be pretty angry and bitter toward him.

Bitter enough to want to kill him?

There was no doubt in her mind. Of course someone who had been assaulted and cheated out of her powers would be angry enough to kill him.

"If I had taken someone's powers, she wouldn't be able to get past my wards," Corvin reminded her, as Reg opened her mouth to tell him that it could have been one of the women he had robbed. "She wouldn't have the power to defeat them."

There was that pesky problem.

"Someone else acting *for* her might. If she had a family member or friend who wanted to get back at you for what you had done."

Corvin appeared unconvinced. "I don't get a lot of death threats. People in the community understand the rules. They know that I'm allowed to do what I have done because it is my nature and you can't make laws against a species' inborn nature. They may not like it, but they know there is nothing they can do about it. Most people don't have... your sense of outrage. Especially when it was not done to them."

CHAPTER THIRTY-EIGHT

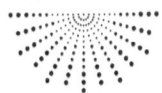

*R*eg was glad that she had gone to see Corvin and that she had left. Corvin had needed the ointment that Sarah had provided to him and, hopefully, it would help his sores to heal faster. She'd saved Sarah from having to go to the hospital. And Reg had satisfied her concerns, seeing that Corvin was, in fact, on the mend and would soon be back home. She didn't have to waste any more thought on him. If he couldn't figure out who was trying to kill him, and Jessup and the police couldn't figure it out, what were the chances that Reg would be able to solve the case? Corvin would have to be more careful and redouble his wards and protections. Maybe if he reinforced them every day, like Sarah had told Reg to do, he would be fine once ensconced in his own walls.

She did need to strengthen the wards, so she took some time when she got home to do so, even knowing that Corvin was probably not going to be trying to get into the yard to see her in the next day or two. She needed to get into the habit of reinforcing her protections every day. If she were diligent and did it, she would be able to keep intruders out.

Or most intruders, anyway. The mortals, at least.

As long as she didn't allow them any other way in.

Someday she would know all of the rules and could be more sure that she was doing everything possible to protect herself and would not slip up and do something like letting someone leave something behind that they could return for later, or handing them her keys to open the door for her. Mistakes she had made in the past.

She was more cautious now. And it would pay off.

She thought about the armadillo as she walked around the yard and the garden in particular. He was there somewhere. If she focused hard enough on his consciousness, she could find him. As he got older, she thought he might get more used to her being around and let himself be seen now and then. If she did not do anything to alarm him, he would decide that she was harmless.

After finishing with the wards, she returned to the cottage and fed Starlight. Searching through the fridge, she found some leftover ribs, which looked good for dinner, and warmed them up in the microwave for herself. While waiting for them to warm, she searched on her phone for armadillos. She ate standing up at the kitchen island, skimming through several articles on fun facts about armadillos. Some people did apparently have them as pets, but they did not do well in captivity. Reg wouldn't want to keep a creature inside that would die from being confined.

Not that she meant to adopt the armadillo in the backyard. She was just curious how close it would let her get to it and whether it would be friendly if she fed it, like the birds and squirrels that ate from the feeders Sarah hung outside.

She was reading about nine-banded armadillos—the kind they had in Florida—always bearing identical quadruplets. Something was niggling at the back of her mind, and Reg tried to put her finger on it. Was it because there only appeared to be one armadillo in the yard? The others might have died soon after hatching. Or the one in the yard might have wandered away from the nest, leaving the others behind somewhere else. Maybe it was orphaned. A predator bird might have picked it up for dinner and then dropped it later when it got too heavy. There were dozens of reasons the little fellow might be alone.

Reg opened a more scientific article, one that detailed several different features of armadillos and their place in the animal kingdom, rather than just a few fun facts, and plowed through some of the drier descriptions.

Armadillos were mammals. Warm-blooded. Somehow, seeing their scaly, armored bodies, Reg had assumed that they were cold-blooded. Lizards or some other reptilian species. It was a surprise to find that they were also hairy or furry and had been classified as mammals. But even some mammals laid eggs, like those weird duck-billed animals. Platypuses. Creatures that seemed to borrow traits from all of the different animal families.

But then she got down to the part that said that armadillos bore live young. Reg read it over a couple of times to ensure that she hadn't misread or misunderstood it.

Forst had clearly referred to the armadillo as a hatchling. She was sure that he wouldn't have made a mistake about whether an animal laid eggs or bore live young. He knew far more about plants and animals than Reg did. More than the internet did, for that matter. If the two disagreed, she would pick Forst as being right.

But it was also possible that Forst had not meant it literally. Like a human referring to children as "rug rats" when they were not rodents or "kids" when they were not goats. She sometimes heard humans refer to a developing baby as "peanut" or some other endearment. Gnomes might refer to babies as hatchlings just to indicate that they were very young rather than that they had actually hatched from eggs.

Reg thought about it for a few minutes, checking a few other sources to make sure that they all agreed that armadillos were live born. Then she went back outside to see if Forst was there. He would quickly clear up her confusion.

She had expected him to be in the garden tending to the plants that had been burned, but couldn't see or feel him nearby. He had said that the fire was good for the garden and that it would regenerate quickly. Maybe he was staying out of the way to give it a chance to heal itself.

She lingered for a few minutes, expecting him to make himself known. Sometimes, she didn't see him right away when he was in the garden until he chose to speak to her. She suspected he might have some kind of invisibility powers. But she should still be able to feel his consciousness if he was there, and she didn't.

She did, however, sense the armadillo.

Reg went over to the bench and sat down, trying to quiet her mind and reach out to the armadillo. If she just charged in and chased him, she would scare him. If she were quiet and still, maybe she could coax him into coming to her.

She closed her eyes and thought about the armadillo and the glimpse she had caught of him. The scaly skin, the long, narrow face. He was cute, in an ugly sort of way. Like bats with their furry little faces could be cute if she ignored the leathery wings and high-pitched squeals.

The armadillo became aware of her, either hearing or scenting her, or noticing her consciousness reaching out to his. She had no idea how intelligent or sentient armadillos were. Did they have a sense of self and the other creatures in their world, or did they just go through life reacting to environmental triggers? Did they have a community? A language?

She waited to see how he would react now that he knew she was there. She made no movement that he might deem threatening and run away from.

Come on, little guy. Let me see you.

There was a definite reaction to her invitation. A sort of a snort and withdrawal to begin with. He had a sense that he should not interact with the other beings in his environment. But even after withdrawing, he kept examining Reg, trying to suss out how dangerous she was to him. They had encountered each other more than once, after all. He must know by now that she was not just passing through, but that they would both keep running into each other.

He crept forward, watching both physically and mentally, to see what Reg's reaction would be.

I'm not going to hurt you. I just want to see you.

He stayed where he was.

I just want to make sure you weren't hurt by the fire.

Fire? There was an immediate response, surprise and increasing curiosity.

Did the fire scare you?

Another snort, but he still drew nearer to Reg, senses on high alert. If he were a cat, his ears would be turning this way and that, twitching as he tried to interpret all of the information he was picking up. It must be challenging to have senses that were so much sharper than hers. Reg knew how overwhelmed she could get at times if lights or noises got to be too much. There was only so much she could handle. She put it down to the ghosts always around her. She had a lot more noise to filter out than most humans.

Eventually, she could hear rustling behind her as the armadillo approached. She waited, her excitement rising. She wanted to turn and look for it, but she didn't want to scare it away with her movement. He knew where she was and he was coming to her. She just needed to sit quietly and wait.

He slowly came around the bench to where Reg could see him. The pinkish-gray, armored body, long face and small ears. It had a potbelly, and Reg didn't know if that was because it was a baby, or how it would still look as it grew up. But it didn't look like any of the armadillo pictures that Reg had seen. It had other horns and spikes on its head and down its spine, and the powerful hindquarters and smaller front legs made it look like it was intended to stand on its hind legs rather than equally on all fours. Its eyes were large and expressive.

Reg stared at it, trying to make sense of him. He was far more reptilian than the pictures she had looked at, which made her think that Forst was right in calling him a hatchling. His upper teeth extended over the lower jaw when his mouth was closed, like a carnivore rather than an omnivorous armadillo.

Hello! Reg reached out to him with her mind, still not moving or making any noise that might scare him away. *What are you?*

Baffled feelings from the creature. He was what he was, and he didn't have a name for that.

Lizard? Reg prompted. *Dinosaur?*

He sat back on his haunches and looked at Reg, tilting his head to the side. Reg looked back, feeling his feelings, trying to understand what she was seeing.

You didn't get hurt by the fire?

The creature snorted and flame flickered out of his nose. Reg's jaw dropped and she stared at him in disbelief. Even after everything she had seen of the magical world since she had moved to Black Sands, she could still be surprised.

You're a dragon?

Drakon, she heard an echo from the creature and he blinked at her, eyes bright.

The hatchling was not an armadillo.

It was a fire-breathing dragon.

CHAPTER THIRTY-NINE

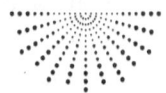

"Oh, my." Reg spoke the phrase aloud, she was so surprised. But that wasn't the phrase that came into her head. She was floored. The dragon tilted its head and looked at her but didn't immediately run away.

Do you have a name?

There was no response from the creature.

My name is Reg. She pointed at herself. *Reg.*

The dragon's tongue flicked out, tasting the air.

How could there be a dragon in her yard? And how was it that no one had known about it or told her that there were dragons in Florida? Sarah's guess that he was an armadillo suggested that she didn't know there might be dragons in the garden, so Reg assumed it was not a common occurrence.

Forst had referred to him as a hatchling, and he practically lived in the garden, so he had known, but hadn't told her what the dragon was. Maybe he thought that she knew.

How long have you been here? How old are you?

If the dragon was still a baby, then even if dragons had spoken language like humans, he probably couldn't answer such a question. How would he know the words that Reg used and how would he know how old he was? Unless some other, older dragon had told him.

Reg looked around nervously for the dragon's mother. Something bigger, stronger, and more sophisticated. She did not want to get between a mother dragon and its baby. That sounded like a recipe for disaster.

She cast her mind around, feeling for some flicker of consciousness from the dragon's mother. But she didn't feel anything. Could the baby have wandered there on its own? And if so, could he survive without parents? Were dragons independent from birth, or did they need a parent to feed and train them?

She visualized an egg with as much clarity as she could. Admittedly, it was a chicken egg. She hadn't ever seen a dragon egg or any kind of reptile egg in person. She knew they were probably rounder and were leathery rather than hard-shelled like a chicken egg. But she pictured what she knew and could visualize most clearly.

The dragon sat looking at her, then formed a picture in his own mind. A dark, enclosed, constricting place. Then tearing out of the ball into the bright, green-smelling world and eating the tough, leathery enclosure. Reg tried to get some sense of the timeline, but had a hard time getting any feeling for it. She had only been aware of the dragon for a few days; she had to assume that was when he had hatched from his shell. There was no image of a mother, so he must be alone. And hopefully, she would not be coming back to take care of him.

"Oh, wow," Reg said aloud.

This was not something that she had expected to encounter. She had been so concerned with other things, the protection of the creatures in the garden had fallen to a lower priority. Orri had said that she needed to protect the garden, and she had been doing what she could to strengthen the charms and ward protecting the yard. Still, she hadn't imagined that there might be some creature already within the fences of the yard that was so dangerous and vulnerable at the same time. Those teeth looked like they could take off her hand, but he was still a hatchling and could fall victim to a human with evil intentions or a larger predator like an alligator. Or if he left the yard, there were the cars. Cats or dogs who ran free were frequently hit by moving vehicles. A baby dragon wouldn't know how to avoid them.

Are you okay? Do you need food? Water?

After looking at her for a moment, the dragon trundled over to the pond and burbled around at its edge. She wasn't sure if he was actually drinking or just playing around, like a child with a straw. Reg giggled at his behavior. After playing for a few more minutes, he turned to face her. He bobbed his head up and down slightly, eyeing her.

A slight breeze stirred the pollens in the plants around Reg and she sneezed without warning.

In a split second, the dragon had rolled up into a ball, protective armor on the outside and no soft body parts exposed. Reg had the impulse to bend over and pick him up, to tell him that everything was okay and to examine him more closely. She had never seen anything like him before. But she stayed where she was and didn't pick him up. Touching wild creatures was not a good idea and, even though he was in a defensive posture, that didn't mean he couldn't switch to offense in the time it would take him to snap his jaws.

You're okay, little fella. I just sneezed. That wasn't on purpose.

It was a moment before he began to unwind himself. He looked around tentatively, watchful for any danger.

I'm not going to hurt you, Reg reassured. She pictured herself reaching out and touching him and stroking the flat scales of his head. She was a safe person. He could trust her not to hurt him.

Ah, Reg Rawlins.

Reg startled at Forst's words coming into her head. She looked around and saw him standing with his wheelbarrow watching her.

Oh, Forst. I was just… Reg realized that the dragon had disappeared. He had fled at Forst's appearance. *I was just meeting the hatchling.*

He nodded, walking up with the wheelbarrow full of dirt. *Few humans see such sights.*

I guess not. Is there anything else in the garden that I should be aware of?

He looked at her and merely smiled. Reg wondered how many other surprises the garden might hold for her.

Is he okay? Does he need a mother around? Is there a mother?

Many creatures live without parents.

Yes. I just wondered. I don't think I want to run into the mother.

He considered this, nodding wisely. *There has not been an adult in these parts many, many years.*

Really? Then… how did he get here?

Eggs remain dormant a long time. Until everything is right. Then they hatch.

So, like… years?

Forst nodded gravely. *Many years.*

Oh. So she laid an egg and then left? And never came back for it?

He continued to nod. *Yes. They do not stay to raise their young. It is too dangerous for several of them to be in one area.*

Danger from humans or other dragons?

He started digging with a shovel. *Both must be considered.*

Are there many in the world? Or are they endangered?

Like so many other creatures she had encountered lately. The nonmagical world was getting larger and stronger, and the magical world smaller and smaller, maybe unable to contain them all anymore.

Forst nodded. *Not many here. Other parts of the world… I don't know. Maybe where there are not so many humans.*

More isolated places like Siberia or the Canadian wild. Maybe there, where, like the bigfoots—or forest people, as they preferred to be called—they could live unbothered by the domesticated humans.

Well… Reg looked around, but the small dragon was nowhere to be seen. *I guess he's gone back into hiding, which is probably the best thing for him. He'll be okay out here, right?*

This is his habitat. Forst made a gesture to take in the garden. *He must make a way for himself here.*

Reg nodded. *Yes. I have to say—your garden is full of surprises! You must have made it such an inviting place that the conditions were right for him to hatch.*

Forst raised one bushy white eyebrow thoughtfully.

Reg walked back around the cottage to her door, her thoughts far away as she considered these new developments.

CHAPTER FORTY

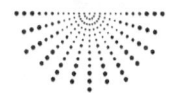

*R*eg opened the cottage door and, as she stepped over the threshold, something brushed past her leg. Reg looked down, expecting to see Starlight there, either begging for food or trying to slip outside unnoticed. But it wasn't Starlight. She didn't see anything there. She closed the door behind her and looked around for Starlight.

Instead, she saw the hatchling a few feet away from her, sitting back on his haunches, watching her. He flicked out his tongue to taste the air and blinked his eyes one at a time.

"What are you doing here?"

He watched her, apparently not scared by her walking around or disconcerted by the new setting, which was far different from the dirt and trees outside. She would have expected him to cower or search for somewhere to hide. But he was focused on her, observing her movements.

"You are supposed to be outside. Come on. Shoo!" Reg opened the door again and moved toward the dragon, trying to herd it back out of doors again. He moved to avoid her but stayed just out of reach and didn't move closer to the door.

"Dragon. Come on. No dragons are allowed in the house."

He kept slipping out of her grasp. Reg pursued him several times but wasn't getting anywhere.

He had come to her before, and he had followed her into the house. So she had done something right in making friends with him. She'd triggered some kind of social response from him. Reg sat down on the couch and was still. That was what she had done outside. Just been quiet and still and let the dragon come to her when he was ready.

She didn't say anything. She closed her eyes for a few seconds to center herself and could hear that dragon moving around restlessly, his claws ticking on the floor. Reg aimed pleasant, happy thoughts in his direction. No need to scare him or make him think that she was some kind of a threat. She was perfectly friendly. No reason he should avoid her.

He was calming, looking around for a place to lie down and go to sleep, maybe. Young animals often slept a lot, and she assumed that a dragon would be more likely to hunt at night and spend most of the daytime hours sleeping.

Then there was a yowl and threatening growl from Starlight. Reg's eyes flew open and her heart raced. Starlight had come out from the bedroom and was looking at the dragon, his ears flattened against his head, crouched low to the ground.

"No, Starlight. No. I'll get the dragon out. Just leave him alone."

Starlight probably couldn't do anything to hurt the hatchling if he rolled up into a ball to protect himself, but he had sharp claws and teeth and could breathe fire. She didn't want him hurting Starlight, who didn't have any armor.

The dragon advanced toward Starlight, looking curious. Did he consider Starlight a threat? Prey? A larger dragon would undoubtedly make a nice meal of Starlight, but the hatchling wasn't big enough. That didn't mean that he couldn't hurt Starlight, though.

"Star, go back to the bedroom. Uh... Dragon, you come with me. Let's get you back out to the yard where you belong." She walked over to step between them. But Starlight was stubborn, refusing to go back to the bedroom, slithering on his belly to get close to the dragon. "No!" Reg waved her hands, trying to make herself big and threatening so that they would both retreat. In different directions, hopefully. "Get back. You guys leave each other alone. I don't want to have to be taking either one of you to the vet! But especially you!" She directed this at the dragon. She had no idea how the vet would react if she took him some mythical animal that, as far as he was concerned, shouldn't exist. Would he just see what made sense to him? Some hurt armadillo or lizard? A bit deformed, but nothing out of the ordinary? And how would he be able to do anything for it? "Go on. I don't want either one of you getting hurt."

Irritated, Starlight jumped up on top of the kitchen island, where he could bare his teeth at the intruder and let out another threatening growl. Reg tried once more to shoo the dragon out of the cottage. "Come on, come on. Just back out to the garden where you belong."

Unexpectedly, the little dragon seemed to grow, unfurling two large wings that had previously been tucked against his sides. He didn't actually fly, but fluttered a few feet at a time, like a fledgling bird, until he managed to get up onto the table.

Starlight hissed and growled again, clearly telling the hatchling off. He had not expected the smaller intruder to be able to make it up off of the floor and thought that he was in a superior position.

"Look…" Reg walked into the kitchen, approaching Starlight on the island. "Just let me handle this, won't you? If you just stay out of the way and don't provoke him, I should be able to tempt him out into the garden…"

Starlight hissed at her. Reg reached for him but quickly pulled back when Starlight snapped at her, trying to bite her. "Hey! That's not nice."

She decided to leave Starlight where he was. He was out of the way. If she just focused on getting the hatchling back out of the house…

She turned away from Starlight and approached the dragon. "Come on, now."

She hoped that if she got too close, he would curl up in a ball again, and she would be able to just pick him up and set him down carefully outside. But instead, the dragon gave her a pretty good imitation of Starlight's hiss and snapped his teeth.

"Sheesh," Reg complained. "You're not supposed to be picking up on his tricks!"

If she couldn't physically remove the intruder, she would have to try another means of persuasion. There was that old saying about catching more flies with honey than vinegar, though she wasn't sure what that had to do with anything. Reg went to the fridge and opened a few containers.

She knew nothing about dragons. Or real dragons, anyway. And she'd had enough experience in Black Sands to know that she couldn't rely on any of the myths she knew as being the truth. But she'd seen those teeth. Those were not herbivore teeth. So salad was out. Probably most soups too. But she quickly found a bowl of leftover tuna. She took it over to the table and waved it invitingly near the dragon, hoping that the smell would convince him to follow her wherever she went.

His nostrils flared and quivered, clearly attracted by the smell. Starlight started yowling and complaining immediately. That was *his* food. Not something to offer an intruder. The dragon drew closer to the bowl. Reg walked slowly along the side of the table toward the door. The little dragon followed her to the end of the table and then stood there, unsure whether to keep pursuing the smell of fish.

"Come on," Reg coaxed.

Eventually, he fluttered down from the table. Crouching, Reg offered the tasty treat just a little closer. The dragon snapped at her again and she jerked away. "No!"

He looked at her, concerned, then craned his neck toward the bowl, seeing if he could reach the contents without moving from where he was.

Starlight went nuts. He jumped off of the island and ran toward the dragon, caterwauling. The dragon spun around. Reg was still expecting him to roll into a ball, but he didn't. He snorted once, then twice, and fire spurted from his nose.

"No!" Reg told him, trying to make him understand that he couldn't use his fire inside the house. But how was she going to stop him? And how was she going to train him not to burn down the garden outside too?

Starlight stopped short, still a few feet away from the dragon. He growled again. A bigger snort from the dragon, and a longer, more sustained flame. Starlight backed away.

"Okay, now you've established who is more dominant," Reg said in disgust. "Now, will you please go outside?"

But the dragon just sat there looking at her. He was not moving anywhere. She tried to tempt him with the bowl of tuna, but he whipped his tail around and knocked it out of her hand, then serenely ate the fish off the floor.

"Hey!" Reg protested. "You're not supposed to do that!"

He snorted at her but didn't produce a flame. Reg pointed at him to scold him and fire burst from her finger, directly at him. He sat back on his haunches, startled, and stared at her. Reg focused. Producing fire when she didn't mean to was not good. Not good at all. She wasn't sure why her fire had gotten out of her control. She hadn't done that since the tribunal with Corvin. Then, even though she didn't know anything about her gift, she had set him on fire more than once. And Damon once too, if she remembered right, but that flame had gone out immediately. And Davyn said he had extinguished the fires she aimed at him. She must have been feeling pretty bad to have set three different people alight. Three men. She had been overwhelmed and had felt like everyone was against her.

This situation was nothing like that. Reg wanted to get a small animal out of her house. It was being stubborn. How often had she dealt with a stubborn cat who either wouldn't stay or wouldn't go, depending on which she wanted? She'd never shot fire at any of them. She understood that sometimes they just needed a little more encouragement.

She built a picture of the garden in her mind, making it look as lush and inviting as she could. The dragon would see how much more preferable it was to be outside and would leave on his own.

The dragon didn't move for a while. Then he started snuffling around the floor, looking for any pieces of fish that he had missed. He turned around and walked toward Starlight, nose held high in the air. Starlight hissed and backed away. The dragon had flight and fire, two things Starlight couldn't fight. At least not without his powers. Maybe he didn't want to tip off the dragon that he had powers. Reg didn't know what kind of relationships normally existed between cats and dragons. Were they automatically enemies? Did they usually just ignore each other? She didn't imagine that many cats lived in the remote places the dragons thrived. Some cats lived in the forest. Wild ones like panthers or ocelots. Not domesticated cats.

Not that Starlight was exactly domesticated. She didn't even know if he could be properly classified as a cat with everything she knew about him.

The dragon wandered around the kitchen, sniffing. It nosed at Starlight's food dish, ignoring his hisses, and ate a few crumbs of the kibble. Starlight hurried forward, growling and trying to get his head into the bowl to eat the rest of the kibble before the dragon could.

"Hey, hey. Don't fight. I can get you some of your own," Starlight told the dragon and hurried over to put some fresh kibble in another bowl. She was going to put it down on the floor like Starlight's but, with much rustling and flapping, the dragon managed to get himself up onto the counter. He nibbled at the food, looking proud of himself. Reg reached for the bag of cat food to put it back away and noticed her fingertips flaming. She extinguished them quickly, then studied them, wondering why they had started to flame without her conscious effort. Just because she was worried about the cat and dragon fighting? Davyn thought it was all of the other stress she was going through, the police being so suspicious of her, her concern for Corvin, trying to figure out who was trying to kill him. There were a lot of things to be worried about.

Not the least of which was that she would unintentionally burn the house down if things kept going as they did.

CHAPTER FORTY-ONE

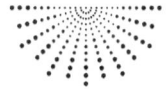

*D*avyn?"

"Reg?" Davyn sounded surprised to hear from her. "Hi, how's it going?"

"Well... I'm having some problems that I need your help with."

"Okay. Shoot."

"Can you come here?"

"Is something on fire now?"

"No."

"Then why don't you just tell me what the problem is, and I can help to walk you through it?"

"It's... I really can't explain it over the phone. I need you to see it and confirm that I'm not going crazy. And then you can help me. I think it might take more than one of us."

"I was already over there today," Davyn continued to hedge. He was the one who had told her to call him if she had any more problems, but now he didn't want to make the trip to see her. Maybe he had other plans. Julian coming into town to have dinner with him. Some hobby or studying he needed to do. Maybe just his favorite show on the TV.

"I need you here," Reg insisted. She wasn't going to back down and she wasn't going to tell him over the phone that she had a dragon in the house and didn't know what to do about it.

"Now?" Davyn sighed.

"Yes. I don't know what to do otherwise. You need to come see and help me out."

"But there's no fire right now."

Reg looked over at the dragon, who snorted, producing a small burst of flame. "Um, mostly. No."

He was irritated and impatient with her. Of course. She would have been irritated in his place too. But she really did need him and, if he came, he would see that.

* * *

The front door to the cottage was still open, since Reg had not yet managed to get the dragon outside. She half hoped that when Davyn arrived, the dragon would be spooked by another person's presence and would run back outside and hide. That would solve at least half of the problem.

But when Davyn stood in the open doorway looking in to see what was going on, Reg was sitting on the couch and the dragon was cuddled up against her leg, making a purring sound.

Davyn glanced around the interior quickly the first time, looking for any danger, any fire or sign of what might have been on fire earlier. Then he looked around again and saw Starlight up on the kitchen island eating kibble from the bowl Reg had gotten out for the dragon and Reg sitting on the couch with the small form curled up next to her. He stepped in closer to get a better look.

"Reg? What's...?"

Reg looked at him, waiting for him to tell her that she was seeing things or to ask her what she was doing with an armadillo. Or with a baby alligator or whatever deformed thing had made friends with her.

Davyn bent down, looking at the dragon closely. He did not flee, as Reg had hoped he would, but opened one eye, revealing this black slit pupil, looked at Davyn, and closed his eye again.

"Is that what I think it is?" Davyn pulled one of the wicker chairs closer and sat down, his attention still on the dragon.

"You see it too, right?" Reg asked. "I mean, I keep telling myself that it isn't and I'm just being silly, but…"

"A dragon?" Davyn shook his head in wonder. "I've never seen one before. This is amazing. Where did it come from?"

"The garden." Reg tilted her head to indicate the direction. "I guess the mother left an egg there a long time ago, and the… this just hatched a few days ago. I knew there was something out there, but Sarah said it was probably an armadillo."

"That's not an armadillo."

"I didn't think so. But I've never seen an armadillo before either."

"Believe me, this is not an armadillo." Davyn looked around the house. "How did you get it to come inside?"

"The real question is how to get it out again. I've been trying, but nothing I do works. He doesn't want to go back outside. He likes it better in here."

"That's incredible. And you've made friends with it in such a short time?"

"Just today. I never saw it clearly before that. Didn't really talk to it. But I was worried after the fire last night and wanted to make sure that it was okay."

Davyn's eyes registered understanding. "The fire!" He chuckled. "Well, that explains it. It wasn't your fire at all."

"I don't think so. I think it must have been his. I told you I didn't think that I'd done it."

"Yes, you did. But you are having problems controlling your fire."

Reg hesitated to agree, even though that was why she had called him. "I guess so, yeah. I keep causing fire when I don't mean to."

"It's because of him. You're reacting to his fire."

"I am?"

"I've heard of it happening before. Firedrakes and firecasters are very sensitive to each other. They can trigger each other's fire. Until they have a common purpose."

"Firedrakes? That's your name for dragons?"

"One kind of dragon. Yes. I assume if he was a water dragon, he wouldn't be triggering your fire."

Reg laughed weakly. "No. Maybe my siren tendencies instead."

"You do have challenges! Most people only have to worry about one or the other."

Reg remembered her teachers and parents trying to explain why things were so hard for her. Why she had problems in a lot of areas rather than just one. Why her brain was so screwed up. Multiple learning disabled. Alphabet soup disorders. Now even as part of the Black Sands community, she still had multiple challenges.

But they were her gifts too, and she didn't wish to be rid of them. She didn't want to have them stripped away as they had been before. Despite having an affinity to both fire and water—or maybe because of it—she could do things that she probably shouldn't have been able to. Davyn wasn't the only one who had told her how strong she was, how quickly she was learning her craft. Her life was completely different from what it had been a year before.

CHAPTER FORTY-TWO

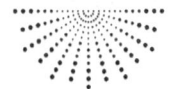

S o, what do I do?" Reg asked. "I can't get him to go back outside. But he can't stay in here."

"Have you tried picking him up and putting him outside?"

"Well, no. I just tried to shoo him out. And then to tempt him out with food. But that didn't go over very well." Reg looked at the bowl still on the floor where the dragon had slapped it out of her hand.

"Or go out ahead of him and see if he'll follow you. If he followed you in, maybe he'll follow you back out."

Reg fleetingly remembered a book she'd read as a child about a small dragon following a boy home from school. And then it kept getting bigger and bigger while people kept saying there was no such thing as a dragon. Reg had loved that book.

"Should I do that now? I'm kind of afraid to wake him up."

"You probably don't want to encourage him to stay inside. Maybe now, while he's sleepy, would be an ideal time."

Reg was still afraid to touch the dragon's scaly skin. It wasn't wet or slimy, but it would feel different. She wasn't a reptile person and hadn't touched very many before. She didn't even like touching handbags made from snakeskin.

Reg leaned over the sleeping dragon and tentatively touched it. The purring noise got louder.

"Hey, little guy, I'm sorry, but it's time for you to go outside, okay? Come on…"

She slid her hands underneath him, unsure how he would react to this. She'd picked up Starlight plenty of times, and it shouldn't be that different picking up a small dragon, but she was very uncertain. What if he had particularly sensitive parts, like a cat's back feet, that he didn't like having touched? What if he jumped away from her or breathed fire and ignited something else in the cottage? What if the manhandling made him angry enough to target her as prey, imprinting her on his brain until he was big enough to eat her in one gulp?

There really were a lot of unknowns.

The dragon let her shift him around and eventually pick him up with both hands, bringing him in to her body to hold him securely. He was larger than a kitten, but not by a lot. Smaller than Starlight. Maybe the size of an adolescent cat, half-grown.

"I don't know about this," she told Davyn nervously.

"You're doing just fine. He doesn't look like he's upset."

"Yeah, until he wakes up…"

Reg stood up slowly and walked toward the front door, shuffling her feet to make sure she didn't step on or run into anything. Davyn stood back to ensure that he wasn't in the way, then followed Reg out the door.

The dragon didn't wake up immediately upon reaching the fresh air of the outside. But then, the door had been open the whole time, so it wasn't a sudden shift in air temperatures or smell. Reg walked toward the bench that she'd been sitting on when the dragon had put in an appearance.

"This is where he was," she told Davyn. "I should put him back in the same spot I saw him in, I think. He'll know exactly where he is and won't be afraid…"

"Dragons don't tend to be very timid creatures," Davyn chuckled.

"He rolled up into a ball when I sneezed!"

"A reflex to a sudden noise, I guess. Probably something that only the little ones have. They must outgrow it as they get older. It wouldn't make sense for a full-grown dragon to roll up in a ball the moment it heard cannon fire or some other munition."

"What happens when a dragon gets hit by a cannon?" Reg asked, her chest tight with anxiety.

"Generally, they move out of the way before that happens. They're quite agile."

Reg leaned down to deposit the dragon in the grass. "This one isn't. You should see him trying to fly."

"He's just a fledgling. I expect he'll be a pro in a day or two."

"Do the mothers just leave the eggs alone and untended? And the hatchlings are supposed to be able to survive on their own as soon as they hatch?"

Davyn nodded. "I admit I don't know much about dragon lore, but most reptiles simply lay eggs and leave. They don't nest like birds, taking care of the young until they hatch."

"But how do they survive?" Reg looked down at the little dragon as she set it down. "He's so small. How is he supposed to learn everything that a dragon needs to know?"

"It's instinct. And then trial and error. Finding out what behaviors will help him succeed and which ones result in pain or hunger."

"That's not very fair."

Davyn shrugged and laughed. "Tell that to Mother Nature."

The dragon was awake. He looked up at Reg after she put him down in the grass, blinking sleepily.

"Don't look at me like that," Reg muttered. She turned away from him, steeling herself and swallowing the lump in her throat. He was a solitary creature. They were supposed to grow up alone. She would be harming him if she tried to help him out. Like people who picked up baby bunnies, thinking they were orphaned, when the baby's job was to be still and wait for the parent's return. Picking them up and taking them home to care for them was the worst possible choice.

The dragon would be fine on his own, just as he had been in the days since he had hatched.

"Okay, let's go back inside," she told Davyn in a low voice, quickening her steps.

There was a flurry of wings and then a whoosh of air and what felt like fingers clasping her shoulder. Reg turned her head and looked at the small dragon perched on her shoulder, looking very pleased with himself. He nuzzled her ear and neck.

"Hey, little guy. You're supposed to live outside. Not with me."

Had she already damaged him by talking to him and encouraging him to come to her? Now he had apparently bonded with her and was determined to stay with her when he was supposed to be alone in the wild.

"Come on. You go on the ground. Back into the garden. Stay there."

Reg carefully detached him from her shoulder, which was not the easiest thing to do, and placed him firmly on the ground.

"You stay in the garden," she ordered. She conjured up the most detailed picture she could of the garden, pushing it to him firmly.

In return, he sent her a vision of the two of them on the couch in the cottage, sitting in front of a crackling fire.

There wasn't even a fireplace in the cottage.

"No. You stay out here. Dragons outside, Reg inside."

She walked toward the house again. The dragon made a gurgling noise. His way of calling her back? She kept walking. With another loud flapping, he launched himself into the air and managed to land on the edge of the roof.

"Fine. You can sit up there," Reg confirmed. "Just as long as you stay outside."

She rounded the side of the cottage and headed for the front door.

The dragon had made his way over the roof to the front corner, and he jumped down as she approached the door, gliding into the house ahead of her.

CHAPTER FORTY-THREE

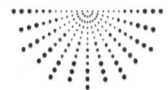

*D*avyn laughed. "Well, he is a persistent little fellow; I'll give him that."

"What am I supposed to do now? Throw him out the window? Shooing him out doesn't work. Leaving him outside doesn't work."

"I don't know," Davyn shook his head, smiling at the dragon, who, after a bit more fluttering was able to get back up onto the counter to see if there was any kitty kibble left. Starlight jumped down with an angry snort and stalked off to the bedroom as if he had been intending to go there anyway and hadn't just been displaced by the little dragon.

"Starlight is going to be impossible to live with," Reg observed. "He does *not* like little Draco."

"Is that what you're going to call him?"

"No." Reg shook her head, frowning. "It doesn't feel right. But I don't know what his name will be, so that will have to work for now. You don't know how to get him to stay outside?"

"I'm afraid not. I'll do some reading tonight and see if I can come up with anything for you. Sorry, I'm just not up on—"

"Not up on your dragon lore. Yeah, you said that."

"It's just not my area. It probably should be, since there have been some interesting stories about dragons and firecasters throughout history. But I never paid that much attention. I honestly never thought I would see one myself."

"Are they that rare?"

He nodded. "They're that rare."

Reg gritted her teeth, looking at Draco. Not only was she now saddled with a dragon, but they were extremely rare creatures, and she would have to be careful not to do anything that might harm it. She couldn't help thinking of the stories she had just been reading about armadillos and how short a time they survived as pets. What if dragons were the same way? He should be out chasing after bugs and small prey, not on her counter eating cat kibble. It was probably the worst possible thing to feed him and just trained him to be more dependent on her, rather than going out and building his muscles chasing proper prey.

"Do you think you'll be able to find anything? Do you have books that talk about how to train them or take care of them? Dragon repellent potions that would keep him out of the house? Do they not like... I don't know, rock music or country and western? There must be something I can do to make the house seem less hospitable."

"I have some books in my library that I think will give us some guidance. You might talk to Corvin about it too. He's the one person I know who has read the most ancient texts. He probably knows more about dragons than I'll be able to find out in a night."

"Okay. I'll try to get him and find out. Is it okay to tell him that I have a dragon? He's not going to come here and try to keep Draco, is he? Or to steal his powers?"

"I don't think so. Besides, he's kind of laid up right now. I don't think he will be doing much traveling or chasing around powerful species at the moment."

Reg thought back to Corvin's state at the hospital. Hopefully, he would be staying there for another day or two. She didn't want him trying to steal Draco or his dragon powers.

"Corvin says he's still going to run for leadership of the coven."

"I don't think very much could dissuade him from doing that. It would take more than a couple of failed murder attempts. He's pretty determined to run."

"And to win."

Davyn's lips pressed together in a thin line. "Yes. He's set a goal and he intends to achieve it. Some people who have big plans and pursue their goals incessantly achieve great things in life for the benefit of everyone around them. And others…"

He didn't finish. Did Davyn just mean that Corvin was working only for his own benefit, or that if he succeeded, he could be pursuing a course that would negatively impact the rest of humankind? Reg shuddered. Hopefully not. Maybe Corvin would serve for a year or two as the leader of the coven and then tire of it when he realized that his focus was supposed on serving everyone else rather than making the changes that he saw himself making or gaining whatever it was he hoped to get from the experience.

"Let's hope he gets bored quickly," Reg said.

Davyn nodded his agreement. "Yes. That would be the best outcome. Give him what he wants and let him get bored of it."

But Reg doubted that was what would happen.

* * *

Davyn left and, once again, Reg was left to herself. And Starlight. And Draco. She really didn't like that name. It didn't fit at all. Reg thought of different names that might be good for a firedrake. Puff? Smokey? Drake?

She tapped a search into her phone to look for more ideas. None of them seemed to fit him exactly. But Reg had time. She probably shouldn't even be trying to name him. She knew that people weren't supposed to name animals they weren't going to keep. It created more of an attachment, and Reg could not keep a dragon there.

There was a knock on the door and then it swung open.

"Reg! I was just wondering whether you were able to…" The words faded into nothingness as Sarah caught a glimpse of the dragon on the counter.

Reg tried to remain casual, as if this happened all the time. Nothing to see here. Nothing to be worried about. Just a little dragon. Nothing that could hurt anyone. She had a mental image of John Cleese. "What's that, dear? Oh, this? What's this, you mean?"

She looked at Sarah politely, eyebrows raised.

"Reg. What's that?" Sarah finally managed to get out.

"It's, uh… the armadillo I saw in the garden."

Sarah looked back at it for a long time. "That is not an armadillo."

Reg ran her fingers through her red box braids, trying to calm herself. She was anticipating a huge explosion from Sarah. She hated shouting and the disapproval of the older woman, reminding her too much of all of the foster homes where she had never failed to disappoint her latest foster mom and got in trouble for talking back at school, not getting her homework done, or "pretending" to talk to people who weren't there. And the countless other things that she had gotten in trouble for. Some of them her fault and some of them not.

"No," Reg admitted. "I guess not."

"Is that… a dragon?"

Reg swallowed. "That's what Davyn said. A firedrake."

"A firedrake? Oh, Reg…" her voice was heavy with disappointment, as if this were something that Reg could have controlled.

"He keeps following me inside," Reg explained. "I've tried to make him go back outside, but he won't."

Sarah took a few steps closer. As much as she didn't want a firedrake in her guest cottage, she was apparently curious enough to want to get a good look. Draco-not-Draco looked at her curiously, flicking out his tongue to taste the air. He used a clawed hand to pick up a few more crumbs of kitty kibble from the bowl and put them in his mouth. He watched Sarah, munching away.

"This must be… he's the one who started the fire in the garden?"

"Yeah. And I think Forst knew that from the start."

"Forst knew about it?"

Reg nodded. "I was asking him about creatures and what I had seen in the garden… what you had said was an armadillo."

"Probably an armadillo," Sarah corrected.

"Probably an armadillo. And Forst said that he knew about the hatchling."

Sarah sighed. "It would have been nice to have been informed about it before now. But I don't suppose that's your fault, or even his, given the communication gap."

"I'm not sure what we could have done even if you had known about him. Do you… know much about dragons? What to do with them?"

"I know some about them. But not what to do with them. They are not usually that friendly to humankind."

"He's kind of made himself at home."

"He can't stay in the house."

"Yeah. I figured that. But if you have any ideas on how to keep him out of the house…"

Sarah flapped her hands at the dragon, barely a token gesture. "Shoo! Get out of here! No dragons in the house," she told him, in what was hardly above a speaking voice. Reg understood that Sarah didn't want to do anything that might make the dragon blow fire at her. And that was a valid concern. Even though Reg was a firecaster, she didn't want to be stuck in the same room as an angry fire-breathing dragon.

Sarah looked at Reg, then spoke more loudly to the dragon. "Out. Come on; you're not allowed in here." She got close enough that she could have reached out to touch the dragon but, instead of doing so, she just leaned in, studying it closely. "It's amazing. Like something that you would see in a movie. A model or digital anima-tion. It's hard to fathom that it is actually real."

"I know."

They both stood there looking at him for a few minutes. The dragon yawned and turned his gaze to Reg. She tried to project an image to him of sleeping under one of the trees in the backyard. She ran into some difficulties, unsure whether a dragon would take a midday nap in the sun or whether he would find a burrow or darkly shadowed place to go to sleep.

The dragon stretched out each of his four limbs in turn and then hunkered down on the counter, legs folded in under him like a cat, wings tight against his body.

"He rolls up in a ball when he's startled," Reg told Sarah. "It's adorable."

"I don't suppose you could…"

Reg shook her head after waiting for Sarah to finish her request. Try to carry him out of the house again? Speak to it telepathically, as she was already doing? Find a way to get rid of it? "What?"

"You know… take a picture," Sarah indicated Reg's phone.

Reg laughed. She framed the sleepy dragon on her phone screen. Sarah got in behind him and leaned close so that they were both clear. Reg snapped several pictures. "Okay, I got it."

She touched the picture roll and flipped through them, picking out the best picture of Sarah.

"You can message it to me," Sarah suggested, which Reg was already doing.

CHAPTER FORTY-FOUR

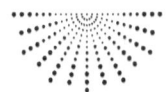

*W*hen Reg had pressed send, her phone rang, startling her. It rang a second time before Jessup's picture was displayed. Reg hesitated. It wasn't the best time to deal with a call from Jessup. Though it would get her out of the conversation with Sarah. Maybe that would be the best after all.

Reg swiped the screen. "Hello?"

"Hi, Reg. It's Marta."

Reg didn't think Jessup had ever introduced herself to her as Marta before. She always either omitted saying who was calling, or referred to herself as Detective Jessup when it was official police business.

This time it obviously was not police business.

"Uh... hi, Marta." She felt weird calling Jessup that after going so long without addressing her by anything but Detective Jessup. "What's up?"

"Well... this is sort of a personal thing to be calling you about. I'm sorry. But I didn't know who else to call, and you have been asking me how everything was and you know about my mom and not many people do..."

"Yeah. What's going on?" Reg wondered whether Jessup's mother was haunting her now. Maybe Jessup was finally coming around to the idea that ghosts were a real thing and wanted to know if Reg would set up a seance to get everything straightened out between them.

"I need to help out with some of the jobs that need to be done after my mom's... passing. I can't just let my brothers and dad take care of everything and pretend that I'm too busy to help out. I know I have responsibilities and I should be there."

"Uh-huh?"

"I need to do some stuff at the house. To help get it ready for sale. I would just go and do it on my own, but... I haven't been there since I joined the academy and my family moved out of town. I'm kind of creeped out about being in the house by myself."

"Oh. So you're looking for someone to come along with you?"

"Yeah. I don't know... would you be free? You don't have to do any cleaning or anything; just be there, so I'm not alone in that house."

"Sure." Reg looked at the time on her phone. "When do you want me there?"

"Would an hour from now be okay? I'm sorry even to ask. I know you must have all kinds of other things going on and this is really short notice."

"No, it's okay. I can move things around."

The truth was, Reg didn't have anything until later that night. Her scheduled activities were, as usual, from after supper until midnight. She didn't keep bankers' hours and, despite Jessup saying that Reg must be busy with a lot of things, she really wasn't. Not scheduled things that couldn't be left. And she didn't mind leaving her current responsibilities to do something else so she wouldn't have to think about Corvin and the attacks against him or what she would do with the dragon. Maybe if she left the house, the dragon would get bored and go back to the garden where he belonged.

"Thanks, Reg. I really appreciate it."

* * *

Sarah headed back to the big house on the understanding that Reg was going out to help Jessup and would ensure that the dragon was out of the cottage before she left.

How Reg was going to accomplish that, she wasn't quite sure.

The only time the dragon didn't seem to object to leaving the house was when Reg left the house. So once she left, it shouldn't take too much encouragement to get the dragon to leave too. It made perfect sense.

Reg picked up her shoulder bag and headed toward the door. "Time for me to go out," she called out to the dragon, even though it was pretty clear that it didn't have the capability of understanding everything she said to it. Some things, maybe, but probably more by her actions and tone of voice than by actually understanding her words. She pictured the garden again, the place where she had initially seen the dragon, back in the undergrowth where he could hide and would not be in danger from any larger predators. She tried to imbue the mental picture with all of the warmth and feelings of safety as she could. That was the dragon's home. That was where he wanted to go back to.

She walked through the doorway and, with less flapping this time, the dragon launched himself into the air and glided onto her shoulder. Reg winced. His grip was a little too tight for comfort. But he was with her as she went out the door, so she turned around and shut and locked the door to prevent him from getting back in again. That was one problem solved.

She tried to pry his claws from her shoulder. "You stay back here. It's nice and safe here."

He transferred his grip to her hand, something like a falcon perching on the wrist of a falconer. Reg tried to throw or shake him off, but he stuck to her like glue.

"You need to stay here. I have to go out, and you can't come with me. You're safe in this yard. You're protected here. It's your home. Your nest." She again tried to encourage him with happy, comforting pictures of the garden and the sights and sounds she enjoyed while sitting on the bench thinking.

But the images were replaced by pictures of herself, her aura glowing, her skin warm and hair flaming red. She felt him squeeze her hand tighter with his claws for a moment and then release to a more comfortable hold.

He might be a baby, but he was pretty good at showing her what he wanted. Not the comfort of a nest, but of another body. Reg in particular. He seemed to have imprinted on her like a baby chick. Now, what was she to do? She wasn't a dragon mommy.

Maybe if she treated him like a mother would, she would have more success. She put her hand down and encouraged him to release her and sit on the ground. "Off. You stay here. Stay," she told him firmly, putting her hand on him and pressing down firmly. "You stay."

She removed her hand and he stayed where he was.

"Good. Good dragon. I'm going out, but you need to stay here."

He looked at her for a moment, then hopped onto her arm.

"No!" Reg was louder and more insistent. "No, you stay here!"

He looked at her with bright, intelligent eyes. But however much he understood, he seemed determined to stay with her. Reg gave a loud growl and pointed her finger at him, producing a burst of flame. He'd seemed impressed by that before. Maybe that was what had convinced him that she was a suitable companion. But she made the flame hotter and made it stay for longer, trying to indicate to him that she was in charge. Her fire was bigger. She was the alpha.

She put him firmly on the ground again, then walked briskly toward the gate. She didn't look back, which she thought might encourage the dragon to follow her. She wanted him to clearly understand that her intention was for him to stay behind and her to go without him.

She made it to the gate and had not heard anything from him. As tempting as it was to look back, she forced herself to keep looking forward and exit through the gate. She practically sprinted to her car and jumped in.

Before she could slam the door, there was a whoosh, and the dragon sat on the passenger seat. He blinked at her with one eye and then the other. She wasn't used to reading dragon facial expressions but thought he looked very smug and satisfied with himself.

She wasn't sure how to force him to stay behind, other than chaining him up like a dog—or maybe getting one of those dog collars that gave a mild shock to train dogs to recognize their yard boundaries. She had an idea that shocking a dragon might not be a good idea. While he might curl up into a ball the first time, she suspected he would be more likely to shoot flames at a shock than be stopped by one.

She looked at the dragon. He looked back at her.

Reg finally pulled the door shut. She was crazy to drive around town with a dragon in her car, but what else was she to do? At least he would keep Jessup distracted from her mother's death and the fact that she was in the house without any of her family when it should have been echoing with their voices.

CHAPTER FORTY-FIVE

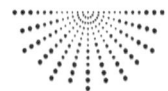

*R*eg had never had an old family home to go to, so she could only imagine what that might be like. What had she felt like when she had been returned to the home of her four-year-old self when Harrison had taken her there? It wasn't a great example of a happy family home. It had been little more than a squat —dirty and rat-infested. There had never been any food and Reg spent much of her time hiding from her mother or the men she brought home. Going back there had felt wrong. And terrifying. Maybe not the same way that Jessup felt going back to her old house, but Reg could at least be empathetic.

Jessup had texted her the address, and it didn't take Reg long to find the house using the GPS. She pulled up to the curb and looked at the dragon. "I really don't want other people to see you. Can you hide?"

She should have thought to bring the cat carrier with her. As it was, she didn't even have a box like she had first carried Starlight home in. All she had was her shoulder bag. She opened it up and looked inside, eyeing the dragon and wondering if she could fit him in it. Maybe if she took a few things out and left them in the car. Her sunglasses. A makeup bag. She wasn't even sure what all was in there.

She didn't clean it out nearly as often as she should. She indicated the open main section.

"Hop in."

The little dragon looked at her face, then its eyes rolled slowly toward the shoulder bag, and he looked at it for a minute without any indication that he understood what she wanted him to do. Then, in a blink, he was inside it.

Reg jiggled the bag a little, ensuring that he was settled and wouldn't be too visible to anyone. He made a comfortable purring noise.

"You like that, do you? A nice little cave for Draco?"

Again, she was struck by the wrongness of the name. It just didn't suit him at all. Maybe he didn't like it. Either way, she felt uneasy every time she used it and needed to find something else.

"Hatchling? Smokey? Berndt?"

None of them seemed to work. Reg remembered trying to find a name for Starlight. He too had not been happy with the first few names that she had suggested, but they had eventually settled on Starlight and he had been happy with that. She had felt that it was right from the moment she said it.

Reg sighed and climbed out of the car, handling the shoulder bag gingerly.

She walked to the house and knocked on the door. It was a couple of minutes before Jessup came to the door and opened it.

"Hi, Reg. Thank you, I'm glad you didn't mind coming over."

Reg nodded. She stepped into the house and waited until Jessup had closed the door. "I didn't come alone," she warned, and indicated the bulge in her bag.

"Did you bring Starlight with you? I know cats like bags and boxes, but did he really—"

Reg held open the mouth of the purse and let Jessup peer inside.

Jessup gave a little shriek of surprise and stumbled back. "What the—what was that? What the heck have you got in there?"

The dragon moved around, growling. He apparently didn't like the noises Jessup was making or the aura she was radiating. She was already emotional from the loss of her mother and being back there in the house where she had grown up, so other feelings were magnified.

"It's just…" Reg looked for something more comforting to say than "It's just a dragon."

"It's just… something that was in the garden?" Reg ended with an upward squeak that made it sound like a question. "When I told Sarah about it, she thought it might be an armadillo." She gave a little laugh, as if Jessup might join in and chuckle about how cute it was.

"That is not an armadillo."

"No," Reg agreed. "But it wasn't that far off."

"How is that not far off. What is that thing? A gargoyle?"

"No!" Reg couldn't help feeling offended. Gargoyles were those ugly goblin-like creatures on Gothic buildings. They were nothing like that handsome young hatchling in her purse. "It's not a gargoyle! It's a dragon!"

Jessup just looked at her with wide eyes.

Reg grimaced and tried to find something more calming to say than that. "I just found him today. He won't leave me alone, so I had to bring him. But no one saw, and I'm sure he'll be very well-behaved while we're here. You said you wanted to be distracted."

Jessup took a deep breath in and out. "I'm not sure I want to be *that* distracted."

Reg laughed. "Well, what was I supposed to do? Wear a clown costume?"

"Not bring *that*!" Jessup pointed at Reg's bag and rolled her eyes.

"Right now, we're a package deal, so… What do you want me to do? Do you want help with the tidying up or do you just want me to hang out?"

"I think your job is going to have to be babysitting. I don't want that thing wandering around the house by itself. What if it lights something on fire?"

"Oh, I don't think he'll do that." Reg felt immediately guilty, thinking about the fire in the backyard. Who knew how often baby dragons started fires? It might be like puppies chewing on shoes, part of their normal development as they figured out how to operate their bodies.

"You'd better keep an eye on it anyway. I'm supposed to be helping to get the place ready to sell. Fire and smoke damage do not do much to enhance property value."

"I'll keep an eye on him," Reg agreed. "But I can probably do other things at the same time." She tried to think of things that might be helpful to Jessup. Having never actually purchased or sold a property, it wasn't an area she had a lot of experience in. "Do you need... cleaning or something done?"

"I have to pack a bunch of books away. And I don't think it's a good idea to have *that* near large amounts of flammable material. Besides, I need to look at and sort each book to ensure it's going to the right place. Some of them are valuable, and some need to go to certain schools or charities." Jessup rolled her eyes. "You'd think that since they've been sitting on the shelves here unused for years, we could just get rid of them in bulk and donate them to a used book store, but my father... that's not how he operates."

"What does he do?" Reg had taken him to be a farmer or some other profession where he did manual labor. But Jessup's words suggested that he was well-read on a number of technical subjects.

"He was a nuclear scientist. Not the kind that designs bombs. Theoretical stuff, technical papers, teaching, that kind of thing. He's quite well-known and respected in the field. Completely unknown anywhere else."

Reg wondered at the note of disdain in Jessup's voice. Was she proud of her father or embarrassed that he wasn't more of a public figure?

"That sounds complicated."

"It is, I guess. Never a field that interested me. My brothers didn't follow in his footsteps either. Me in law enforcement. Harker in investment banking. William... has been in a lot of things. Gets too restless to stay in one thing for long, I guess. So Dad didn't have anyone to give his books to. None of us are the least bit interested in them, no matter how valuable they are. He reads in a lot of other areas as well. I don't know if it was because they were related or just because he has wide-ranging interests. And he has a lot of classics too.

Literary stuff. Maybe some first editions, so I have to check everything over carefully."

"Why isn't he doing that? Wouldn't he know more about them?"

"I asked for something to do to help out. Because I felt guilty about staying away and not doing anything, letting him and the guys take care of it all. Not just since Mom passed... but before that too."

"Oh." Reg nodded. "Well... I guess I'll take a look around and see if there is anything I can see that needs to be done. And keep an eye on... Drake here."

Drake didn't sound any better to her ear than Draco, even though Davyn had said he was a firedrake. She still hadn't hit on the right name. Nothing was resonating yet.

"Drake?"

"Just trying it out. It doesn't really work. I'll hit on a name sooner or later."

Jessup nodded. "Okay." She paused. "I really do appreciate you coming. Just having someone in the house makes me feel better. Even if we're not doing something together. I hope you don't mind. You'll probably be bored to death."

"No," Reg laughed. "I'll be fine. I've got my phone if this little fellow doesn't keep me entertained. That's what I end up doing at home anyway. Even though I have a big-screen TV, I always end up scrolling through stuff and watching it on my phone."

CHAPTER FORTY-SIX

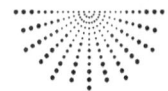

*J*essup went into her father's study to review the books lining the shelves. And from what Reg glimpsed through the open door, there were a lot of them. It would keep Jessup busy for quite some time. Probably longer than Reg could stay there. Despite her assurances to Jessup, she wasn't sure she would be able to keep the dragon entertained for very long. Right now, it was sitting quietly in her shoulder bag, but that wasn't going to last forever. Sooner or later, he would get restless and would want to explore. Or to go outside, back to Sarah's garden, or something else that Reg hadn't thought of.

She settled herself into a comfortable chair in the living room and opened her bag to have a look. "How are you doing in there?"

The dragon was curled up around Reg's wallet. He made a purring noise. Reg reached in to move the wallet so that he could make himself more comfortable. He nipped at her finger and snorted. No burst of flame, luckily. She didn't want all of the receipts and lint and accumulated detritus in her purse to ignite. It might not bother the dragon, but it would make a mess of her purse.

"I'm just trying to move it out of your way," she told the baby. "That doesn't look very comfy."

He made purrs and clicks, seemingly trying to communicate

something to her. Reg focused all of her senses on him, reaching out and trying to catch the nuances of whatever he was telling her.

She was probably making too much of it. He was just a baby. Even if dragons had a spoken language, he wouldn't know it yet. He hadn't even had contact with any other dragons. Just how could a species that was so rare and did not congregate together manage to develop and retain a language?

But she tried anyway, trying to connect with him. The visual images had seemed to work in the past, so she tried that again, picturing herself taking the wallet out of the purse, giving him more room to curl up and go to sleep.

The impressions she got back from the little dragon were not as clear and crisp, but she got images of him sleeping in a pile of gold coins, like a pirate's booty. How could he even know about something like that? She had heard the term "genetic memory" before and wondered if that was how the hatchling dragon seemed to know about things he couldn't possibly have been told or read about. He was a dragon. Alone, without any other dragons around. There was no one to teach him dragon language or history. How could he look at or smell her wallet and know that there were coins in the zippered side? They were not as valuable as gold coins, but that apparently didn't matter to him. He knew that they were money, and he wanted the treasure. Or to sleep with it, anyway. The beginning of his own little hoard.

"Do you want me to get them out? I can take them out of the wallet for you so that you can touch them." She imagined doing this, hearing the clink of the coins and that distinctive smell of coins when she had a lot of them together or had handled them a lot. The dragon lifted his head and tilted it to the side slightly, looking at her inquiringly. "Do you want the coins?"

He stayed still. This time, when Reg reached in for the wallet, he didn't nip at her, but watched with bright eyes as she opened the zippered side and scooped out a few coins with her fingers. She wondered if she should put them on the floor to get him out of the purse, or whether keeping him inside the bag would be better. Holding the coins in her palm, she lowered them into the purse.

Using his clawed front paws, he took the coins one at a time and examined each, smelling them, occasionally flicking a tongue out over them to taste them, and then putting them down underneath him. When he had taken them all, Reg shook the wallet to free up any coins that had stuck in the tight corners of the pocket and took them out as well. Eventually, the dragon had all of the coins. He had formed them into a little pile in the center of the purse, and now he curled up on top of them, murmuring and purring to himself.

* * *

Reg played with her phone while the dragon slept. She wasn't doing anything to help Jessup, but the woman had made it clear that she was more concerned about Reg keeping track of the dragon than doing anything else to help. What she had asked for was some company, not physical labor. After a couple of hours, Reg got tired of all of the sitting. Her eyes were starting to get heavy and she didn't want to go to sleep. She went back to the study to see how Jessup was doing with her job.

She knocked lightly and stuck her head into the room. "Hey. Just thought I'd see how it's going."

Jessup's face was smudged with dust. She looked at the books lying all around her, some of them sorted into boxes or stacks, and shook her head. "Well, I have books off of the shelves… but I'm not sure if I've made any progress. Moving books from one place to another doesn't seem very helpful. I'm sure Dad would be able to do it much faster himself. In fact, he'll probably reorganize everything after I do anyway, so what's the point in even doing this?"

"Sounds frustrating."

"How's the you-know-what?"

Reg shook her head. "The dragon? Why won't you say that?"

"I don't know." Jessup laughed. "Fear of making it too real, I suppose. I can take the stories about dragons, no problem, but seeing one in front of me and realizing that they exist, they're not just some myth or bedtime story, that seems to be a little harder."

"You know that he exists."

"I'd prefer for it just to be speculation."

Reg laughed. "I was pretty shocked. I had no idea that they were a real thing."

"Yeah. You get used to saying that this creature or that is just a figment of people's imaginations... that they saw a bear or gorilla, and that's what they thought was Bigfoot. Or that Nessie was just a bunch of tires tied together. That dragons were just a story made up after seeing a big lizard. Maybe a morality story to get kids to behave."

Reg nodded. She hadn't even thought about dragons in that way. They were no different to her than comic book superheroes or *The Cat in the Hat*. She hadn't even thought about their being inspired by an animal sighting or crafted for a specific purpose. She opened her purse and looked inside. The hatchling stirred and sat up.

"I found out that he likes coins," she told Jessup. "I guess that's treasure to him. Dragons collect treasure, right?"

"Like magpies collect shiny things, I guess," Jessup said with a shrug. "It isn't like they can do anything with them. Buy dragon food or a new cave. They don't have dragon commerce."

"He just instinctively likes shiny things?"

"Right."

"Why?"

Jessup raised her brows. "What?"

"Why do they like shiny things? If they aren't food or shelter... would they use them to impress a mate? Is that why magpies collect shiny things?"

"I think... they just like the way they look."

"Hmm." Reg wondered. She supposed there didn't have to be a reason to explain animal behavior. Or not a *human* reason. She liked to think that other creatures thought and felt the same way as she did, but knew that most people would tell her not to humanize them. Animals were animals, and they had their own motivations and brains that were completely different from humans'. But were they? Maybe those people just didn't like to admit how similar they were to the "lower-order" animals.

CHAPTER FORTY-SEVEN

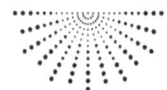

The dragon stretched its legs one at a time and flicked its tongue out. He must have realized that they were in a different environment from the one they had been in when he had fallen asleep. He poked his head out the opening of the purse and looked around.

Jessup watched him anxiously. "He is kind of cute. In an ugly sort of way."

"Ugly? He's not ugly at all!"

Reg remembered how startled she had been the first time she had seen him in the dark undergrowth. How surprised and scared she had been, just catching a glimpse of him. But he had grown on her since she had started to communicate with him and she was exposed to his strange appearance and behavior more. He wasn't cute like a cat, but he had his charm. And he had that baby innocence and simplicity around him. A wonder at the world. She didn't sense any evil or anger from him. No negative feelings. It was nice to be around a creature so new and unspoiled.

"Well…" Jessup drew the word out. "He is a lizard, and I've never been partial to reptiles."

"I haven't either. But he's not ugly."

"Okay," Jessup conceded. "Not ugly. Just… reptilian."

Reg couldn't argue with that.

She put the shoulder bag down on the large desk nearby and, as she expected, the dragon climbed slowly out, stretching each limb carefully and looking around with interest. He started to creep along the desk slowly, like iguanas that Reg had seen on Animal Planet.

"You shouldn't let him out," Jessup warned. "Especially in here."

But Jessup didn't make any move to stop him and appeared to be just as interested in his explorations as Reg.

Reg didn't think that he would blow fire or try to ignite the books. Not like when he was confronting Starlight and had used his fire. That had just been self-defense. Not wanton destruction.

She tried to tear her mind away from the thought of lighting books on fire. She knew from experience how well paper burned, how quick and hot, and the thought of all of that fuel excited the fire within her. Davyn had warned her that her fire and the dragon played off of each other, making it harder for her to control her fire around him. That seemed to be true here in the library. She tried to tamp down those feelings and just watch the dragon to see what he was interested in.

In a few minutes, Jessup went back to sorting the books, maybe reassured that he wouldn't do anything harmful. Reg stuck close to the dragon as he explored the desk, one of the bookshelves that Jessup had cleared, and crawled along the carpet, following the walls around the room.

After a second time around the room, he stopped at the closed door and waited.

"I guess he's bored in here," Reg said with a shrug. "You don't mind if he explores a little out here, do you?"

"Probably less for him to harm out there than there is in here."

Reg took that to mean it was fine. She opened the study door and the dragon exited.

He was more interesting to watch than random videos on Reg's phone. But she quickly grew tired of his having to crawl around all of the baseboards. It was the same in every room.

He did find a few lost coins, teasing them out from cracks and crannies where they had become wedged. Reg placed each of them into the pile in her purse, which seemed to please him. He stuck his head into the bag once or twice to examine his growing hoard, but didn't crawl back in to go to sleep.

In a bedroom occupied by one of Jessup's brothers while they were in town, the dragon crawled through the closet and under the bed and eventually pushed a metal box out from under the bed to Reg. She looked at it and didn't touch it. "That's not yours, Smokey. We should leave it there."

Smokey didn't feel right either. He pushed it toward her insistently.

"What's that?"

Reg startled at Jessup's voice but didn't move. She hadn't done anything wrong.

"Cash box," she said. "I didn't open it."

Jessup entered the bedroom. She sat on the bed and bent down to retrieve the box. The dragon growled, but Reg pointed at him warningly and he stopped. Jessup thumbed the latch and opened the top of the box. There was a black plastic cash tray like the one in a cash register drawer. It held a few coins, a ring, and some small documents Reg suspected were birth certificates or other family records.

Jessup removed the plastic tray, revealing the storage space underneath for larger items. There was a thick, stiff envelope along with a few other papers. Jessup picked up the envelope and turned it over.

Marta was written on the back in a looping script. Feminine handwriting.

Jessup looked at the top edge of the envelope where it had been torn open. "This has been opened," she said accusingly.

"I didn't open it. I didn't touch the cash box. The dragon did. But he didn't open it either. You are the only one who opened the cash box."

"And whoever opened this."

"Or whoever stored it here. It might have been opened long before that."

Jessup looked at her, frowning.

"I just mean that the person who opened it and the person who put it in the box could be two different people," Reg clarified.

"Yes," Jessup admitted. "Or another person could have accessed the box afterward and opened it."

"But it wasn't me."

"I heard you," Jessup said evenly.

Not "I believe you" or "I know you wouldn't do anything like that."

Reg chewed on her lip. She was there to help. She had come at Jessup's own request. And the woman still couldn't trust her. Immediately jumped to the wrong conclusion the instant something went wrong. But she knew Jessup was going through a difficult time. Her mother had died. Committed suicide. Jessup had been estranged from her family and felt guilty for not having stayed close to them. Her emotions were near the surface. It was only natural that she would be more reactive to anything Reg said or did.

And Reg had been blamed plenty of times before for something that she had not done. It was not a new experience by any stretch. If Jessup wanted her to carry some of the load, then why not? What did it hurt?

Jessup was the first to look away. She had been trained by the police in interrogation techniques, but she was the one who dropped her eyes.

She looked down at the envelope she held in her hands. Maybe accusing Reg was just a delaying tactic. She didn't want to see what was in the envelope with her name on it. It wasn't likely to be anything good. Even if it were an emotional letter saying how much Lily had missed her daughter, it would still make Jessup more upset. Bereaved because of what she had lost. The fact that her mother had written to her rather than talking to her in person. That someone had opened the envelope, violating it, before Jessup had had the chance to read it. Someone else knew of the letter's existence and had kept it from her—all negative, even in the best-case scenario.

"I can go out," Reg suggested. Maybe Jessup would want to be alone for this revelation. She needed time and space to react without being judged and without having to put on a mask for Reg, pretending she was tough and didn't care what that letter said.

"No. Stay here, please. I don't think I can do this by myself."

"Okay."

They both just sat there, Reg on the floor and Jessup on the bed. And the dragon sniffing around the cash box and eyeing the top tray beside Jessup on the bed.

CHAPTER FORTY-EIGHT

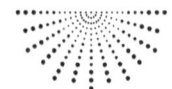

*E*ventually, Jessup slid her fingers into the envelope and pulled out the several items it held. Photographs. Notes or a letter on lined school paper.

Jessup unfolded the lined paper and glanced over it. "It's dated the day I was born."

Reg had a bad feeling about this. She looked for a way to divert Jessup's attention from the letter. "Maybe we should leave this until later. You must be hungry. You've been working hard."

Jessup shook her head. "No. I need to do this."

Reg waited. If she were in a TV movie, maybe she would have pulled the note from Jessup's hand and read it aloud to her. But Reg was a terrible reader. Especially of cursive. And she didn't think that taking charge was the right response to Jessup's dilemma. Jessup needed to work it out on her own.

Jessup sighed and looked down at the page. She blinked a few times, scanning the lines.

"Despite what happened, the baby seems healthy and normal. Only time will tell what the long-lasting effects will be."

Reg frowned and scratched her scalp, then fidgeted with her braids, not sure what any of this meant. "Despite what happened?"

"I don't know," Jessup shook her head.

Reg thought back to Lily's anger, her railing accusations and the demands for vengeance. "You said that she had always been depressive, always had mental health issues?"

Jessup nodded.

"Was that only after you were born? How about before that?"

"I don't know. I never asked. I just assumed so."

"Maybe something happened when she was still pregnant with you that affected her later. And she was afraid that it would affect you too."

"But what?" she stared down at the page. There was a lot more written on it than she had read aloud. If she didn't want to read out all of what was written there, that was her right. Reg didn't want to infringe on Jessup's privacy.

Jessup nodded slowly as her eyes moved back and forth across the page. "Yeah... she refers to the 'assault,' the 'attack.' What happened to her?" She frowned at the pages. "Do you think she was... why didn't anyone ever tell me about this? Dad had to know about it. Clearly, it was something very violent, very traumatic."

"Maybe she didn't want you to know."

"I guess. She had years to tell me about it and never did. This envelope... did she prepare it all years ago and then just not share it with me? Or did she do it knowing what she was going to do?"

"Looks old. I think she's had it for a while."

"Then why didn't she tell me about it? Why couldn't she reach out?"

Reg could hear Jessup's mental self-recriminations as well. *And why didn't I?* She put her hand briefly on Jessup's knee.

Jessup picked up the photographs. One of Lily and Arthur and a small boy who must have been Harker. Lily with her hand over her protruding belly, looking somber. Another photo was of a baby in an incubator, swaddled tightly. Marta Jessup, obviously. Tiny pink hat. Black hair poking out from under it. Golden skin. Jessup looked at them for a long time.

"What happened?" Reg murmured.

There were more papers. Not just the single sheet of lined paper, but other pages of other sizes and colors that indicated that they had been written at different junctures.

"I still struggle to understand what happened," Jessup read aloud. "How I could have been tempted. How I could let myself be led astray by him." Jessup swallowed. "She cheated."

"Maybe," Reg said. "But it's together with the other, so… maybe she was lured."

"How is that any different?"

Reg shook her head slightly. "It is," she insisted. "It's very different. Especially if…" Her heart sank, but she couldn't say it until she knew more. Until her suspicions could be verified. "Umm, look… I've got to go. I'm sorry I can't stay for longer, but…" She looked over at the dragon. "Scorch and I have somewhere we need to be."

Scorch. No. Definitely not.

Jessup looked surprised and hurt. She held the papers against her body. "I'm not kicking you out," she said. "I could use someone here…"

Reg nodded. "I wish I could stay. Another time."

Jessup's injured eyes followed Reg as she got to her feet and reached for the dragon. He didn't like being touched, and she hadn't picked him up before except when he was asleep, so she wasn't sure how firm she could be with him. He pulled away from her and squirmed, trying to escape her grip. Reg let go.

"Here," she said, picking up the purse and putting her hand inside to stir the coins around. They clinked and rubbed against each other, making a tinkling, musical sound. The dragon's ears pricked up and he turned his head to follow the sound. "Are you getting in or not?"

When she held it open toward him, he obligingly hopped inside, and she could hear him moving the coins around, sorting them or putting them back into a comfortable pile.

"I'll call you later," Reg said hurriedly. "And you can tell me what else you find."

She hurried out of the Jessup family home as quickly as possible, climbed into her car, and carefully put her purse down on the passenger seat. Pieces of the puzzle were falling into place, and she didn't like the picture they were forming.

CHAPTER FORTY-NINE

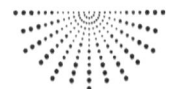

$\mathcal{R}$ eg didn't know whether he would be back at home or not. She assumed that he was because that was the simplest place for her to go to and she didn't think he would have wanted to stay in the hospital any longer than necessary. He would demand to be released and go home where he could rest without being bothered by intercom pages and starry-eyed nurses.

She might have broken a few speed limits on the way to Corvin's house. She didn't know why she felt such a sense of urgency when the matter had lain dormant for so many years. Maybe it was just because she wanted to deal with him before Jessup figured it out, and Jessup would probably have it in another ten minutes. Even if there was no identifying information in that little folded packet of papers, it would click in sooner or later.

She screeched to a halt in front of the house, ending up at quite an angle to the curb, but she didn't care. She needed to get to him and find out if it was true.

She didn't even knock before trying the doorknob on the front door. It turned in her hand and she entered, barreling on ahead without heed to whatever wards and protective spells he had guarding the place.

"Corvin? Are you home? Where are you?"

He had to be home. The door had been unlocked. But she didn't see him right away. Reg looked around frantically, straining her ears to hear his voice or anything else of importance. He could be sleeping in bed and disoriented. Drugged to combat the pain of his burned throat. Or to prevent escape.

She saw feet through a doorway. Not the feet of someone standing or sitting in the kitchen, but toes pointing up like he was lying on his back. Reg hurried to him. "Corvin! Wake up!"

She was hit with a feeling of breathlessness and nausea. Ignoring it, she grabbed his hands and tried to pull him over the slick tile floor. He was too heavy for her. Reg took deep breaths, trying to get enough oxygen into her lungs to perform the task, but she just felt dizzier.

She saw movement through his patio doors. Someone was out there. She hadn't been quick enough to see who. Something sailed toward her. It smashed through the glass of the door and Reg recognized what it was an instant too late. She didn't have enough time to get a psychic shield around Corvin but, somehow, she did. It wasn't big enough to shield herself, only Corvin himself. The Molotov cocktail smashed on the floor, but the air around them exploded even before that.

There wasn't time to transport them all out of there. Reg couldn't think of where she wanted to go or the steps she needed to follow to port them to another location.

Davyn had warned about what could happen if a firecaster were taken off guard and didn't prepare herself for a fire. For an instant it felt like every cell in Reg's body was burning, and then the sensation was gone, and she just felt pleasantly warm and comfortable. The fire raged around her.

Corvin unconscious on the floor near the gas stove. The dizziness that Reg had felt. The firebomb sailing through the air toward them. Whoever had attacked Corvin had done everything he could to ensure that Corvin would not survive this time. And without the shield around him, he wouldn't have. Even with it, she couldn't be sure that he would survive. How much natural gas had he breathed?

There was a yowling noise from her shoulder bag and she realized much too late that she had not done anything to shield the dragon from the blast. She swore and, while retaining the shield around Corvin, she opened the purse to peer inside.

The dragon pushed his way out, climbing up one of the bag's straps to perch on her shoulder. He didn't appear to be harmed. Just angry that he had been inside the bag and had missed the initial blast.

Like she was, he seemed to be perfectly comfortable with the firestorm in the kitchen.

Dragons. Why would a little fire bother him?

But it was still a danger to Corvin. She needed to keep the shield around him, which made moving him out of the house or giving him any kind of first aid rather tricky. She'd had plenty of instruction and practice in extinguishing fires, so she went to work calling the fire to her and gradually reducing it in size and strength. She could have done it faster, but that would have taken more energy and not been nearly as much fun. If she wasn't allowed to start fires herself, she could at least enjoy one that someone else had started.

She could hear sirens in the distance—fire engines. Looking around, Reg had a sudden moment of panic. The firefighters were going to show up, take a look at what had happened, and immediately fixate on the fact that the fire had disappeared by itself.

A bright red fire extinguisher was mounted on the wall near the stove. Reg plucked it from the brackets holding it, pulled the pin, and sprayed the contents over the flickering remnants of the fire on the floor, emptying the fire extinguisher. That would look a bit better. Even if it wasn't perfect, they could see that she had put out the fire with an extinguisher, not her magic.

The dragon looked around at the glowing embers and made a pouty, whining sound. Reg laughed. "I know, little guy. You wanted to play some more too. But the firemen are here, and they can't see you. Come back in the bag."

She stirred the coins around to make them clink, and the dragon sulkily made his way down her arm and back into the purse.

"Just stay there while I deal with everything else. I don't want anyone to hurt you."

Who knew what people would do if they saw him. People didn't react well to things that they couldn't understand. They would think that he was some dangerous deformed lizard and shoot him. Or capture him to study or put in an exhibit. She couldn't bear it if anything happened to the little guy. What had he done to hurt anyone?

Other than starting a small fire, and he couldn't help that.

CHAPTER FIFTY

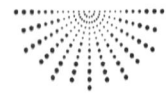

The fire engines pulled up to the house, their sirens blaring. Reg winced at the painfully loud wail and pinched the top of the shoulder bag closed, hoping it would muffle the sound to protect the dragon's sensitive ears.

Boots stomped through the house. The firefighters burst into the kitchen then looked around, disappointed.

"Sorry," Reg said. "Just a little kitchen fire."

"A little kitchen fire?" one of them growled, putting his face shield up and looking around. "This was clearly not caused by someone leaving the macaroni on the stove."

"No," Reg admitted. "But everything is out now. He'll need a good interior decorator…"

"He'll need to gut the kitchen and start over," the fireman corrected. "Assuming that there isn't any structural damage."

One of them knelt over Corvin and reached for him. When his hand encountered an invisible barrier, Reg quickly dropped the psychic shield. Too many things going on at the same time. She had forgotten that.

"Is he okay?" she asked.

"I haven't had a chance to look yet," the firefighter growled. He proceeded to examine Corvin, taking his pulse and checking his breathing. "How long was he in here?" He looked toward the stove. "Someone had better shut the gas off or we're going to have more problems."

One of the others stepped forward and bent over the stove to do whatever was necessary.

"He's breathing," the fireman kneeling by Corvin said. "But who knows how long he was in here." Reg hadn't even had a chance to speculate. "We should get oxygen on him right away."

They relayed the information back to whoever was still outside. In a few minutes—longer than Reg felt like it should have taken—a paramedic brought in a gurney and load of equipment. She slapped an oxygen mask over Corvin's face.

"Gas?"

Everyone else nodded.

"What else? Did the gas knock him out or did he sustain a head injury or something else?" She looked at Reg inquiringly.

"I got here just before the explosion. I didn't have a chance to check him out," Reg said.

"You weren't with him before that?"

"No. I just… had a feeling that something was wrong and came to see him." She was going to add some detail like having called him, but he failed to answer his phone, but that was the type of thing that a savvy investigator could check and, if they discovered that Reg was lying about just one thing, there would be trouble and a lot more questions. Best to offer less and avoid any awkward questions.

Corvin groaned and started to move around, trying to pull off the oxygen mask.

"You need to leave that on, sir," the paramedic told him loudly, close to his ear. "You need oxygen."

Corvin's eyelids fluttered like he couldn't decide whether to open them or close them. It was still smoky in the room, and he was probably overwhelmed by everyone around him, confused about how he had gotten there and if he was okay.

He turned his head toward her. "Regina?" he asked huskily, his eyes still closed most of the way. Did he see her or just feel her presence?

"Hey. You had a little fire."

"What?"

"An accident," Reg explained. "The pilot must have gone out."

Corvin tried again to get up, but the paramedic held him down. "Please stay still, sir, until I've had the opportunity to examine you for any other injuries."

"No, no," he tried to push her away. "I'm fine. Leave me alone."

"I need to see—"

"No," Corvin insisted. "Don't touch me."

The paramedic was hesitant and didn't withdraw immediately. She still really wanted to make sure he was okay. But a patient could refuse treatment. Corvin was at least alive and talking.

Corvin tried to prop himself up on his elbows, then lowered himself back to the floor with a groan. But when the paramedic tried to move back in, he swatted at her. "Leave me alone."

They all stood around looking at him, trying to figure out what to do next.

"Should we wet this down?" suggested one young-sounding fireman. "Make sure that everything is out? There could be hot spots under the floor that could flare up again."

"Don't you dare," Corvin protested. "I don't want water damage too."

"We need to make sure everything is completely out."

"It is," Corvin insisted. He turned his head slightly to look in Reg's way again. "Right, Reg?"

She explored the house with her mind, thinking about glowing coals still under the floor, any little embers that might feed on the fuel and grow into something more. She quashed every tiny glowing speck she could find. "Yeah. It's good. It's all out."

"We still need to check and monitor it," one of the older firefighters said. "We don't want to be back here later with more tragic results."

Corvin shook his head.

There was a rustling and crunching noise from Reg's shoulder bag. She readjusted it and coughed, trying to cover up the noise.

Which wasn't such a great idea, because that turned the paramedic's attention to her and concerns about smoke inhalation.

"Let me take a look at that," she told Reg, and made her open her mouth so that she could shine a light down her throat. She then put on her stethoscope. "Let's have a listen. Can you breathe deeply, please?" She glared at the firefighters, who were beginning to talk among themselves, quieting them with her look. "Again? Again?"

Reg rolled her eyes and tried to breathe normally and, at the same time, prevent the woman from hearing the noises coming from her purse. But the paramedic was focused on her lungs and didn't seem to notice anything unusual.

"You should get checked out anyway, but you seem fine." There was a note of disappointment in her voice. Two patients, and no one to treat. "Do you have a sunburn?"

Reg looked at her hand and arm, which were definitely pinker than usual. She had been surprised by the blast initially. Apparently, the split second before she realized what was going on had resulted in her sustaining a mild burn from the explosion.

"Yes," she told the paramedic. "You'd think that with this red hair, I would know not to spend too much time at the beach."

"You should wear sunscreen."

"Oh, I do. But you can still get burned, especially when you have such fair skin."

There were more sirens. It didn't sound like they were big trucks. Police cars, maybe. Reg suddenly remembered Jessup. Reg hadn't even said goodbye; she had just run for the door without explanation. She would have to call Jessup and explain what had happened. Or maybe not. She wasn't sure it was a good idea for Jessup to know what Reg had instinctively grasped.

But it was too late for that.

CHAPTER FIFTY-ONE

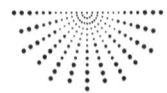

*J*essup was in the kitchen a couple of minutes later, getting a report from the firefighters as to what had happened. "Hunter has been the target of several attacks lately," she told them tersely. "I'll be the point person on this one. I'm already investigating the other attacks."

The firefighters talked to her about what they had found. The stove leaking gas. The glass on the floor from the patio door and a Molotov cocktail. They agreed that it was a suspicious scene that warranted further investigation and that forensic evidence would have to be preserved.

"Let's take the discussion to another room," Jessup suggested. "Hunter...?" She hesitated, looking at Corvin and then at Reg.

Corvin raised his head, and this time when he propped himself up, he stayed up. "We can use my study," he told her. At first, he just stayed there like that, then eventually pushed himself up to a more upright position. He was probably pretty woozy after all of that natural gas. And the blast. Reg had done her best to protect him, but there was still the possibility of a concussion.

"You need help?"

"No. I'm fine. I can manage."

It would probably make the paramedic happier if she saw that he could get to his feet independently.

"Okay…" Corvin rose unsteadily to his feet. He braced himself on the counter for a moment. "You see? I'm just fine."

"You don't look fine," Reg said.

He rolled his eyes at her. "I'll be okay once I'm sitting down. Ears are just ringing a little bit."

Reg and Jessup walked him to his study, and he settled himself into the big chair behind a beautifully carved antique desk. He sat there for a moment, hands on the top of the desk to steady himself. He looked at Reg and then at Jessup. Reg snuck a glance at Jessup. Even with her complexion, she seemed a little pale. Maybe just the shock of finding her potential victim the target of yet another murder attempt.

But maybe not.

Reg rubbed her temple and looked back at Corvin. Her brain was buzzing with questions, but she didn't know where to start. And she didn't want to say the wrong thing with Jessup in such a fragile mental state.

"What just happened?" Corvin asked finally.

"You were knocked out and the gas left on your stove. Then someone threw a lit Molotov cocktail through the porch window," Reg summarized. "Or maybe you weren't knocked out; maybe you were just overwhelmed by the gas."

He shook his head. "Who would do such a thing?"

"Someone who had a grudge against you." A major grudge. Reg looked at Jessup and then back at Corvin. "Maybe it's time to tell us who that was."

He shook his head. "I have no idea," he said faintly.

Reg didn't believe he could have gone so long without figuring out who it was and why.

Corvin followed Reg's eyes to Jessup. His brows drew down.

"Hunter," Jessup's voice was hard. "Ever since I got onto the police force, you've been around. A pain in the neck. Putting your nose where it isn't wanted, but also helping out with cases where you can provide some background or insight."

He nodded.

"But only *my* cases."

Reg remembered how Jessup had once classified her relationship with Corvin. Not as friends, but as "respected adversaries." She had always wondered about what was between them. Jessup seemed to hold something over Corvin and, even though he was many times more powerful than she was, he gave her respect and did not disobey her. Not outright, anyway.

Corvin gazed at Jessup for a moment, then shrugged. "You're one of the only ones investigating cases with certain... abnormalities. There have been other practitioners on the police force, but they are few and far between and, like you, find it necessary to keep a low profile and not attract too much attention to themselves."

"And you've always been..." Jessup searched for the right word, "Cooperative? Courteous? Even outside of our professional... situation. Not like I've seen you with Reg and others you have pursued. You've never given any sign of *interest* in me."

Corvin shook his head. Reg bit her lip to keep from jumping in. Corvin wouldn't have shown any interest in Jessup if she had been any other non-gifted person either. He was attracted to magical powers. Not exclusively, maybe; he enjoyed the package they came in too, but his interest in Reg had always been because of her powers before anything else.

"You knew who I was when you first came to the police force as a consultant, didn't you?"

Corvin considered the question. He licked his lips. "What do you mean, I knew who you were? A rookie cop? Yes. Someone with a magical family who would be open to my more *unusual* suggestions. Yes. Certainly."

"The daughter of the woman you attacked."

Corvin swallowed. He looked over at Reg to see her reaction to this question and she didn't give anything away. Or she hoped she wasn't giving anything away. He was too expert in reading her sometimes, catching a fleeting thought that she couldn't keep to herself.

He turned his chair slowly on the swivel and opened a cupboard behind him. There was a decanter full of amber liquid and several sparkling crystal glasses.

"I need a drink. Anyone else? Marta? Reg?"

Neither of them said anything. Reg could have used a drink too, but thought she'd better keep her wits about her. She would be dehydrated after all of the work putting out the fire and adding alcohol would be a bad idea.

"Do you have water?"

"No," Corvin snapped. He poured himself a drink and swiveled back to face his desk and his visitors. "What makes you think I knew your mother?"

"She named you." Jessup looked over at Reg to fill her in. "You figured it out before that, though, didn't you? You knew exactly who was behind the attack. Mom didn't know who it was early on. Tried to forget everything, to deny that it ever happened. But that didn't work. She included more details in the later notes." She looked back at Corvin. "Including your name, when she figured it out."

"*Attack* is a misrepresentation," Corvin said with distaste. "There was no physical violence. Just a woman who consented and later changed her mind. It happens." His eyes flicked to Reg.

"You're a liar," Jessup snapped. "You always have been. You attacked her and stole her powers."

"I followed the rules," Corvin insisted. "And that means that I give something in exchange for the powers I take. And that I never do it without consent."

"You seduced Lily with your charms. She was happily married to my father. She would never have had an affair without your spells."

"She could spin the story however she wanted to. Of course she would try to make herself look innocent, just the victim of a random attack. But you know that's not the way I work. I didn't force her into anything. It was her own choice."

Reg knew just how strong Corvin's charms were. He was impossible for most women to resist. But she also knew that he had broken the rules in the past. That was how he had ended up before the tribunal.

"You *haven't* always followed the rules," Jessup told him, echoing this thought. "And you've been caught."

Corvin looked at Reg. "Maybe you could give the two of us some privacy. This is not the type of thing that is discussed in polite company."

Reg barked out a laugh. "Since when am I polite company?" The magical community's silence concerning what Corvin was and the danger he posed made them complicit in whatever he did. She wasn't going to be party to a cover-up.

"Regina, please."

Reg looked at Jessup to see if she wanted Reg to leave so that the discussion about her mother would go no further. Jessup shook her head. Reg stayed where she was.

"What about me?" Jessup demanded. "How exactly are you going to excuse *that*?"

He shook his head. "What are you talking about?"

"The fact that you stole my powers before I was even born. Explain to me how you get consent from a fetus."

CHAPTER FIFTY-TWO

*R*eg felt sick. *That* was why Lily had been so worried about Jessup when she had been born. Because she had been pregnant at the time of the attack. Corvin looked at Reg, apparently looking for someone who would be on his side. But Reg was not on his side.

"I had no idea your mother was pregnant. She never said anything to me. By the time I realized, it was too late."

"Because you don't give powers back," Jessup sneered.

Reg saw why Jessup was so angry. Corvin *had* given stolen powers back once before. Just once. To Reg.

But not to Lily and little Marta Jessup. Not while Lily was still pregnant, and not once Marta was born, lacking anything but the most basic gifts.

"No, I don't," Corvin agreed stolidly. "If I did that, then I would never be filled. How does one satiate his hunger if he has to return everything consumed?"

"You could have. When you found out you had stolen my powers as well as my mother's, you could have returned them."

Corvin shook his head. "I have only ever been able to do that once. Believe me, if I had thought it possible when you were still a baby, I would have." He spread his hands out in a gesture of helplessness. "But that was long ago; what little magic I drew from you is long since diminished."

Reg wondered how much of what Corvin said was true. He was blocking her, to the best of his ability, from reading him, and his walls were strong. But she could feel his vulnerability, the guilt over what he had done. The place inside of him where he had chosen greed and his own comfort over the rights of someone else. Just like when he had tried to steal Reg's powers without her permission. When she had expressly denied him.

Was he a good warlock with an unfortunate curse, doomed to steal what he could not produce himself? Or was he evil, with no regard for anyone else, who feared being discovered and proven to be what he was?

"And what... you kept track of me?" Jessup demanded. "How is it you were there as soon as I joined the police force, just waiting for me, offering your services? You can't tell me that was just a coincidence."

"Well... no. I do regret what happened. I never intended to take your powers too. I wanted... to make up for it in some way."

"And you thought hanging out with me and consulting for the police force made up for that."

"There wasn't much else I could do for you," Corvin said, his tone petulant.

"Oh, brother."

Jessup was silent for a while, taking it all in. Reg felt sorry for her, suddenly discovering these secrets from her past. The assault on her mother, theft of her own powers, and the fact that her sort-of friend and trusted consultant was the person responsible for both.

"Marta," Corvin tried. "I've really done everything I could to make up for what happened. I am sorry."

"You're sorry? I don't think you are. Do you know that my mother killed herself because of you? Because of what you did to her? What you did wrecked her. She was never the same again. She wasn't there for me. She wasn't a person I could rely on emotionally. I had to prop her up, to support her mental health. Take care of things at home because she wasn't able to. Cover for her problems. Deal with holidays with her gone, in the hospital for treatment."

Corvin poured himself another drink and downed half of it immediately.

"How did you keep your identity a secret from her all these years?" Jessup demanded. "How could she have only figured it out a year ago? Black Sands is a small town. I know she hasn't lived here for a while, but she lived here for the first twenty years of my life. How could she live in the same town with you for twenty years and not run across each other? You're not exactly a recluse."

"She might not have known who he was," Reg supplied, "but *he* knew her. So he could avoid her if he happened to see her somewhere." She frowned at Corvin, who was scowling at her, not liking her interference. "He could confuse her with his powers. Block her from noticing him. The question isn't how could she not find out who it was. The question is—how *did* she find out? Did he just not see her coming one day?"

Jessup put her palms over her eyes and didn't answer for what seemed like an eternity. Reg could feel the anguish pouring off of her. Could see the shifting blue and red auras as Jessup tried to wrestle with both her grief for her mother and her anger at Corvin. Reg had just saved Corvin's life; should she have stayed out of it? Let the avengers take their vengeance?

"It was Corvin's tribunal," Jessup said finally.

Of course. It would have been impossible for Corvin to notice everyone who had come to the hearing and, even if he did see Lily there, using his charms to keep her from recognizing him as her attacker would have been noticed by the tribunal. They would have wanted an explanation of what was going on. They had shunned him indefinitely for what he had done to Reg. If another woman had been disclosed that he'd done the same thing to decades before, not only stripping away Lily's powers without consent, but also the powers of her unborn child, they might have kicked him out of the coven forever, with no chance of reinstatement.

Corvin seemed to have aged. His skin had a grayish tinge and seemed stretched thin. Was it the result of being exposed to natural gas? He gave a tired nod and sat there with his head bowed as if he were actually repentant.

So he knew. He had seen Lily there and had known there was nothing he could do about it but hope that she would keep quiet. And she had. But even if she had gone away quietly then, she wouldn't let him get away with it forever. She had named him in the papers she had left for Jessup.

Had she hoped that once Jessup read them, she would arrest Corvin and see that he was punished for his actions? Of course, it hadn't been criminal under the legal system. Jessup could have accused him before his coven, brought him before a tribunal for the second time.

Or had Lily merely wanted her daughter to know the secret she had kept all of those years? The cause of her emotional instability and inability to nurture her little girl like she had wanted to. Why the baby had been born with no or minimal powers, doomed to a normal, nonmagical life working in law enforcement.

"Are you okay?" Reg asked Jessup. "I'm so sorry for all of this. I wish the dra—I wish he hadn't found that box."

"No." Jessup waved this apology away. "That package was supposed to come to me. They weren't supposed to open it and read it themselves. They were supposed to give it to me unopened, and then I could decide what I wanted done about it. Not *this*." She motioned to Corvin.

"What?" Corvin asked, raising his head and frowning at her.

Reg didn't want to make any unjust accusations. She kept her mouth shut.

"*This*," Jessup said again. Her dark eyes drilled into him. "Trying to kill you."

"*You* have been trying to kill me?"

The gas must have muddled him.

"Not *me*," Jessup snorted. "Though we'll see about that after I've had a chance to process everything. My brothers. One or maybe both of them have been trying to kill you."

Understanding flooded Corvin's features. "To avenge her. And you."

"Yeah. Seeking their own justice."

Corvin nodded his understanding. Like maybe he would have done the same thing. He was very calm. Reg would have expected him to pound the desk and demand justice, demand that both brothers be arrested and locked away for the rest of their lives for what they had done. But Corvin seemed resigned to it. Like everything finally made sense and now he could stop trying to figure it out.

"Do you know which one it was?" Reg asked hesitantly.

Jessup looked at Corvin as if he might know. Corvin shook his head. "I never saw them."

Jessup shrugged. "I don't know. Probably both of them. I'll have to pass the case off to someone else. Let them try to get evidence of which one it was."

"No, don't," Corvin protested. "I don't want them arrested." He swallowed. "Your family has been through enough. What good would putting them in prison do?"

"It would keep them from trying to kill you," Jessup pointed out the obvious.

"Just tell them you know. Tell them to leave if they don't want to be arrested. I just want... I want this to all go away. It has been too long. I just want to forget about it." He rubbed his temples tiredly. "I was relieved when they moved out of town, and you were the only one left. It made it so much easier. Not having to worry about running into her at the grocery store. Hearing other cases of women coming forward and making accusations after years of silence. And people listening to them. Trying and punishing the men that they accused. I was always worried that sooner or later... she would show up. And the accusations would be made."

Reg shook her head. He had been lucky. Lily could have chosen to come forward instead of killing herself. She could have decided that punishing Corvin was the only way for her to find peace. She had certainly been intent on retribution *after* she had died. Stripped of everything else, only her anger had remained.

They were all quiet. There were more munching sounds from Reg's purse. She opened it to look at the dragon, worried about what he might be destroying. He'd found packages of snack crackers and was working his way through them. He stopped and looked at her, crackers held in his front claws. Like he was wondering why she was interrupting his snack. Reg couldn't help smiling. She shook her head.

Corvin sat forward in his chair, looking at her. "What have you got in there? The cat?"

"No, not the cat. The dragon."

"The *what?*"

Reg scooped the dragon up with one hand. She was getting more used to touching him but was still a little nervous about it. She held him high enough that Corvin could see him.

"A dragon?" Corvin repeated, blinking as if to clear his vision.

Reg thought about the fire that had started in the kitchen—reaching out with her mind to smother all of the live sparks and coals to make sure that it didn't reignite.

"Ember," she tried, looking down at the dragon and smiling encouragingly.

He made a soft squawk. It felt right. Like it had always been his name and she had finally figured it out.

"Ember," Reg repeated with satisfaction.

EPILOGUE

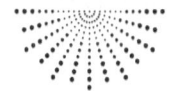

*a*t The Crystal Bowl, Jessup stirred the soup in her bowl for a moment, thinking, before she looked at Reg.

"That was why they were able to get past Corvin's wards," Jessup explained. "It never occurred to me before. It's called *probity.* You can set wards against your enemies, against people trying to break in to harm you or your possessions. But if they are in the right, seeking retribution for an injustice you have caused or to set something right, then even though they might harm you, probity allows them safe passage."

"Who decides whether they are trying to get retribution for an injustice or just to hurt someone?" Reg asked, baffled. She slid a package of soda crackers from the table into her purse before opening another package to crumble over her soup. The restaurant was busy enough that her actions and any suspicious movement in her bag would not be noticed, but quiet enough that they could still talk without raising their voices.

"Nobody *decides*," Jessup said patiently. "It's just whether you are in the right or not."

"But how can the wards determine that by themselves? They're not sentient."

"No," Jessup agreed. She gave a little laugh. "It's called magic, Reg."

"But what if they said they were seeking justice and actually weren't?"

"Then they couldn't get past the wards."

Reg shook her head. "I don't understand."

Jessup shrugged.

"So where are your brothers now? Is everyone really just going to let them get away with it? I mean, nothing against your brothers, but trying to kill someone *is* against the law."

"It was… done in a moment of extreme emotional disturbance," Jessup said slowly. "If they had succeeded then, at worst, it would be manslaughter. But they didn't, and they're not going to try again, so…"

"How do you know they won't try again?"

"They won't," she said firmly. "I've had a word with them. They are leaving town, and they won't be back."

"You trust them not to come back and try again?"

Jessup nodded. "I'll make sure of it. I would have turned them in, you know. But Hunter didn't want me to."

"I know. That would have been really hard."

"So was all the rest of it. Losing my mom, finding out what happened to her all those years ago. Finding out that it was Corvin Hunter. And that my own brothers were the ones who were trying to kill him." Jessup shook her head. "They should have just given me the envelope like they were supposed to. Then none of this would have happened. Mom knew that. She only wanted me to know. And they go and open it without telling me anything about it and decide to seek retribution themselves. It's *all* been hard. I can't even process it right now. I don't know how long it will take for things to go back to normal."

"Sorry that you had to go through all of that." Reg picked up her drink and swirled it in the glass before taking a sip. "What did they put in Corvin's drink? Why couldn't the lab find anything?"

Jessup gave a little laugh and shook her head. "Would you believe holy water? It's supposed to be able to kill his kind."

"Well… it just about did, so I guess I believe it. Water. I guess water wouldn't come up on a tox screen."

Jessup murmured her agreement.

"So even though it isn't proper to talk about power drinkers and what they do in polite company, there are still legends about what is supposed to kill them?"

"Of course. Why do you think there are so few of them around anymore?"

"If you aren't allowed to talk about them, how would you find out?"

"There have always been places where such dark things are discussed. Nowadays, it's mostly on the deep web. But once upon a time," Jessup smiled at her use of the phrase, "it might be around a campfire or in the backroom of some saloon. You don't discuss such terrible things in the open, but there are places to go."

"How do you stop someone like him? Is there any way other than killing them? Is that really the only choice?"

"We can't make rules against something that is his nature. You can't rule that lions aren't allowed to hunt anymore. That all animals have to become vegetarian."

There was a burp from Reg's shoulder bag. She looked at it, giggling.

"Just like the rules for sirens," Jessup said. "That they are not allowed to hunt on land. We can't stop them from claiming their territorial waters and hunting the humans who use them. We try to put reasonable limits on them. And on power drinkers like Corvin."

"Saying that they have to have consent from their victim is ridiculous." Reg tried to keep her voice steady and not raise it above the hum of the conversations around them. "No one would ever give consent to having their powers stripped away. So he tricks women or ensorcels them to get them to say yes. But it's a sham. That's not consent. Consent has to be freely given."

Jessup sighed. "I wish we had the perfect system, but we don't."

"Do you think your mother gave consent for what happened to her? Having her gifts stolen? And yours? Do you think she ever would have given Corvin consent to do that? If she even knew what he was, don't you think she would have told him that she was pregnant, have begged him not to harm her baby? He said he didn't know. Either she told him and he's lying, or he overwhelmed her so that she couldn't."

"Do you think I don't know that, Reg? Does it matter at this point whether he knew before or not? You can bet that he knew when he took whatever gifts I might have had. I don't believe for a minute that he couldn't tell the difference between what he took from her and what he took from me. That he could enter my mind and not know that I was a separate entity from her."

"This whole thing about getting consent is just about making his crimes look less offensive to the public," Reg pointed out. "There's no difference between charming and ensorceling someone and getting them drunk or high. It's not really consent."

Jessup pushed her bowl away from her slightly. Her meal was hardly touched.

"I never knew that she'd had powers. They didn't tell me that. I grew up thinking that she didn't have any. That it was a mixed marriage, with my father holding all of the gifts. I thought that it was just the genetic lottery. My brothers took after Dad and had powers. I took after Mom and didn't. Or have so little it's hardly even worth mentioning. Mom never talked about what had happened to her. I hate knowing what she suffered in silence. In the notes she left… it's pretty obvious that she was devastated. She couldn't just live a normal, nonmagical life as if she'd been born that way. She couldn't live with having her gifts taken away."

Reg could remember the hollow, echoing feeling she'd had when she awoke and discovered that Corvin had stolen her gifts. The emptiness and ringing silence that filled her head, which had always been filled with voices. It was painful. Reg had only had to deal with it for a short time. Lily had lived with her loss for decades. And it had just been too much.

* * *

Ember was getting restless in Reg's bag. They had been at the restaurant for long enough. He'd been very good about being quiet and remaining out of sight, but she didn't want to push her luck. Sooner or later, he would want to stretch his legs and people would see him.

She paid for the dinner and said an awkward goodbye to Jessup. "I wish I could do something to help you feel better."

"You did. You listened. I don't know how I would do it if I didn't have anyone to talk to about it. I don't want everyone to know what happened to Mom. She didn't want anyone else to know, so I can't justify taking it public. But I at least have *someone* who knows. Other than Hunter."

"What's going to happen to him? Nothing? He's just going to go on doing what he's doing, being himself?"

"Pretty much, yeah. I can tell you I probably won't be using him for any more police consulting." Jessup gave a grim smile. "I don't want anything else to do with him. But I can't stop him."

Reg wondered how Lily would feel about that. Was it enough that her daughter now knew the story and wouldn't have anything more to do with Corvin? Enough that her sons had tried three times to kill Corvin, even if they had failed?

"Can't you report Corvin to his coven?" Reg demanded. "To Davyn? Say that he stole your powers before you were born?"

"Hunter will say it was an accident. That he had no way of knowing. And I can't prove that he broke any rules in what he did to Lily. The coven forgave him for what he did to you. They're not going to do anything about something that happened decades ago."

Reg shook her head. She gave Jessup a brief shoulder hug. Reg wasn't a hugger and she and Jessup had been through some rocky times in their relationship. But she felt like it was necessary at that point. There was nothing else she could do to comfort her friend.

When they touched, Reg could feel Lily's presence. Not raging this time. Closer to being at peace. Maybe she would soon be able to move on in her afterlife. "I'm sorry for what happened to you, little one," Lily whispered in Jessup's ear. "I'm sorry for everything he took from you."

There was a noise of protest from the shoulder bag. "I've got to get going," Reg apologized, withdrawing. "We'll talk more later if you need to."

Marta Jessup squeezed her arm and nodded. Reg went on her way.

* * *

Once the car was in motion, she opened the top of the bag and called to Ember. "You can come out now. We'll be there soon."

Ember crawled out of the purse, making an eager squeaking sound.

"You'll like it there," Reg told him for probably the hundredth time. But Ember kept wanting to hear it over and over again. Like a human three-year-old who kept repeating 'why?' until it drove his mother crazy. "He has a great big fireplace in the middle of the house. You can see it from all of the rooms on the main floor. And Davyn is like me, so he loves fire as much as you do. You'll have a great time there." Reg formed a picture in her mind of the dragon snoozing beside a roaring fire in Davyn's huge fireplace. Ember squeaked some more and looked out the window.

"We'll be there soon," she assured him.

When they arrived at Davyn's house and Reg opened her door, Ember immediately took flight and circled her and the house, exploring the area. Davyn came out of the house and watched, smiling.

"I really appreciate you taking him," Reg told Davyn. "I don't know what else I could have done. I think he really needs to be with a firecaster, but he couldn't stay with me in the cottage. And he wasn't happy staying in the garden. Here, he'll be able to play and have fires and you can look after him. As much as dragons need to be taken care of, I mean. They're supposed to be able to be pretty independent."

"It's an honor to have him," Davyn assured her. "There aren't very many of his kind left in the world."

They both stared up into the sky for a few minutes, watching the dragon's graceful circles.

"Ember," Reg called. "Let's go inside and look at the fireplace."

The dragon swooped down and landed on her shoulder. Even after just a couple of days, she had seen significant improvement in his ability to fly and land softly, so it didn't feel like he would rip her arm off in the process. Reg followed Davyn into the house, and they made their way to the big central fireplace. Reg could feel Ember's disappointment at finding it cold and empty. Davyn opened glass doors big enough to accommodate a man's height and started to move logs from a large indoor woodpile into the fireplace. Reg joined in and helped to stack the wood inside. After a few minutes, it was ready.

"Do you want to do the honors?" Davyn asked, with a bow to Ember.

Ember squeezed Reg's shoulder, and she sensed that he did not understand. Figuring out human behavior was hard enough. Davyn using archaic language didn't help. She pictured Ember stepping into the fireplace and blowing flame at the logs. Almost instantly, he glided from her shoulder to the fireplace and did just that.

The dry firewood went up like a torch. Reg enjoyed the blossom of heat that washed over her. The fire roared and crackled and was a thing of beauty.

"Come on out now," Reg said. "We'll just sit by the fire and enjoy it for a while."

It was a few minutes before Ember moved out of the fireplace, allowing Davyn to shut the big doors. Reg's own fire pulled within her. She glanced over at Davyn.

"Yes, you can join in," Davyn agreed. Reg sat down and, with Ember sitting on her feet, she played with the fire, making it grow and shrink, cool and heat as the urge hit her. It was lovely not to have to do any of her firecaster exercises or perform under Davyn's critical eye, but just to play with the fire as she pleased, like running out of school at the end of the day to the playground. *Not* the one at the school where she was expected to follow all of the rules and be supervised, but the one between the school and her house where there were rarely any adults and no one who knew her well enough to report to her foster family that she was being too loud or too wild or staying there after dark.

As it got later, Reg knew that she had to go back home. She couldn't just sit there basking in the light of the fire with a dragon lying on her feet forever. She sighed and stood up, easing her feet out from underneath the snoozing Ember.

"He can have the basement?" she asked, making sure of the arrangements.

"Yes, of course. I'm not using it for anything."

Reg walked over to the stairs. Ember scrambled to his feet to follow, wondering what she was doing. "Come on," she invited him, with a pang of disappointment. "Let's show you your lair."

The stairs that led down to the basement were old and worn and felt a little spongy, as if she shouldn't trust them to hold her weight. She slipped down them as quickly as she could to avoid landing on any one stair for too long. She had turned on the switch at the top of the stairs, but the light coming from the bulb was very dim, casting a yellow glow over everything. There wasn't much there to make a dragon comfortable. But Reg had come prepared.

"This is your place," she told Ember. "Your very own. Starlight likes to sit in the sunshine on the windowsill, but you don't like the sun, do you? A dragon likes somewhere dark and still."

Ember walked around, stretching each of his legs out, smelling the corners of the room with interest. Reg delved into her purse and removed the handfuls of coins that were weighing it down, making a pile in the middle of the room. Ember immediately came over and started to paw through them. Reg took out a small plastic zip-top bag and poured the contents, a few small gems, into her hand. She let Ember snuffle her hand for a moment, then sprinkled the gems on top of the coins. Ember pushed everything around until it was the way he wanted it. Then he curled up on top of the hill of treasure and started purring.

Reg stroked the top of his scaly head. "I'll be back to see you in a little while. And I meet with Davyn every week for firecasting. He said you can come too. As long as we are going somewhere safe for dragons. I'll see you again soon, okay?"

Ember closed his eyes and was still, his purr still rumbling away.

* * *

Get the next book! *Cloaked Campaign,* Book #18 of the *Reg Rawlins, Psychic Investigator series* by P.D. Workman can be purchased at pdworkman.com

Did you enjoy this book? Reviews and recommendations are vital to making a book successful.

Please leave a review at your favorite book store or review site and share it with your friends.

Don't miss the following bonus material:
Sign up for mailing list to get a free ebook
Read a sneak preview chapter
Other books by P.D. Workman
Learn more about the author

Sign up for my mailing list at pdworkman.com and get
Gluten-Free Murder for free!

PREVIEW OF CLOAKED CAMPAIGN

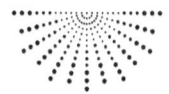

REG RAWLINS, PSYCHIC INVESTIGATOR #18

CHAPTER 1

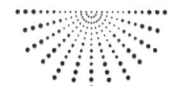

*R*eg was eager to see Davyn as she drove down the highway toward the isolated area he had directed her to. To be honest, she was more excited to see Ember, but that seemed unfair to her mentor. Reg had, after all, only known the dragon since he had hatched a few weeks earlier in the garden behind the guest cottage Reg rented, and she had known Davyn for almost a year. There were no other firecasting witches or warlocks in Black Sands as far as Reg knew; none that had made themselves known to her. But Davyn had been helping her learn control of her craft, and they had become pretty good friends. She had helped to rescue Davyn after he had been kidnapped not that long ago, which had cemented their friendship even further.

So why was she looking forward to seeing the dragon so much more than her teacher?

She felt that it was a bit of a betrayal of Davyn, after all the time and effort he had invested in training her, for which he charged her nothing. But Reg imagined it was like going home at the end of a long day to the eager greeting of a loyal dog. Ember didn't judge her or care what she was doing, whether she made small talk or had been following all the rules. He was just happy to see her. And Reg was happy to see him, even if Davyn said he had been getting into things and not listening. He was a dragon. What did he expect? The creatures were not well-known for being house trained.

Reg could feel her connection to Davyn and Ember strengthening, so she knew she was going the right way. She watched for the old Carroll Property sign Davyn mentioned and turned onto the small road. The vegetation was thick around her, rubbing against the sides of the car as she drove deeper into the wild. Eventually, she broke into a clearing and saw Davyn's car parked off to the side. She parked her car alongside his.

She couldn't see either of them and peered into the thick green foliage. "Davyn?"

There was a loud flapping of wings. Reg froze in place until she felt claws grasp her shoulder. She turned her head to look at Ember, who was looking very satisfied to have found her.

"Hello, there, handsome," she greeted, grinning.

Davyn walked out of the trees. He was cloaked, with his hood up, so she couldn't see much of his face, but she could see the corner of a smile as he surveyed Reg and the dragon.

"I see you found each other."

Reg reached up her hand to rub against Ember's jaw. He rolled his head into her palm like a cat begging for more scratches. Reg obligingly scratched his neck and round his small round ears. "I can't believe how much bigger he is every time I see him."

Before long, she wouldn't be able to support him on her shoulder. His grip was much more comfortable than the first time he'd landed on her shoulder, still an unsteady fledgling. But his weight was getting to be too much, even though he occasionally flapped to get some lift and lighten the load.

"He's growing fast," Davyn agreed, surveying the young dragon, who had also changed color from the pinkish-grey he'd had when he first hatched to a blue-green sheen. "Sometimes, when I get home at the end of the day, I could swear he's bigger than when I left that morning."

Ember puffed out his chest and made a rumbling noise. Reg could see the picture of the adult dragon Ember aspired to be in her mind. Huge and magnificent. She felt a pang of worry, wondering what they would do when he got that big. Where was he going to live? How would she be able to ensure that he would be safe from hunters or other dangers? Would she even be able to see him?

He squeezed her shoulder and bent down to rub the side of his face against hers, making coaxing noises. Reg patted his neck and scratched his ears some more.

"How has he been?"

She really shouldn't ask. She didn't want to hear complaints about what Ember had gotten into lately or the trouble he was causing Davyn, who had been happy to take the dragon in without any expectations of payment for pet boarding.

"He's been amazing," Davyn said affectionately. "I've never had a familiar, but he is quickly becoming… indispensable."

Ember jumped off Reg's shoulder and strutted around. Reg and Davyn laughed.

"He's like a puppy or a toddler, though," Davyn said, giving a little sigh. "Not that he's teething, but he gets into things and makes a mess or destroys things. I need to keep an eye on him all the time he's in the house. And I worry about him leaving the property when he's outside. We do not need him menacing Black Sands and bringing the villagers down on us with pitchforks and torches."

"I wouldn't suggest torches," Reg said with a laugh. Fire wasn't likely to harm a firecaster and a firedrake. "We just have to… convince him to stay where he's safe."

"And have you ever tried to explain that to a toddler?"

Reg shrugged, conceding the point. She reached out to Ember with her mind, trying to form pictures that would warn him of the hazards of leaving the property without Davyn. But the prospect of danger seemed to excite him. Like a child who had just watched a superhero movie and thought that he would be able to kick butt just like his favorite character if he had to face off against bad guys. Reg rolled her eyes and shook her head.

"You have to be careful," she told Ember aloud, even though he was less likely to understand the English words than the pictures she had given him. "I don't want you to get hurt."

Ember snorted, shooting flames from his nose. Reg reached down to pat his head, hoping she had not hurt his ego. "I know. You're going to be bigger than any of them, and you have fire. But humans can still be dangerous, even to full-grown dragons. There aren't very many of your kind left in the world."

That seemed to give him pause. Maybe he was thinking of his parents and wondering where they were and what had happened to them. Davyn assured her that dragons didn't normally raise their young, but that didn't mean that the young dragon didn't have questions about where he had come from and what had happened to his mother after laying her egg many years before. Ember seemed to have a lot of knowledge that he had simply been hatched with. He knew things that he had never been taught by a mother, including a few English words. She and Davyn had agreed that it must be genetic memory, something that scientists had only speculated about.

"Well… are we ready to begin?" Davyn asked.

"Yes. Sorry. I know you don't have all day."

"Well, as the guardian of this little fellow, I fully expect to need to take time to discuss him. But we can talk more while we're working."

"Playing," Reg corrected with a grin. How she loved to play with fire. Her sessions with Davyn were the only time she could safely explore her abilities. He had recently agreed to allow her to light a small, candle-sized flame for meditation in the cottage where she lived behind Sarah's big house. She had to only do it in the bathroom with all the flammable materials removed, just in case she was to get distracted or let it get out of her control. But at least she could now have a small flame in her home when she was alone. It was a step.

"Playing," Davyn agreed. He held his hands apart as if cupping an invisible basketball between them and started to kindle a small ball of fire between them. Reg mimicked him and, watching the development of his flame, tried to copy each change he made precisely. Making it larger and smaller, hotter and cooler. It was a familiar warm-up exercise. She could do it in her sleep. But she didn't complain about having to do the same thing over and over again. After all, even the most advanced athletes still had to stretch and do proper warm-up exercises before performing. In their case, it helped to prevent injury. The firecasting warm-up exercises would, she believed, help her to focus and gain greater and greater control over the fire that burned within her and was always so eager to get out and cause destruction and chaos. A fire could be helpful. It could be controlled. It could be used as a tool.

But it didn't always want to be.

CHAPTER 2

*H*ave you met the new witch in town?" Davyn asked.

"New witch?" Reg shrugged. "I don't know. Not that I've noticed."

But there were lots of witches and warlocks in Black Sands. Reg certainly didn't know all of them and wouldn't necessarily know if she had met someone who had just moved into town. Unless the witch mentioned being new, Reg would assume it was just someone she hadn't met before.

"I think you would have noticed her."

"Oh? What was so special about her?"

"She appears to be young and inexperienced, but I got the feeling that her powers are much stronger than she would have those around her believe." He paused, looking for something else to say, then just repeated, "Much stronger."

"Did you get her name? Or where she lives or works?"

"Verity. I don't know where she is living or working, if she has found work yet. She's only been around for a day or two."

"Verity." Reg shook her head. "No, I don't think I've run into anyone with that name."

"You would remember her."

"So who is she? Is she related to someone here? Or just came to Black Sands because…" Reg shrugged. Because Black Sands had the highest number of witches and other practitioners than any other town in the country. The same reason Reg had initially come to Black Sands. Knowing that there was a high density of psychics and people using their services, she had figured it would be a good place for her to run a fortune-telling con. But things had turned out very differently than she had expected.

"I don't know. Didn't get much of her history," Davyn confessed. "I was trying to be polite. Sometimes people don't want to share their reasons for moving to a new town. If she got run out of the last place she lived… a lot of people are anxious about anyone finding out what happened, worried that Black Sands will run them out on a rail too."

Reg held the glowing ball of fire in her hands, letting its warmth seep into her. She was glad to have "found her tribe" in Black Sands. She had always moved frequently from one place to another as people discovered her talents. Constantly watching out for the police or anyone that she had run into previously. Changing her name, her scam, making up a new history. That life had ended with her arrival in Black Sands.

She startled as Ember leaped across the clearing and snatched the fireball from her hands, appearing to swallow it and then breathing out a long stream of fire that reached from one side of the clearing to the other.

"Ember! No, bad dragon!" Reg couldn't help laughing. "You have to let me practice with Davyn!"

Ember sat looking at her, not the least bit sorry.

"You'll need to stay focused," Davyn told Reg, chuckling. He was always trying to think of new ways to distract her focus from her fire, forcing her to strengthen her skills and her ability to stay on-task. Apparently, he had not planned for Ember to jump in and distract Reg, but it was a good challenge. "We don't usually have to defend against someone stealing our fire, but who knows, maybe one day you will, and you'll be glad for this trial. You'll have to keep your attention on *both* your fire and your dragonlet."

Reg eyed Ember as she kindled another fire between her hands. "You'd better stay there. It isn't going to be easy to do that again," she warned him.

She shifted her focus to the fire and tried to remember what she and Davyn had been talking about before the interruption.

"I'll watch for this Verity. I guess. If you think it might be important."

Davyn shrugged. "Maybe the two of you won't have anything to do with each other. But I got the feeling that she might… make some waves while she is here in Black Sands."

"What kind of waves?" Reg was always happy to have someone else in trouble. As long as they didn't involve or accuse her. Growing up in a series of foster homes, she tried to stay under the radar of the authorities and to divert people's attention to the other foster children in the home rather than her. Even if it had *occasionally* been Reg who had caused the trouble.

Very occasionally.

"I don't know what her special gifts or interests may be," Davyn admitted. "She was asking me about the coven, which of course, is odd because it is not a mixed-gender coven."

"Did you send her to Letticia? Or someone here in town?"

Letticia was the head of the witch's coven that Reg was aware of. She knew there were others, but those were the ones she had acquaintances in. Letticia didn't live right in Black Sands, but like Davyn, outside the town limits. She had a little house on the edge of the Everglades that looked like something out of a fairy tale. Not a gingerbread house, though Letticia did make wonderful cookies.

"Since she doesn't know her way around yet, I sent her over to Sarah. So you may see her while she's over there."

Sarah was Reg's landlord, a grandmotherly witch who was apparently centuries old, despite looking like she was in her sixties. She had rented the guest cottage to Reg on the day she had arrived in Black Sands, and Reg had been pretty happy there. Though she sometimes resented Sarah's meddling in her affairs, she had to admit that she didn't mind Sarah finding her additional clients, tidying up, or feeding Starlight, Reg's tuxedo cat, if she was away.

Sarah hadn't wanted a dragon living in the cottage, which was perfectly understandable. Starlight hadn't been too impressed with Ember's presence there either.

"Okay, I guess I'll keep an eye open for her. What does she look like?"

Davyn didn't answer immediately, and after a period of silence, Reg glanced at him. She was having to split her attention between her fire and Ember. Looking at Davyn, she realized he was flushing pink. She raised her brows at this.

"Davyn?"

Davyn's voice was measured and steady when he spoke. "She is… very attractive. Dark hair. Slim. Very pretty."

"I see." Reg laughed. "Does Julian know that you are ogling women this way?"

Davyn's eyes widened. "I'm not! I can't help recognizing that she was pretty. What do you want me to say? That I didn't notice? People who say that are just lying. It doesn't mean I was attracted to her, just that…" He raised both eyebrows and rolled his eyes upward. "She is… stunning."

"Uh-huh. But Julian doesn't have anything to worry about?"

"Of course he doesn't." Davyn turned even redder. "And he knows that."

"Did you tell *him* about this stunning woman you saw?"

"Not yet. Focus on your fire."

Reg turned her gaze back toward her fire. "Are we going to do some more today? I don't want to just do warm-ups."

"Only once I'm sure that you're prepared. We don't want to make any mistakes today."

That sounded like he had something challenging in mind. Reg tried to tamp down her excitement to keep it from making her make a mistake or inadvertently grow her fire too much. No mistakes. She would be sure to do everything right so that Davyn would let her do whatever he had in mind.

* * *

Cloaked Campaign, Book #18 of the *Reg Rawlins, Psychic Investigator series* by P.D. Workman can be purchased at pdworkman.com

ABOUT THE AUTHOR

Award-winning and USA Today bestselling author P.D. (Pamela) Workman writes riveting mystery/suspense and young adult books dealing with mental illness, addiction, abuse, and other real-life issues. For as long as she can remember, the blank page has held an incredible allure and from a very young age she was trying to write her own books.

Workman wrote her first complete novel at the age of twelve and continued to write as a hobby for many years. She started publishing in 2013. She has won several literary awards from Library Services for Youth in Custody for her young adult fiction. She currently has over 90 published titles and can be found at pdworkman.com.

Born and raised in Alberta, Workman has been married for over 25 years and has one son.

* * *

Please visit P.D. Workman at pdworkman.com to see what else she is working on, to join her mailing list, and to link to her social networks.

* * *

If you enjoyed this book, please take the time to recommend it to other purchasers with a review or star rating and share it with your friends!

facebook.com/pdworkmanauthor

twitter.com/pdworkmanauthor

instagram.com/pdworkmanauthor

amazon.com/author/pdworkman

bookbub.com/authors/p-d-workman

goodreads.com/pdworkman

linkedin.com/in/pdworkman

pinterest.com/pdworkmanauthor

youtube.com/pdworkman

Find P.D. Workman's books at

PDWORKMAN.COM

Scan the QR code below